Easton at the CROSSROADS

The *Easton* Series
—Book Three

Endorsements

A fascinating story about a modern-day Easton historian whose discovery of centuries-old family secrets helps her confront a complicated mix of family, professional and romantic challenges.

—**Scott L. Reda**, Managing Director/Executive Producer, Lou Reda Productions

Easton at the Crossroads is a captivating and factually accurate account of the fighting on Long Island in 1776. It captures the experiences of men preparing for and experiencing battle, as well as the plight of American prisoners of war in the Revolutionary War. A thumb's up for a work of fiction that might easily be confused with a historian's account of the ordeal of George Washington's soldiers.

—**John Ferling**, author of *Apostles of Revolution: Jefferson, Paine, Monroe and the Struggle against the Old Order in America and Europe* (2018)

A fitting continuation of Ms. Price Janney's charming story lines, that weave together modern and Revolutionary War Easton. Brings to life the issues of both times—complete with a battle scene not-to-be-missed!

—**Richard F. Hope**, Historian, *Author of Easton, PA: A History*

Janney's love for American and Pennsylvania history shines through every page of Easton at the Crossroads to enrich this story of intrigue and overcoming false accusations on the journey to true freedom. This gentle read interweaves past and present to craft a story that makes you feel as if you've come home to Easton, even if you've never been there before.

—Marlo Schalesky, award-winning author of *Reaching for Wonder*, Executive Director, Wonder Wood Ranch.

Rebecca Price Janney's *Easton at the Crossroads* grabs you with wonderful detail, transporting you from her heroine's new home to a fledgling country seeking its independence. Janney has told a story of lives that parallel and is sure to satisfy both the contemporary and historical reader.

—Debbie Lynne Costello, author of the #1 Amazon bestseller, *Sword of Forgiveness*, a medieval romance, and two other series.

Easton at the Crossroads is a fascinating and fast-paced historical novel that provides the reader with an accurate and personal view of members of Easton's Revolutionary community. The juxtaposition of well-developed local historical people with 21st century Easton citizens provides the reader with local color and allows one to see the impact 18th century heroes have upon their descendants.

—J. Michael Dowd, Senior Pastor, First U.C.C., Easton, PA (formerly the German Reformed Church)

Easton at the CROSSROADS

The *Easton* Series
—Book Three

Rebecca Price Janney

Elk Lake
PUBLISHING, INC.
PLYMOUTH, MASSACHUSETTS

Cover Design: Jeff Gifford
Photography: Paul Stikwerda, Randy Janney
Interior Design: Derinda Babcock
Editor: Deb Haggerty
Published in Association with WordWise Literary Services.

PUBLISHED BY: Elk Lake Publishing, Inc., 35 Dogwood Dr., Plymouth, MA 02360

Library Cataloging Data
Names: Janney, Rebecca Price (Rebecca Price Janney)
Easton at the Crossroads. The Easton Series—Book Three / Rebecca Price Janney
262 p. 23cm × 15cm (9in × 6 in.)
Description:
Identifiers: ISBN-13: 978-1-948888-02-8 (trade)
| 978-1-948888-03-5 (POD) | 978-1-948888-04-2 (e-book.)
Key Words: History, Revolutionary War, Pennsylvania, Colonial America, Genealogy, Ancestors, DAR.
LCCN: 2018938426 Fiction

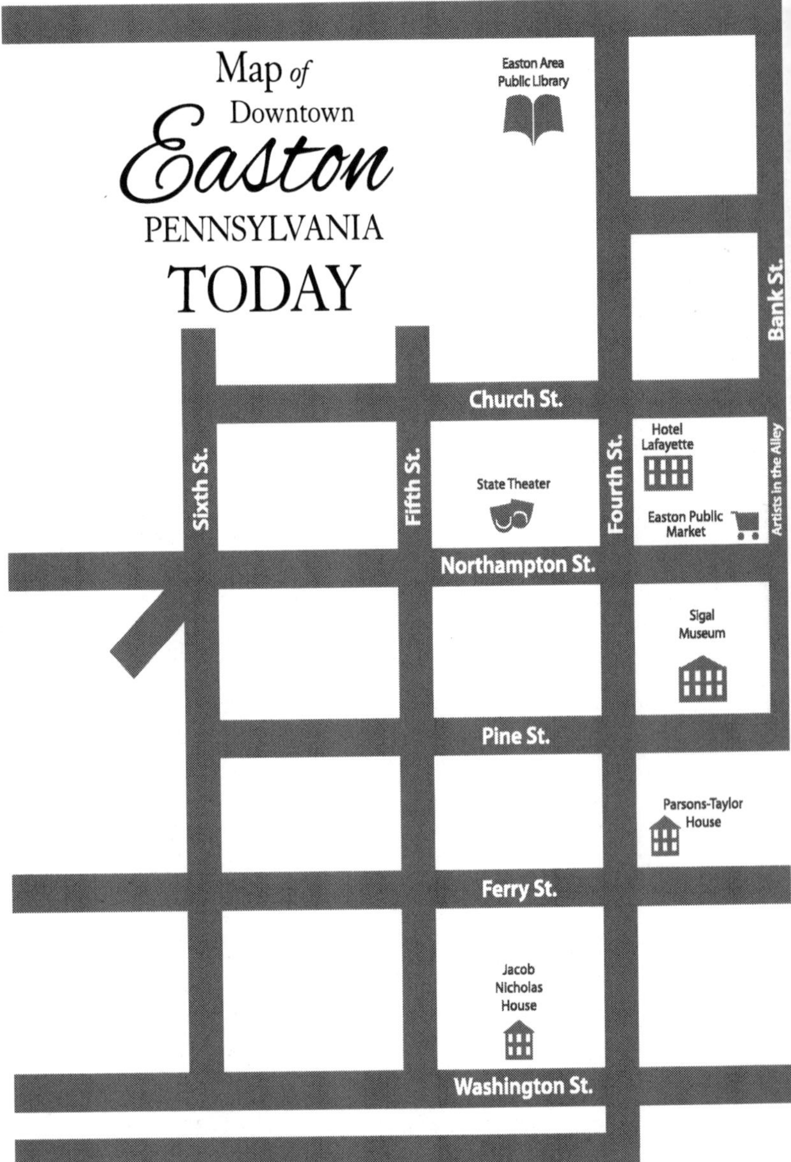

Map of
Downtown
Easton
PENNSYLVANIA
TODAY
Easton Area
Public Library
Bank St.
Church St.
Hotel
Lafayette
Sixth St.
Fifth St.
State Theater
Fourth St.
Easton Public
Market
Artists in the Alley
Northampton St.
Sigal
Museum
Pine St.
Parsons-Taylor
House
Ferry St.
Jacob
Nicholas
House
Washington St.
Lehigh River

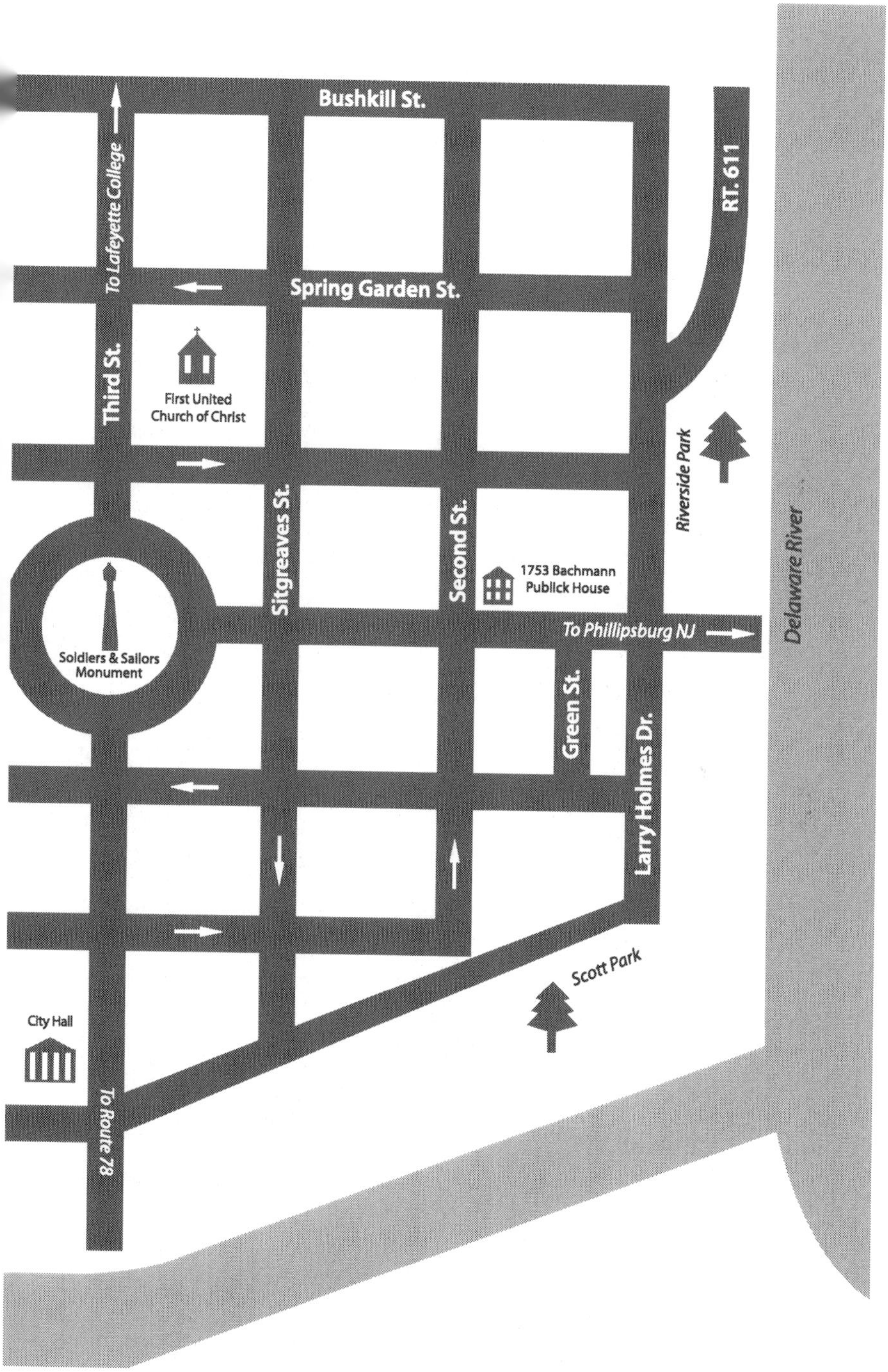

Bushkill St.

To Lafeyette College

RT. 611

Spring Garden St.

Third St.

First United
Church of Christ

Riverside Park

Sitgreaves St.

Second St.

1753 Bachmann
Publick House

Delaware River

Soldiers & Sailors
Monument

To Phillipsburg NJ

Green St.

Larry Holmes Dr.

Scott Park

City Hall

To Route 78

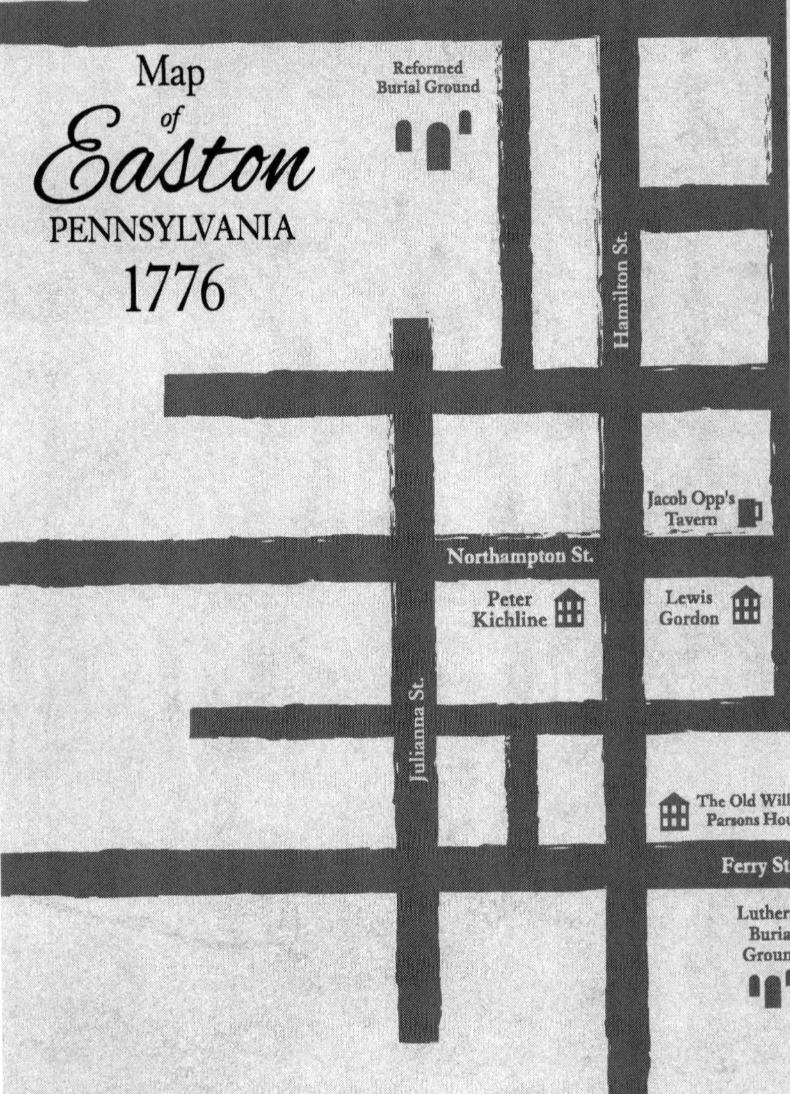

Map
of
Easton
PENNSYLVANIA
1776
Reformed
Burial Ground
Hamilton St.
Jacob Opp's
Tavern
Northampton St.
Peter
Kichline
Lewis
Gordon
Julianna St.
The Old Willi
Parsons Hou
Ferry St.
Luthera
Burial
Groun
Lehigh River

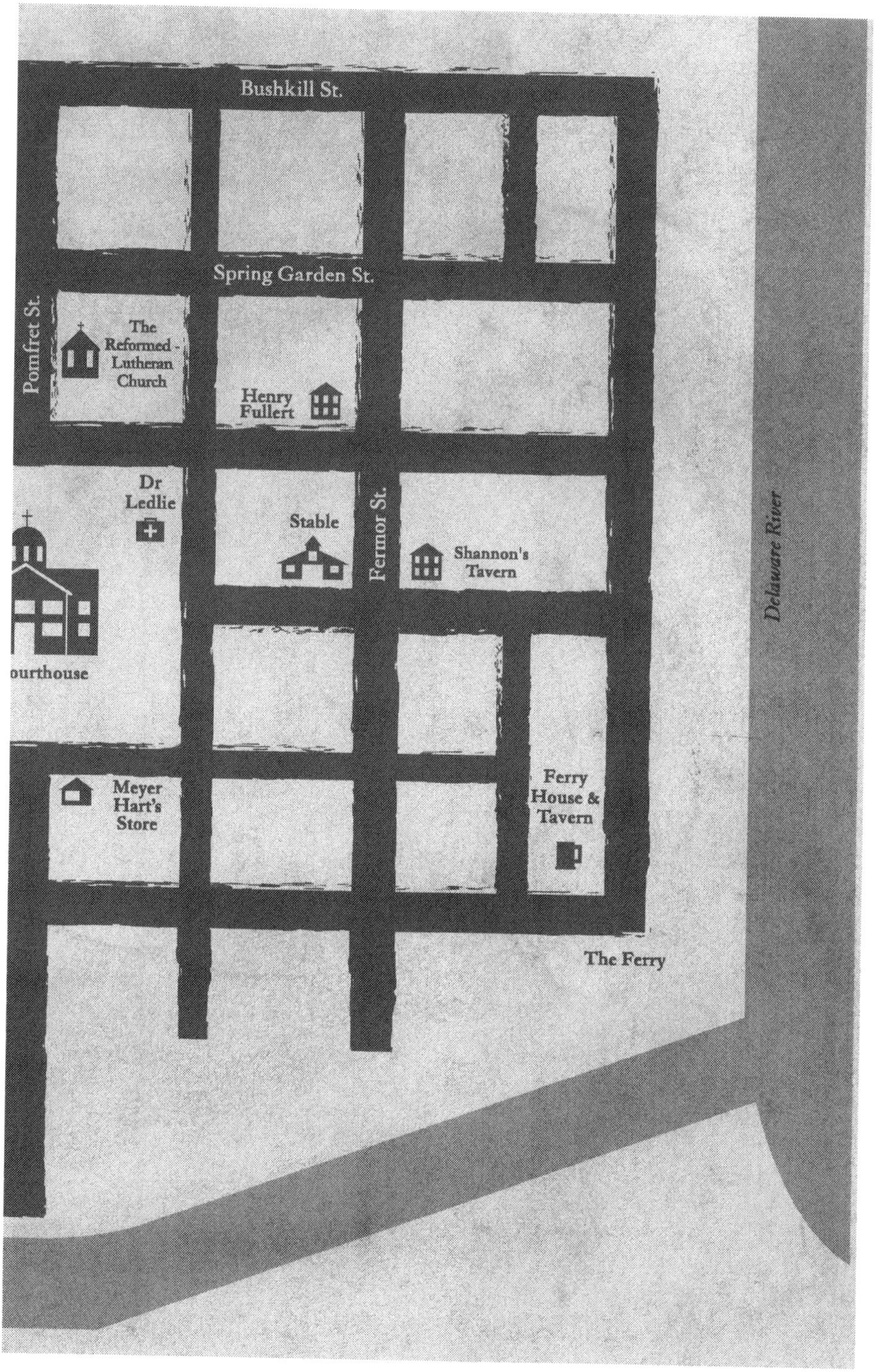

Bushkill St.

Spring Garden St.

Pomfret St.

The Reformed - Lutheran Church

Henry Fullert

Dr Ledlie

Stable

Fermor St.

Shannon's Tavern

Delaware River

ourthouse

Meyer Hart's Store

Ferry House & Tavern

The Ferry

"In you our ancestors put
their trust;
They trusted and you
delivered them.
To you they cried out and
were saved;
in you they trusted and
were not put to shame."
Psalm 22:4-5 (NIV)

Dedication

For those who served in the Northampton County Flying Camp,

and their descendants—

"O beautiful for heroes proved

In liberating strife,

Who more than self their country loved,

And mercy more than life!"

Acknowledgments

Writing this book has been a source of tremendous joy for me, as well as a great honor. Like my fictional character, Erin Miles, I am awed by the sacrifices the people of Easton made during the American Revolution. My gratitude especially goes to the men of the Northampton County, Pennsylvania, Flying Camp, commanded by my six times great-grandfather, Colonel Peter Kichline. They endured great hardship and loss to win freedom for their families, friends, and the generations who would come after them.

If Peter Kichline could read *Easton at the Crossroads*, I would hope he could look beyond any errors I've made to see my purpose, which was to present him and his men with the honor they so deserve. For the facts I did get straight, I have many people to thank:

◊ My dear and most helpful friends, Christopher Black, Richard Hope, Sharon Gothard, and Kichline cousin Miles Dechant.

◊ Katherine Ludwig, Librarian of the David Library of the American Revolution.

◊ Historian and author Dr. John Ferling.

◊ Brittany L. Merriam, Curator, Northampton County Historical and Genealogical Society.

◊ My friend, Paul Strikwerda, for his great cover photo of Peter Kichline and the Northampton Street Bridge.

◊ Ellis Finger, *mein lieber Deutscher* Professor.

I would also like to thank Carey Birgell, Executive Director of the NCHGS; my editor, publisher, and "sister," Deb Haggerty; my darling husband, Scott, beloved son, David—and devoted Perry, who stands vigil while I write. I'm also thankful for my "Street Team" and dedicated readers, who keep asking for more stories about Peter and Erin.

Chapter One

Ethan seemed to be taking an undue amount of time in his new bathroom. He'd run the water in the shower, though briefly, followed by a ten-minute lull, as if he were observing a long moment of silence for the dirt he'd apparently scrubbed away. Was he brushing his teeth? Washing his face? She strained to hear, wishing for a moment her ears had the capacity, if not the size, of her bassett hound. Just how long did a ten-year-old boy need to get ready for bed? She'd been more hands on in Ethan's earlier years, when a mother's touch was still necessary in the lav, but then Jim had taken over, guiding their son into a modicum of independence. A year-and-a-half later, Erin was still figuring out this part of being both mom and dad. Back home, she'd let her son pretty much do his own thing, except for insisting he wash his hair at least every other night and brush his teeth for as long as he took to sing "Three Blind Mice" in his head. But this was now. A new home, a new start.

She sat stroking her dog's back on the edge of the blow-up mattress in the room her cousin Laura had occupied four decades ago. Erin vaguely remembered photos of horses interspersed with images from *Tiger Beat* magazine covering the walls as well as the sliding closet door. She was a little kid when Laura had worked through a series of crushes on the Davids—Jones, Cassidy, and Soul—all of which had seemed very grownup to Erin. Now, the room featured Crayola Blue paint and glow-in-the-dark stars winking from the ceiling with a border of soccer balls thanks to her brother's efforts. Ethan had eclectic interests.

She gazed out the window into the emerging late-summer night wishing the new blinds could've been in place by now. She wondered if the glow of streetlights would keep Ethan awake. Another kind of glow warmed her, settling into her shoulders. After three weeks of living in separate places,

Erin was at last reunited with her son. Because she was renting her Lansdale home, there'd been no settlement date to delay her move. She did, however, need all of August and the first week in September to clear out and pack twenty years' worth of possessions. Unfortunately, Ethan had been required to report for the start of sixth grade in Easton on August 28th, the same day her classes began at Lafayette.

Erin didn't mind commuting to Easton for the initial two weeks of teaching on Mondays, Wednesdays, and Fridays, but Ethan had to be at school by 8:03 every morning. When she considered the amount of stress and effort involved in getting him up at five a.m. to drive an hour to school in heavy traffic, then bringing him home again after three o'clock, she dismissed such a plan as cruel and unusual for her son's inaugural days of middle school.

Enter Alana and Neal. When Erin's brother Allen told his oldest daughter what Erin and Ethan were up against, Alana texted her aunt. *Neal and I would like to have Ethan stay with us until you move to Easton. It just makes sense! Zoe will be in eighth grade this year, and she's on the same schedule at the same school as Ethan. They can ride the bus in the morning, and since she stays for field hockey after school, I can either pick him up, or he can take the bus. I'll be home from work by three each day, so he won't be alone. Neal likes this idea, and so do Zoe and Charlie, who would love to share his room with his cousin for a few weeks. Please say yes!*

Erin had said a very grateful "yes," although she disliked the idea of being separated from Ethan for the start of middle school. He already didn't have a dad, and now, his mom wouldn't be there. During that time, she had at least been able to pick Ethan up at school on Mondays and Wednesdays, and though she planned to take him back with her to Lansdale on weekends, he balked. "I want to stay with my cousins," he'd said. "We're going to the Farmers' Market and a hay ride and to pick pumpkins." Although she'd hated to admit to such a feeling, Erin was relieved to be able to pack up two decades' worth of memories without interruptions. She'd also indulged in a good cry when she found two unused boxes of Pyrex she and Jim had received for wedding gifts, and the time she opened a box full of cards he'd sent her over the years, tied with a fraying red ribbon.

She emerged from her reverie when the bathroom door finally opened. Accompanied by a veil of steam, Ethan trotted into the room in Avengers pajamas, hair sopping wet—the part and sides at cross-purposes.

"Hey, Toby, old boy." He bent over to pet his dog, scratching a certain spot which resulted in the rhythmic thumping of the dog's right rear leg. "Can he still sleep with me, Mom?"

Erin had hoped for the company of her good dog tonight, but of course, Ethan needed Toby more. "You bet." He crawled under a sheet and comforter, which spilled over the low mattress onto the carpeted floor. Then he patted the side of the bed for Toby, who lumbered up next to him. Erin held her breath, wondering whether the whole thing might cave in on itself, or Toby's nails might puncture the mattress.

"So, all the furniture is coming tomorrow?" Ethan asked.

"All the furniture is coming tomorrow."

"Including my bed?"

"Including your bed and your dressers and the new couch."

He smiled. "I really like that couch."

"Me too." She smoothed back his bangs.

He simultaneously yawned and asked, "When are the movers coming?"

"First thing in the morning. They put everything from our old house onto the truck yesterday, and they'll be here early tomorrow to unload." Her mind wandered as she struggled to remember whether she'd labeled the kitchen boxes or not. Would she be able to find her new spoonula and Grammy Ott's mixer? Her dear friend Melissa and mother-in-law Pat had packed the kitchen, both of them promising to put everything in a similar order at the new house. Maybe she'd go downstairs and put sticky notes on cabinets and drawers to show where various items belonged. Ethan was saying something, but Erin hadn't heard a word. "Sorry, hon, I was daydreaming."

"How can you daydream at night?"

She gave his arm a little shove. "I can daydream anywhere, at anytime. It's a gift." She was surprised when Ethan blew a large bubble. "Are you chewing gum?" She didn't wait for an answer. "Get back in the bathroom and brush your teeth."

"I already did. Then I put the gum back in."

She pointed toward the bathroom. "March."

"Heck, Mom, I hated to waste the gum," Ethan said after returning. "Grammy Audrey always puts hers on the side of her plate while she eats so she can keep chewing afterward."

Don't remind me. "Yes, and Grammy Audrey has false teeth. Do you want false teeth?" She mussed up his hair.

Ethan laughed as he hunkered down under the covers. "You're funny, Mom. Why does she save her gum anyway? Is she poor?"

"No, she's not poor." She looked up at the ceiling, thoughtful. "When she was growing up, though, people didn't have as much as we do now, not as many things anyway. They tended to hold on to what they had longer."

Ethan's eyes suddenly opened wide, and he pulled the comforter up to just below them. "What was that noise?"

Erin listened, hearing a clunk, then a low hum, as if the house were a band warming up. "That's the air-conditioning unit. We're going to be hearing all kinds of new sounds as we get used to the house." She looked down at him. "Are you sure you're okay in here tonight? You could stay in my room if you like."

He twisted the side of his mouth. "Mother, I am not a baby."

"You are not. You also have Sir Toby to protect you. Do you want to read a little before you go to sleep?"

"Um, Mom, would you mind reading out loud—you know, like we always did in the old house?" He reached into his LL Bean backpack and produced a dog-eared copy of Redwall.

Erin smiled to herself. He wasn't such a big kid after all. Not just yet. "I would love to!" *Then we'll say ours prayers, and I'll go to my new room and collapse—after I put those sticky notes in the kitchen, and maybe grab a snack. Then I'll try to get some sleep.*

♛

She stood before the cream-colored cabinets studying the red notes which gave them the appearance of a medieval pox. Smiling, she reached into the Igloo cooler she'd brought from Lansdale and located a half-eaten tub of kalamata hummus, dripping from a leaky bag of ice. She rummaged through her purse and found a flattened chocolate mint protein bar under the house and car keys, and tearing off the wrapper, dipped the bar into the hummus. Erin carried the snack into the living room where she studied what appeared to be the half-moon's reflection on the Delaware about a hundred feet below her College Hill home. In several weeks, leaves would no longer obscure the vibrant view, a prospect she very much looked forward to, just as she had when she was a little girl coming to this house to visit her aunt.

She scooped out the last of the hummus, put the empty container on a windowsill, and made her way upstairs. Tomorrow would be here soon enough.

Erin slowly emerged from a cloud of sleep, incorporating her cellphone alarm's relentless buzzing into her present surroundings. Fumbling, she finally located the device under an excess of covers on the floor down by her feet. She snatched the phone, and when she tried to sit up, the air mattress gave a small bounce, nearly catapulting her across the room. She slid her finger across the screen to silence the bell and lay back against the wall, gathering her thoughts into a manageable basket. This was her aunt and uncle's former bedroom. She was no longer in Lansdale. Glancing around, she noted this room was a tad smaller than the one she'd shared with Jim. So was the master bath, but as she'd told herself several times, there'd be less cleaning to do.

Her phone informed her the time was five-thirty. She needed to be showered and dressed in an hour since the movers had said they'd be there as early as seven o'clock, maybe before. She would let Ethan sleep until six and in the meantime, dig up the donuts and juice pouches she'd bought at Wawa the day before. She had also brought her Keurig with the last car load from Lansdale, because there was no way she could face this day without java. She carefully rose from the bouncy bed, took a shower, and put on a pair of shorts with an Easton Middle School tee shirt. She decided minimal jewelry would work best today—her watch, a pair of medium-sized hoop earrings, her grandmother's small locket. Looking down at her wedding band, she paused. *I don't want to lose any of the stones. I'll just put the ring in my suitcase for today.* She nestled the gold band in a side pocket next to her engagement ring, which she always removed before bedtime.

While walking down the hall to get Toby from Ethan's room, she heard someone at the front door. *That couldn't be the movers already!* She peered over the railing and saw the back of someone go down the porch steps, get into a silver SUV and drive away, smoke from the tailpipe softly catching the morning mist. *The paper boy maybe? Did I even order the paper?*

Erin quietly opened Ethan's door and found Toby waiting for her, his eyes large with purpose. "C'mon, old boy. I'll take you out." He thumped beside her down the carpeted stairs, and Erin found his leash by the front entrance. When she unlocked the door to take him out, she found a square basket the size of a laundry hamper on the porch.. Inside, she discovered warm muffins and bagels, containers of cream cheese and butter, and a half-pound of crisp bacon wrapped in foil. To the side of the hamper was a box of coffee from a donut shop.

"Amazing!" She looked at Toby. "Who could have brought this?" Immediately, her mind ran to Paul, but would a guy have put together such a breakfast using layers of bright pink tissue paper and a matching bow tied to the handle? Not likely. Looking closer, she found a small card attached to some ribbon. "Welcome home, Erin and Ethan!"

Chapter Two

February 10, 1776

As thin sunlight retreated to the west, the wind rose, then hovered and swooped onto Easton's shivering villagers completing their Saturday marketing. There was something almost personal about the way this gale pursued the Forks of the Delaware's inhabitants. *Frau* Fartenius pressed her small *Tochter* against her legs as they hobbled home in tandem, their full basket swaying in the wind.

"*Guten abend*, Colonel Kichline!"

He stopped to tip his tricorn hat with a bow. "*Frau* Fartenius. *Fraulein* Maria." Since Elizabeth understood a little English, and he had wanted to encourage this, he asked slowly, "May I assist you?"

"No, *danke*." She smiled through cracked lips. "We hurry to house!" And she was off, the wind at least blowing her and her daughter in the general direction of their home.

To most of the Germans in Easton, Peter Kichline stood tall, and not just literally. He'd built a bridge over the Bushkill Creek, served as Northampton County Sheriff—twice—helped found Easton's first school, and erected its first dedicated church edifice. He'd also fought in the French and Indian War, acted as Justice of the Court of Common Pleas and Quarter Sessions, served on the Committee of Observation, the Pennsylvania Provincial Convention, and the Pennsylvania Assembly. Now, he worked as colonel in charge of the Northampton County militia.

He enjoyed the high esteem in which the Germans of this adolescent town held him, always mindful of his mother's continual counsel over the years, "To whom much is given, is much required." He had much, and he gave much, desirous to elevate the condition of the Palatine German community, the majority of Easton's citizenry. Many who came from English and Scotch-Irish descent, who made up the political and social establishment, looked unfavorably upon the *Deutsch*. Across more than two decades, Peter had encouraged German literacy, so his people could prosper in this new world where old barriers were constantly being challenged. Every week, he'd taken his Philadelphia newspapers to the courthouse where villagers could increase their reading skills while keeping up on current events. Many German families had taken what advantage they could of the school and the periodicals. Others couldn't afford to have their sons and daughters learn about Milton and Shakespeare when they were needed to provide labor for family farms and businesses.

Peter glanced at what remained of the small bundle he held carefully in his gloved hands. He'd spent the better part of the afternoon distributing a remarkable new pamphlet to the taverns and businesses, and his last stop would be the courthouse. While he looked forward to seeing his old friend Ziba Wiggins, his chest swelled at the prospect of his own hearth and his family's company.

He nodded and greeted a handful of other townspeople, then walked past the pond, which had congealed into a dark mass of frozen animal dung. He carefully avoided a pile of fresh sheep manure from which steam ascended. As if he'd been anticipating the visit, Ziba Wiggins opened the door and admitted Peter, who was at the gate.

"Hello, my friend! Come in out of this cold." Wiggins glanced at the sky which featured clouds so low they almost could be touched. He held his fist at the crook of his back. "My bones tell me we're going to have another storm."

Peter entered, closing the door against the wind. "I wasn't sure if I'd find you still here."

"I was just about to close up for the night. My good woman has promised me pepper pot, and I'm more than ready for my supper."

He grinned. "She makes a wonderful pepper pot. I'm not going to keep you." He handed two of the pamphlets to Wiggins. "These have recently arrived from Philadelphia, and I believe they're as important to distribute as any newspaper I've ever shared."

Wiggins read aloud, *Common Sense*. He looked up at Peter—way up. "What exactly is this?"

"This is a wonderful case for why the colonies should be independent from Great Britain. Beautifully written, highly logical."

"I believe Mr. Levers was talking about this at the tavern."

Peter nodded. "When I read the copy he brought up from Philadelphia, I was so moved I decided to purchase more to distribute throughout the village. Every citizen should read this to better understand the course we've been taking and where we are heading."

Wiggins pursed his lips, nodding. "*Common Sense,* eh? Do you mind if I take one home to read while I'm having my supper? I know you said my good wife has a copy at the tavern, but by now, people are probably borrowing it."

"Not at all, Mr. Wiggins, and thank you."

He made a "no problem" sign with his hand. As Peter turned to leave, Wiggins spoke up. "Uh, Colonel Kichline, if you would please let me have a word before you go."

"Yes, of course." He studied the earnest face, the encroaching wrinkles and nearly-gray hair.

"I've been thinking about something. Do you believe … that is, does it make sense … oh, I might as well just say what I need to say." He shook his head, then met Peter's eyes. "I want to do my part, to join the, uh, militia, that is, if you think I'm not too old."

Peter winked. "Ziba Wiggins, do you think I am too old to lead the militia?"

He drew himself back. "Why, certainly not! You're in the prime of life, sir!"

"If I understand correctly, you're a few years younger than my fifty-three."

The keeper of the courthouse's face brightened.

"Although I believe you have answered your own question, you are already serving by all you do right here. No one could easily replace you if you were needed in the field of battle."

Wiggins leaned his head to one side. "Then I just don't know."

Every time he came through the door, without fail *Frau* Hamster appeared, her timing certain and precise. Joe was always right behind, mimicking the old woman's footsteps and gestures as he continued finding his place in the Kichline household.

"Good evening, *Frau* Hamster." He smiled as she accepted his hat.

The tiny woman bowed her head and deftly passed the object to Joe. "*Bürsten Sie den Schnee vom Hut.*"

Joe's shoulders straightened. "*Ja*, ma'am!" He hurried down the hallway for a brush to clean the snow from Peter's hat.

He shrugged out of his coat, feeling the heavy wool slip into the *Hausälterin's* bony hands. "*Vielen dank.*"

"*Bitte.*"

The house smelled of burning wood tinged with the fragrance of beeswax candles, accented by cinnamon-laced *apfel* cider. Sniffing, he detected something else, like burnt milk, which was odd since the women in his family were excellent cooks, every one of them. Maybe he was smelling tobacco and wondered if they had a visitor, perhaps Robert Traill or Nicholas Tatamy, whom he was hoping to see soon. He could hear the hesitant cadence of a man reading aloud in the parlor, William perhaps. Susannah had been teaching him to read and write, so when he finally became free, William could get on in life. Peter regretted not being able to imbibe of this domestic ambrosia more frequently, but he wouldn't fill his spirit with laments, he'd just enjoy his family, including his beloved Catherine, who matched the cheering fire glow-for-glow.

"Good evening, husband. Did I hear something about snow?" She dropped her knitting into her lap, still holding the needles.

"Yes, my dear. I got home a few steps ahead of what promises to be a heavy storm."

He kissed her cheek, then greeted the others. "Susannah, dear. Jacob." He felt momentarily baffled—when had Jacob begun smoking a pipe? How old was he? Peter quickly calculated—nearly eighteen. For the life of him, he didn't know how such a thing was possible.

"Hello, Phoebe. How are you feeling today?"

His niece smiled as she ran her right hand over her enlarged abdomen. "I'm doing well, Uncle Peter."

"Very good. Has there been any word from your William?"

"Yes, he's told me our new home will be across the river in Greenwich, near the largest of the churches we're serving." She burped, giggled, and flushed. "Do pardon me. He's been able to get the foundation laid, and perhaps during the slower times this winter, he can complete the inside. He said to tell you how grateful he is for letting me stay here until the baby comes."

"You may stay as long as you need to, my dear. Let your family and Dr. Ledlie look after you." He didn't know how much Phoebe was aware of the controversial physician's private life, so he checked his own opinion at the threshold of their conversation. Andrew Ledlie may not have been a paragon of virtue, but he was a good doctor. Of course, Phoebe might only need a midwife, but just in case, Ledlie was available.

Jacob looked up, just barely, from his own copy of *Common Sense*. "Hello, Father."

"Hello, son." He nodded toward the pamphlet. "Are you enjoying your reading?"

"Very much." All the weight of his convictions seemed to hang on those two simple words.

"Papa, this writer makes such strong arguments for independence." Susannah pointed to her own pamphlet. Then she turned to the man sitting next to her, a slave Peter had rescued from the block the previous year. "William has been reading aloud for us. He's come such a long way in his study of English." She beamed in his direction, and Peter saw William's cheeks redden.

"You and Mistress Catherine are good teachers."

"And you are a fast learner," Catherine said.

"Well, then, let me hear what you're reading." Peter eased himself into his favorite chair, feeling the fire's warmth seep slowly into his chilled body. When he'd retired from his second term as Sheriff of Northampton County two years ago, he'd expected to be in just this position more often. Then duty called, and he knew he couldn't be selfish enough to sit around his hearth and his mills just when the fledgling nation needed him the most.

When William opened his mouth and nothing came out, Peter encouraged him. "Do continue, son. I've been out all afternoon and would like to hear you read."

"Yes, sir." William cleared his throat, ran a finger down the right side of the page he'd been reading from and took up the story where he'd left off. "No man was a warmer wisher for a re, re ..."

Susannah looked over his shoulder. "Reconciliation."

"Re-con-cil-i-a-tion than myself, before the fatal nine-teenth of April, 1775, but the moment the event of that day was made known, I re-jected the hardened, sul-len-tempered Pha-raoh of England for ever; and dis-dis-disdain the wretch, that with the pretended title of FATHER OF HIS PEOPLE can un-feel-ing-ly hear of their, their …"

"Slaughter," Susannah said.

"… slaughter, and com-pos-ed-ly sleep with their blood upon his soul." William plodded through the text as if it were covered in molasses.

Peter saw Jacob nod in agreement, his eyes as tightly fixed as his jaw. When William paused, Phoebe spoke up. "Uncle Peter, can there be reconciliation, or do you think most people believe as this writer does?"

Susannah interrupted. "Who, by the way, is the author?"

He looked into the fire, then at his niece. "There certainly is no shortage of opinions. Even in Pennsylvania, some still agree with the Assembly's efforts at trying to resolve our differences peacefully." He thought back to recent boisterous sessions he'd attended as a member of that body.

"Who are those people?" Phoebe asked.

"The Assembly is Quaker-dominated, and Pennsylvanians who came from England and Scotland tend to side with them."

"Yes, Father, but there are also Germans who disagree with our quest for independence—Moravians and Mennonites."

"You're right, of course, Jacob." Peter leaned more deeply into his chair, allowing his muscles to relax after a long day in the saddle and on foot. When Frau Hamster appeared with a mug of hot cider on a small tray, he gratefully accepted her offering. Catherine moved her chair several inches away. "Does the smell bother you, my dear?"

"I'm afraid so, but do have your drink. You must be half frozen."

He reached out and patted her hand. "As for the Germans who are reluctant to break away from the Crown, the Moravians and Mennonites would like there to be a peaceful solution to the conflict. Regarding other Germans who disagree with our push for self-determination …" Peter shrugged. "Many of them have enjoyed a peaceful lifestyle since they left the homeland with its wars and religious oppression. They signed an oath of loyalty to the Crown and don't believe they should renege."

"Father, listen to this," Jacob said. Lifting the pamphlet he read:

> And when a man seriously reflects on the idolatrous homage which is paid to the persons of kings, he need not wonder that the Almighty, ever jealous of his honour, should disapprove of a form of

> government which so impiously invades the prerogative of heaven ... The children of Israel being oppressed by the Midianites, Gideon marched against them with a small army, and victory, through the divine interposition, decided in his favour. The Jews, elate with success, and attributing it to the generalship of Gideon, proposed making him a king, saying, RULE THOU OVER US, THOU AND THY SON AND THY SON'S SON. Here was temptation in its fullest extent; not a kingdom only, but an hereditary one, but Gideon in the piety of his soul replied, I WILL NOT RULE OVER YOU, NEITHER SHALL MY SON RULE OVER YOU. Words need not be more explicit; Gideon doth not decline the honour, but denieth their right to give it; neither doth he compliment them with invented declaration of his thanks, but in the positive style of a prophet charges them with disaffection to their proper Sovereign, the King of heaven.

Peter nodded, sipping the hot beverage, letting the tankard warm his hands.

"I just want to read this other part too," Jacob said: "'That the Almighty hath here entered his protest against monarchical government, is true, or the Scripture is false ... For monarchy in every instance is the Popery of government.'"

Peter saw his daughter nodding in tandem, his good wife and niece sharing a glance of agreement.

Susannah asked once again, "Papa, who wrote this pamphlet?"

"No one knows, although I've heard some speculation Benjamin Franklin might be the author."

She frowned. "I've read his work, and he's more humorous than this."

Someone knocked at the front door, and Peter watched Frau Hamster trundle down the hall, Joe at her side. *Who in the world would be out on such a blustery evening?*

"Oh, Papa, I forgot to tell you, someone came here today looking for you," Susannah said. "He didn't give his name, but he was a stout German, and a farmer."

Peter nodded, then he, Jacob, and William rose when the housekeeper ushered a snow-dusted man into the parlor.

Susannah whispered behind her raised palm, "That's him."

"*Guten abend, Herr Kichline.*" The man did not offer his hand, but he took Peter's when extended. The farmer's words and manner were stiff, more required than genuine.

"*Guten abend.*"

"*Ich bin Stefanus Drunkenmiller.*"

Peter looked the man in the eye. *This could be trouble.*

Chapter Three

"Hey, lady, where do you want this desk?"

Erin saw the nose ring, stretched ear lobes, and a heavy eye piercing before she saw the mover. She sincerely hoped the trend to mutilate oneself would end before the next sighting of Halley's Comet. "What desk?"

He pointed an index finger downward. "This desk."

Obviously, she hadn't thought of everything. Even her extensive diagram showing the movers where every numbered and labeled box went, as well as every piece of furniture, had not been all-inclusive. She'd forgotten about the desk she'd bought for Ethan for his new computer, which would not go to his room behind closed doors where cyber bullies, violent video games, and predators could stalk him. No sirree Bob, as her Uncle Howard used to say. She could put the desk in the family room or living room. The family room could work if she weren't watching a cooking show or the latest episode of *Who Do You Think You Are?* while Ethan was trying to do homework. The living room could work rather nicely, quiet enough but not too private. The only thing was, she had already laid out the furniture scheme.

"Erin! Oh, there you are." Melissa appeared, her face shimmering from the heat. What use, though, was putting on the air conditioning with the doors constantly open for the movers? "I'm not sure where you want your measuring cups and bowls."

The pierced man's mouth shifted to the left, and he rolled his eyes, a look not lost on Erin.

"First, I need to make a decision about where to put this desk. I forgot to figure this in when I made my diagram."

"Oh, your diagram is amazing, like a floor plan you'd see in a home magazine. Did I tell you about the new issue of *Better Homes and Gardens?*

There's a really cool layout of a porch just like yours. I think I brought the issue with me, but I'm not sure because I was trying to remember to put garlic on my grocery list before I headed out this morning."

The mover's sigh might have been heard all the way to the Soldiers and Sailors Monument, and back again.

Melissa clapped her hand to her chest. "Oh, sorry! So, you need help positioning the desk."

"Yes. I think it should go in the living room, but where?"

"I agree. Let's go see."

"Bring the desk to the living room," Erin told the man, who followed her and Melissa. She did a quick survey and decided the desk might just fit along the wall running parallel to the stairs. "Try there," she said, pointing to the spot. The man placed the desk close to the railing, leaving too much wall showing. "I think you need to move it about four feet to the right." Erin tilted her head. "What do you think, Melissa?"

"I think so, , but a little more to the right would be more centered."

Erin nodded, the man obliged. "Perfect! Thanks." The guy headed toward the front door to bring in more furniture. She had a sudden remembrance of something her Grammy Ott used to say whenever Erin left for college in the fall, then came back home in the spring trailing boxes—"Movin' in, and movin' out!" Since no one else would understand except her mom, who was currently in the kitchen, she cherished the memory in her heart.

"So then, Erin, can you come to the kitchen and tell us where you want the measuring cups and bowls? Your mom and I think the Lazy Susan by the sink, but we're not sure from the way the box is labeled."

They were standing to the side of the entryway while three moving men blew by them with cartons whose contents caused the guys to bow slightly.

"Hey, lady, where do you want these books?"

Erin bit back a sarcastic retort. *Can't they read?* "In my office."

"We don't know where the office is."

"Behind the living room, to the right of the family room. There's a sign above every doorway saying which room is which."

"Guess we must've missed that."

"No problem." She turned to Melissa, who'd asked something about her measuring cups. As she opened her mouth, Paul Bassett appeared in the doorway wearing a Lafayette tee shirt and a pair of jeans. His ball cap read

"Lehigh Valley Iron Pigs." She wondered how he could manage to look crisp and put together with a heat index in the mid-90s?

"I brought someone with me," he said.

A man stepped into the hallway bearing a clipboard. "I have your washer and dryer from Tierson's Appliance."

"Oh, right!"

"Where do you want them?"

"In the laundry room, next to the garage. You can bring them through the garage. You're going to install them too, right?"

"No, ma'am. Just delivery."

"But I paid for installation." A sudden image of laundry rising to the height of the landfill off Route 78 sent her blood pressure off to the races.

The sandy-haired man consulted his work order while the movers staggered past them under the weight of Erin's personal library. "Sorry, but there's nothing about installation on here."

Where do you want the desk? Where should the measuring cups go? Where is the office? Where was the receipt for her washer and dryer in all this mess?

"Don't worry, Erin. I'll take care of this," Paul whispered. "Do you have the name of the salesperson on your receipt?" he asked the delivery man.

The guy reviewed the paper. "Hmmm, yeah."

"Well, let's just get out of the way here, to the porch. I'll call the store, and we'll confirm Dr. Miles paid for installation."

"Oh, sure."

Erin mouthed "Thank you."

"You're welcome," he mouthed back.

"Okay, so you want to know where to put my mixer," Erin said to Melissa.

"Not the mixer, the measuring cups and bowls."

"Right. I do know where they go."

They started down the hall, whose carpeting had been covered with a thick, clear runner. "When was the last time you had something to drink?"

Erin pursed her lips, which felt like sandpaper. "I can't remember."

"You, my friend, need a bottle of water with electrolytes. Come with me."

Erin grabbed a donut from the gift basket and, spying a packet of mayonnaise from a fast food restaurant, opened and squeezed the creamy insides onto the top of the chocolate glaze. Then she sprinkled some pepper on for good measure. She nearly choked when her mother pulled Erin's Wedgewood teapot out of a box and saw Melissa make a dive worthy of Greg Louganis for the top, which hung by a tiny piece of bubble wrap.

"Got it!" Melissa exclaimed. She put the small piece on the counter and exchanged a wide-eyed look with Erin.

Audrey held out the teapot. "What do I do with this?"

Erin put her donut down and took the valuable piece from her visually-impaired mother. "Thanks, Mom. The teapot belongs in the china cabinet."

"Okay. Maybe I should lay shelf paper in your cabinets." She glanced about her.

"Uh, Mom, I decided not to do shelf paper."

"Not do shelf paper? Everybody does shelf paper."

Maybe they did in the 70s. "Actually, Mom, shelf paper is pretty optional these days. I can keep my cabinets cleaner this way."

"I don't know how, but then I'm not up with these new-fangled ideas." Audrey shook her head.

Erin had a sudden glimpse of her Grammy Ott and wondered whether she, like Audrey, was destined to become her mother.

"Here you go, Mrs. Pelleriti," Melissa said. "Why don't you clean out the refrigerator? Mr. and Mrs. Miles are going to be here soon with the contents of Erin's fridge in Lansdale." She handed Audrey a roll of paper towels and a bottle of spray cleaner.

"What's this?"

"Spray cleaner and paper towels."

Audrey frowned. "In my day, we used rags and Mr. Clean in a good soapy bucket."

"This is Mr. Clean, just more convenient."

"Well, alright." Audrey opened the refrigerator door and started spraying and wiping. "Did I tell you, Erin, I talked to your cousins last week?"

"Yes, you did."

Audrey went on as if she hadn't heard. "They are absolutely thrilled you're living in their old house. Emma said she should come home and see the place."

"She's welcome to stay here," Erin said, trying to figure out when the last time was she'd seen her older cousin.

Audrey switched the subject. "Where's Ethan? I haven't seen him since he moved up here." She sounded like a wounded bird.

"He and Toby are with Alana until later this afternoon when things settle down."

"Will I get to see them?"

"Probably."

"Erin." Paul opened the door from the garage and peaked into the bustling kitchen. "Everything is straightened out. The salesman told the delivery guy you paid for installation."

"Oh, thank God! And thank you."

"I'm happy to help. Would you like me to stay with him—to oversee the process?"

"Would you please?"

He grinned and before disappearing called out, "Hello, Audrey!"

"Well, hello. Is that Allen?"

"No, it's Paul."

"Hello, Paul." When the door closed, Audrey said, "That is a nice man if I ever saw one. Are you two serious?"

"Mother!"

"Well, he certainly seems to have taken his place."

She felt like someone had stuffed her in a blender, hit "liquefy," and walked away to answer the door. Her thighs burned as if she'd had a hard workout and her sore back would've made an excellent subject for an infomercial.

"So, you went to church this morning?" her father asked across the table.

The waitress at his favorite South Main Street eatery had just taken their order, and Erin tried to keep her mouth shut. Her dad, who was supposed to be watching his cholesterol, had requested three eggs over easy, home fries, and a side of buttered toast.

"Yes, we went to the church Mom grew up in."

"The same church my seven times great-grandfather helped build," Ethan added, not a little too proudly.

Tony appeared not to have heard, staring toward a TV mounted on the back wall featuring a football pregame show. "So, how is your mother?"

"She's doing well, still adjusting to not driving."

"Her eyes are pretty bad, aren't they?"

"I'm afraid so."

A moment later. "Is that the church on North Third Street?"

"Yes." Erin moved back slightly when the waitress delivered their drinks.

"You know, that was a hospital for Revolutionary War soldiers."

"Uh, yes, I know." She'd told him the story of Peter Kichline before. *Wasn't he listening?*

"So, how did you like the church?"

"I liked being there." Sort of. Erin was thrilled to have sat in the same building where her mother, aunts, and uncles had gone and where generations of her family had worshiped over the course of four centuries. She imagined her "Grandfather Peter" sitting there, saying the same creeds, singing the same doxology. Then there was Beverly, who'd known her mother when they were young, and who'd encouraged Erin's spirit during a Heritage Day tour right after Jim's death. The pastor, of late middle age, had given a compelling sermon. Still, the choir was the size of a postage stamp. Erin was used to her Lansdale church where the pews held about two hundred people for each of two services, and Ethan's Sunday school class had enough kids to field a baseball team.

"How about you, Ethan?"

"It was okay, Pop Pop." Ethan shrugged.

"Just okay?" Tony sipped his coffee and leaned forward.

"Yeah. There were only four kids in Sunday School."

"Four kids?" He looked at Erin. "Don't many people go there?"

"Not too many, Dad, maybe fifty all told." *Maybe more like thirty-five.*

"That used to be a big church. What happened?"

She drank a swig of iced tea, put the glass back down. "I really don't know."

"Do you think you'll be staying there?"

She wanted to say "yes." She'd been counting on going to the church of her ancestors and taking her and Ethan's places among the generations. The truth was, she didn't know. The experience hadn't been what she'd expected.

She woke up in her own bed at six on Monday morning, pleased by the general absence of kinks and soreness. Over the weekend, she'd managed to hang some pictures, and thanks to a lot of help, the ubiquitous boxes had been emptied to a manageable level. Allen and Tanya had come by Sunday afternoon, and her brother had broken down the empty containers in the garage while her sister-in-law put up window treatments. The house was looking amazingly settled. A few more pictures here and putting items away there, and she'd be completely moved in.

After taking a shower, she dressed, then went to her jewelry box where her wedding ring glimmered in the light from the overhead fixture. *I'm starting a new chapter in my life. I wonder if now is the time to keep this here. How does anyone know when to stop wearing a wedding ring? Are there any rules or guidelines?* She slipped the ring onto her finger.

She finished getting ready and went to Ethan's room to wake him. "Hey, Toby." She patted the dog on the head. "Good morning, Ethan. Time to get up!" She kissed him on the forehead and opened the blinds, which had arrived on Saturday. What a manic day that had been!

"Hi, Mom."

She stood by his bed. "Did you sleep well?"

"Uh-huh." He yawned wide enough to swallow his pillow.

"Are you ready for school?"

"I think so."

She realized she didn't even know if he liked middle school, if he'd made any friends, or how he felt about riding a new bus. There just hadn't been time for a heart-to-heart talk. She would make time at dinner tonight. As for herself, she was the new kid at school as well, still getting used to the other professors and her students. One in particular. She knew the saying was cliché, but entering Ramer History House, she felt like Dorothy Gale in the *Wizard of Oz* after she was swirled away from Kansas.

Chapter Four

Frau Hamster held her hands out to receive the large man's cloak, but his back was turned to her. Peter guessed she'd tried to take his coat in the hallway, and this was a second attempt. When she glanced up at Peter, he nodded a dismissal then watched her and Joe retreat down the hall.

Peter motioned toward the parlor. "*Bitte, nehmen Sie Platz?*

The man shook his head, clearly uninterested in taking a seat. He addressed Peter in broken English. "Vat I haf to say can be standing said. I haf waited all the day to see you."

"Very well." Peter crossed his arms and stood straighter, feeling a small popping at the base of his spine. Although the man outweighed him, Peter had the usual advantage of height. He wasn't afraid he and the farmer would come to blows, but he anticipated an unpleasant encounter just the same—in fact, had wondered why this hadn't happened earlier.

"You may be a powerful *mann* in this county, but you haf no right to take a man's son from him."

"Your son came to us of his own accord."

Jacob appeared, stepping next to his father.

"Jacob, this is Herr Drunkenmiller frm Lower Saucon. His son has joined the militia." As Peter spoke, his gaze remained firmly on the farmer.

"My son does not his own mind know."

"Are you sure you wouldn't like to sit down, *Herr* Drunkenmiller?"

"Wouldn't you like some hot apple cider?" Catherine asked, standing next to her husband.

"*Nein, dank*. This vill not take long."

This was one stubborn Dutchman.

"Your son has strong convictions," Peter said, "like yourself." When Drunkenmiller opened his mouth, Peter raised a hand. "I am not finished, sir. You raised him to have the courage of his convictions. Unfortunately, they are not your own in the matter of the current conflict between the colonies and Great Britain. You can still be proud of him for his strength of character."

The man's nostrils flared, and a small amount of snot dripped from his nose onto his boots. "I do not call walking away from ze faith any kindt of courage."

"Your son has proven to be a fine Christian man and a credit to my unit."

The large cheeks, already red from the cold, purpled. "He has no business engaging in var. Ve are a peaceful people who seek with all men harmony, to preserve life, not take it."

"I, too, was hopeful our problems could be solved without taking up guns and swords. My good sir, there are times when a man must defend his homeland and his family from aggressors."

"I cannot with you agree." Drunkenmiller took a deep breath. "My son iss very young, and I need him on the farm. When he iss not there to do ze verk, his family suffers. Does he not care for his own family?" He spoke the last words in staccato bursts. "Do you not care if my family suffers, you a family man?"

Peter noted the manner in which Drunkenmiller trickled a steady course of melting snow on the floorboards. Frau Hamster would not be pleased. "Kind sir, won't you please come in? You must be frozen."

"*Nein*. I must be to home."

Catherine spoke again, as if she were addressing their toddler. "But, sir, the storm is just beginning, and you have such a long way to go. You are very welcome to stay here." She looked at Peter. He noticed her slightly green shade, and suddenly, Drunkenmiller's presence faded in importance. "My good wife is right. You are very welcome to stay with us."

The Mennonite may have been a man of peace, but he was a force to be reckoned with. "I vill not in zis house stay aanother minute. I haf said my piece." He waggled his right forefinger at Peter. "You stay away from *mein* son!"

Catherine suddenly clasped her hand over her mouth and rushed out of the room. Drunkenmiller's eyes popped.

After she fled, Peter faced his adversary. "Won't you reconsider, sir? I don't want you to freeze to death."

"You control much in this county, but me you do not control." He turned swiftly on his heel and stomped out of the house into the swirling white gale.

"Father, what do you think will happen to him?" Jacob asked.

"I hope he has enough sense to stay at a tavern." He smiled to himself. *Andrew Drunkenmiller certainly has his father's fiery spirit.*

The others had retired, William bunking with Joe so he didn't need to venture to the saw mill house in the storm. As Peter reread parts of *Common Sense*, his eyelids kept closing until he found himself pulling up his head with a jerk. He glanced about the room, seeing Jacob bent over his own copy, his lithe body draped over the chair closest to the fire.

"Father? Are you awake?"

"Uh, yes, yes, of course." Peter sat up and pressed his shoulders against the top of the chair.

He tapped the booklet with the back of his right hand. "This is brilliant. I have read no better arguments for independence."

Andrew Drunkenmiller wasn't the only young man in Northampton County harboring strong beliefs. Peter studied his youngest son, whose profile mirrored his deceased mother's, albeit more masculine. He had a fine intellect, and Peter regretted not having sent him to Yale or the College of New Jersey to give him the benefit of his own Heidelberg education. For now, however, he was needed at home. The thought startled Peter into complete wakefulness. Maybe he wasn't so different from Stefanus Drunkenmiller.

"Come in, Colonel Kichline." John Van Etten welcomed him into his home. This had once been the tavern owned by his in-laws, the Lefevres, and he had welcomed Peter to gather there on county business. "Your friends are waiting for you."

"As always, I appreciate your hospitality."

"My wife has some refreshments for you. I'll leave you to your business."

"I am most grateful." Peter wondered at a certain stiffness in his friend's manner. Putting this aside, he turned to his other friends in the community north of Easton, who were drumming up militia enlistments and the acquisition of ammunition. This area wasn't nearly as challenging as the townships near Bethlehem where Moravians and Mennonites lived. He looked forward to hearing mostly positive news.

"Good day, Peter!" Caspar Doll rose from his chair, and they shook hands. "How was your journey?"

"Quite pleasant, thank you." He detected not only a fresh set of wrinkles around Doll's eyes, but something slightly off in his manner. "How is my good daughter, Sarah, and her Peter?"

"They are well and send their regards." He turned to John Arndt, leaning across the table to shake his hand. "Good day, Jacob."

"Good day, Peter. I am glad you came out today." He sat erect, not at his usual ease.

Why is he being so formal?

Doll continued talking about his daughter and son-in-law back in Easton. "I hear the fulling business is going well."

"Yes, and I'm also grateful he sometimes is able to help at the mills when we're especially busy."

"Have they any news yet?" Doll leaned closer, his eyes expectant.

Peter smiled. "Not yet, Caspar."

"I understand Catherine is with child," Arndt said. He looked up after Mrs. Van Etten had served mugs of hot cider and plates of pumpkin pie. "Thank you, dear lady."

The other men echoed their gratitude, and she blushed.

Peter responded to Arndt's earlier remark. "Yes, my wife is expecting and doing quite well."

"And Baby Elizabeth? Is she a year old yet?"

"A year and four months to be exact. She's learning to walk and getting into everything." He pictured her making a mad dash after a stray cat. The creature had wandered into the kitchen and when Elizabeth gave chase, the cat upset a bowl of porridge, which trickled down the girl's head and face like a mop. "Actually, my niece is also staying with us until the birth of her child." At the wistful look on Doll's face, Peter said, "Don't worry, my friend. Your time will come." He was beginning to feel the ground beneath him leveling after a slanting welcome.

Once they'd polished off two plates each of dessert, they set about discussing numbers—enlistments, oaths of allegiance, guns acquired for the Cause. Then they calculated how many men and materials were yet needed. In the end, Peter was satisfied. "I'm pleased with your diligence.

If every township fared this well, there would be no shortage of men or munitions."

"We will need these soon?" Doll asked.

Peter nodded. "Perhaps this spring. Maybe the summer."

"How are you dealing with townships not meeting their quotas?"

"Well, Caspar, I go to those places and do my best to be persuasive, without being overbearing." He laughed and looked down at his hands resting on the rough-hewn table. "There's a fine line sometimes."

Van Etten answered a knock at the door, and Peter smiled upon seeing his old friend.

"Tatamy!" Peter stood and clapped him on the back. "How very good to see you. Can you join us?"

Nicholas Tatamy stepped away from Van Etten, nodding toward Doll and Arndt. "I just came to visit my neighbor. Beside, I'm not sure my friends would want me to sup with them."

"And why not?" Peter asked.

"Mr. Tatamy thinks he's too old to join the militia." Doll leaned back in his chair and thumped his ample chest. "We're not exactly spring chickens."

"Nevertheless," Arndt said, "he has generously contributed toward our arms and ammunition." He waved the man over to them. "You are always welcome among us, Mr. Tatamy. We're through discussing business, so if you'd like to join us ..."

He looked at Peter, who tried interpreting his friend's demeanor. Cautious perhaps? Tatamy definitely had something on his mind. They all seemed to have something on their minds. He placed his hands on the edge of the table. "My friends, I suspect there is news you haven't shared with me."

Doll looked at Arndt, who looked at Tatamy, who looked at Peter. "Apparently you haven't heard the rumors, then?" Doll asked.

Peter frowned. "What rumors?"

"Maybe they've just been circulating up here and haven't reached the rest of the county."

Tatamy nodded, leaning closer to Peter. "Unfortunately, there is a story afloat that you have accepted a gift of many acres to prop up support for the Pennsylvania Assembly."

If not for the downward thrust of feelings running through his gut, Peter would have shot up from the chair. Indignation filled his thoughts, those he was able to keep straight. His voice was a growl as he fought to maintain self-control. "Who, may I ask, has said such a thing?"

John Van Etten walked over to the table and stood near Peter. Although he no longer ran a tavern, he still knew all the area's business.

"My friend, in recent weeks, some younger men have come this way from Easton, on what business I do not know. They've been telling anyone who would listen you're not wholeheartedly committed to the Cause but are acting as a puppet of the Assembly." He cleared his throat. "This is so you can enrich your landholdings."

The words settled between them like a freezing rain. Peter remained quiet, listening to his pulse thumping in his ears. "Who, may I ask, started this report?"

"I think his name is Musch," Tatamy said.

"John Musch? Peter pictured the young man. "He's in his early twenties, dark hair, dark eyes. He signed up for the Easton Company, then proceeded to cause trouble for Isaac Sidman when he was drilling one day."

"How so?" Doll asked.

"I wasn't there, but Sidman told me Musch kept giving voice about our half-hearted response to Great Britain. He said we should've declared independence long ago but were too indebted to the Crown and too cowardly to fight."

"What did Sidman do?" asked Tatamy.

"Told Musch if he didn't fall in line, he couldn't remain in the militia."

Doll sighed, his shoulders relaxing. "And did he—fall in line?"

"No. Musch wouldn't accept our authority."

Arndt exhaled long and slow. "I figured the story wasn't true, my friend, but I am still vastly relieved to have heard your account."

"You must forgive me, Peter, but for the sake of snuffing out this vile tale, has the Assembly offered you land, or anything ese, in return for your loyalty and using your influence to persuade others? Not that you would have accepted," Doll said.

Peter looked into the face of his long-time friend and relative, understanding his need to ask. "No, Caspar. There is no truth in any part of this. I have never been approached by agents of the Assembly to do such a thing, nor would I entertain them for a second if any tried. I simply do my duty as a member of that body."

A giant bellows seemed to have expelled the air previously fouling the room.

Doll reached across the table and gripped Peter's hand.

Arndt repeatedly shook his head. "I don't understand how this could happen to someone with the purest motives, who sacrifices so much to do the right things."

"How in the world do we put an end to this loathsome report?" Caspar wanted to know.

For the moment, no one seemed to know.

Chapter Five

Monday morning had gone off without a hitch until she and Ethan saw the bus pull away just before they arrived at the corner. She waved like a windmill in a hurricane to attract the driver's attention while Ethan broke out in blotches. The driver stopped on a dime and swung the door open.

"Hello! This is Ethan Miles, and he's on your bus now. I thought pick up was at seven-twenty-three." She looked at her phone. "It's seven-twenty." She'd been so proud of herself for being on time.

"Well, ma'am, we ask the kids to be here five minutes early. I've been running ahead of schedule."

She turned to Ethan, who was bounding up the steps as if to disown any association with this crazy woman. "Bye! Have a good day." He barely nodded as she saw him negotiate the kids and the seating arrangement, a known middle-school minefield. As she watched the vehicle disappear, she prayed he'd find someone nice to sit with.

She returned to the house for her book bag, then locked up and walked the few blocks to campus, autumn's first fallen leaves padding her footsteps. After her Monday morning classes, Erin hoped to do some research at Skillman Library, then take her mother for groceries.

"Hello, Dr. Miles!"

She slowed her pace to greet one of her students, a light-haired girl with dimples and an easy smile. "Good morning, Mia." She hoped she'd remembered the student's name correctly. "How are you?"

"Pretty good." She looked down for a moment. "I'm just going to my English class."

"Well, then, I'll see you later."

"Okay."

She veered off to the left and a minute later, opened the door to the Ramer History House. On the way to her third floor office, she bumped into Herman Weinreich.

"Well, good morning, Professor! How are you this fine day?"

Erin liked how her favorite teacher's smile had deepened over the years. For some strange reason, however, she thought there was something beside joviality behind his brown eyes. "I'm just fine, and you?"

"Never better." They fell in tandem on the staircase. "Do you have a minute before your class?"

"Sure."

"This won't take long."

They walked past the main office and waved to the secretary. Erin waited for Herman to unlock his door and turn on the overhead light, revealing a tight space lined with floor-to-ceiling book shelves. His desk was a veritable archaeological site containing uneven stacks of books, magazines, papers, notebooks, discarded coffee cups, and family photos. For some reason, she thought she smelled chocolate pudding.

"Have a seat, Erin." When she looked at the leaning Pisa of books on the chair, he laughed. "You can just put them on the desk."

"Uh, where?"

"Anywhere will do."

She did as she was told, trying her best to prevent a landslide.

He put his briefcase on the floor and sat across from her. "How's it going these first few weeks?"

"Pretty good." His manner signaled caution, and she gripped her bag. She tried not to let her imagination go from zero to sixty in less than ten seconds.

"I've heard from most of the students they like your classes a lot."

"I like them, the classes, and the students." *Most of them.*

"I always knew you were a good teacher." He cleared his throat. "Unfortunately, one of them isn't too happy with you."

Erin's shoulders felt suddenly pinned to the back of the chair. Since when had Herman Weinreich been taking lessons in bluntness from her father?

"Do you know who I might be talking about?"

"Marty Lee."

He pursed his lips, nodding. "He claims you're insensitive to him because of his ethnicity."

She wanted to shout, "What!" Instead, she managed an open-mouthed backward croak.

"Of course, this makes no sense to me, Erin. However, since Lafayette places a high value on diversity, I needed to bring his complaint to your attention."

She felt ready to unleash a howl of frustration but thought restraining her response would be more in her favor. Surely Herman would believe her side of the story. She crossed her right leg over her left. "Marty has been rather cold toward me since our first class."

"What happened?" Weinreich produced a pack of peppermint gum from a drawer and offered her a piece.

"No, thanks."

He popped one in his mouth and began chewing.

"After each student filled out an information form, I went around the class and made introductions—you know, asked their names and where they were from. I also told them a little about myself. When I got to Marty, I thought he might be Korean, which made me really happy because I taught so many Koreans at Hatfield. I said hello to him in Korean, and he just glared at me. I thought maybe I'd been mistaken, so I asked, 'Are you Korean?' He sort of gritted his teeth and said, 'My parents were born there. I don't know the language or care to.' I didn't know why anyone would be so angry about what had been a friendly gesture on my part, but he won't participate in class, and what's worse, he stares at me the whole time." She shivered. "Actually, Herman, it's made me quite uncomfortable. I feel like a little doll he's sticking pins into with his eyes."

He waved his hands in front of his face. "Oooh, I'm going to forget I heard you say that."

"I don't understand." She was open-mouthed, disbelieving.

"Erin, he's feeling singled out for being a minority, something he thought wouldn't happen at Lafayette. Now you just made an ethnic reference."

"I did?"

"I don't think you even realize it."

"Well, I don't." She didn't try too hard to keep her irritation from showing.

"You said you felt like someone was sticking pins into you, a reference to Voodooism."

Who was this man, and what had he done with her friend? "Oh, Herman! I just meant to convey how threatened I feel sometimes."

"Because he's Korean?"

"No! Because he stares at me unrelentingly."

She'd never been knowingly insensitive toward any student. She honored their backgrounds, even had them over to her house for study parties in which they shared some of their special foods. What craziness was this?

"I thought Lafayette celebrated diversity, allowed people to be who they were," she said.

"Absolutely, the school does. But we want students to set the tone for themselves, to discover who they are within the context of their backgrounds, whether they be religious, ethnic, or gender-based. Marty felt you were calling attention to something he didn't want to highlight about himself."

Erin sighed. "I wish he'd come to me first."

"Yes, he should have, but when I asked why he didn't, he said he couldn't trust you."

She sighed. "So, where do we go from here? Do I need to talk to him or just let the matter drop?"

"Let it drop for now. I told him I would speak to you and encouraged him to give you a chance. I assured him you meant nothing hurtful or embarrassing."

"What about the way he's been treating me, Herman? Not participating. Glaring at me."

He lifted his hands. "Just give the whole situation time. I think both of you need to adjust to Lafayette since you're new here." He smiled. "Well, you aren't completely new, but you haven't been on campus for, what is it, twenty years?"

She rose from the chair. "Alright then." On the way out, one of her colleagues smiled as he walked past her with a poster, "Support the Antifa." Erin clenched the hand railing. No, Toto, she definitely wasn't at Hatfield anymore.

Audrey was sitting on the bench under a maple tree when Erin arrived. "Hi, Mom." She bent down to kiss the softly powdered cheek.

"Erin! What time is it?"

"Twelve-forty-five."

"Oh, okay. I didn't expect you until after one."

"I know. I hope my being early isn't a problem." There was no way she was going to the library after her last class, still stewing in her own juices after the meeting with Herman. Taking her mom food shopping would help get her mind on something entirely different, like coffee ice cream and chicken tenders. Besides, she'd be sure to meet Ethan's bus on time.

Audrey reached up and took Erin's hand. "How could being with you for more time be a problem?"

Unexpectedly, she felt the corners of her eyes sting.

One of the residents came outside and sat on the second bench. "Hello, Audrey."

"Why, hello. Mae?"

"Yep."

"Mae, do you know my daughter?"

"I don't think we've met before." The gray-haired woman looked at Erin, squinting against the sun.

Erin shook her thin hand while her mother spoke. "Mae just moved in a week ago from upstate. Mae, this is my daughter, Dr. Erin Miles. She's a professor at Lafayette."

"Well, then, I'm very glad to meet you. What do you teach?"

"History."

"How nice for you."

"She's taking me food shopping."

"Have a good time. It was nice to meet you, Doctor."

"Same here, and you can just call me Erin."

As they walked to the minivan, Audrey started chattering about her grocery list. "Oh, and don't get those big cans of green beans and carrots. Allen got me a bunch of them last time, and they're just going to sit on my shelf. I have no use for big cans. I like the little ones with the pop tops. I have one of those every night with my microwave dinner."

"Couldn't you use the other ones too? Either save the rest for the next night or throw away what you don't eat."

"I can't afford to throw away food."

"Well, then, give them to a neighbor or a food bank at church."

"Just be sure to get me the small cans with the pop tops."

"I will, Mom." She grinned to herself as she unlocked the doors with her remote key. At least she was thinking of something other than what had happened at school.

"Erin, you're somewhere on this planet, but I can't quite figure out which continent."

"Huh?" She looked up at Paul as they sat on the porch with glasses of iced tea. He'd come over after dinner to help her adjust the automatic settings on her air-conditioning unit and to empty the last of the boxes. Ethan was in the family room doing homework, Toby at his side.

"You just seem preoccupied. Is everything okay?

She looked at his earnest face without quite seeing. Should she tell him? She hadn't said anything to her mother, and when her dad called in the late afternoon, again she mentioned nothing about her meeting. She was almost too embarrassed to relate what now, in the umpteenth telling in her mind, seemed preposterous. Maybe, however, Paul would understand. Maybe he would be able to give her some sort of reality check. After spilling the story, she absently sipped her iced tea, waiting for his response.

His blue eyes met hers. "This student … is he threatening you?"

"I, I don't think so, not directly anyway."

"Has he said anything sounding like a threat?"

"He doesn't say anything at all, not to me anyway." She was surprised, and not a little pleased, how Paul was looking out for her safety. Jim would've done the same thing and to heck with the school. "He just sits and stares. When I walk around the room, his eyes follow me." She shivered. "His behavior is pretty creepy." She remembered an incident from the previous week when Marty had turned to another student and said something while gazing at Erin. The other fellow had just shrugged.

"Listen to me, Erin. There are a lot of scary people out there these days. I don't give a rip about you being 'insensitive' to this little twerp." He made air quotes. "That's a lot of nonsense. Herman should be more concerned about having your back." His eyes sparked. "If this kid continues his nonsense, and you feel intimidated, tell the campus police. If they won't do anything, call the Easton police. Do not think you have to cater to him. In my opinion, he's nothing more than a jerk or a bully."

"Or a snowflake."

Erin and Paul turned toward the open front door. Apparently Toby wasn't the only one in this house with big ears.

Chapter Six

Something about his two mills grounded him, gave him a sense of oneness with the land and the village he'd come to with his bride a quarter of a century ago. He stood along the left bank of the Bushkill breathing sharp air into his lungs, listening to the creek persist in its journey to the Delaware past melting layers of ice. He'd made a success with these enterprises, and Easton had benefited from the fruit of his labors. His sons had done well by him since he'd been less involved in the day-to-day operations. Peter considered himself blessed to have Andrew and Jacob's talents, as well as Hans, whom he'd hired years ago after his indenture expired, and Peter Horeback. Now William was here too, and he wasn't only good at cutting wood, his skill in carpentry and natural leadership had contributed to the building of Easton's new church.

Purple finches flitted among a ragged-looking bush while Peter considered what might happen if—no, when—he was called to duty. The Committee of Observation hadn't been entirely clear about his role beyond the initial start-up. He only knew he was ready to serve in any way he could. He tossed a small rock toward the creek, watching the object bounce off some ice. Jacob had made a strong case for joining the militia, but Peter had told him his services, for now, were needed at home. Still, he'd consented to allow his youngest son to drill. With Andrew in charge, assisted by Jacob at the mills, there was Peter Horeback to consider, whose seven-year obligation to Peter was about to expire. Would he stay on, join the militia, or go elsewhere? He wondered whether finding new help would be more difficult in these unsteady times.

Peter became aware of someone walking toward him and turned upstream, seeing a brawny man with a lanky boy of about eight.

"Good day, *Herr* Kichline!"

"Good day to you, *Herr* Schmidt." Peter smiled at the boy with dusky skin and straight dark hair, marks of his mixed parentage. "Good morning, Johann."

"*Gut* morning."

Hans looked up at the blue sky along whose seas clouds sailed. "I do believe we soon have spring, *ja*?"

Peter nodded. "I believe you're right, my friend. And how is your fine family?"

"We are good, *danke*—all that I know of anyhow." Sadness tinged Han's expression.

"You haven't had any word then?"

He looked down. A crow cawed in the trees. "Not for a very long time."

Once again, Peter wrestled with the desire to tell him Greta was alive and well. He had never told Hans about seeing his daughter Greta in Philadelphia a year ago, how she'd been in the company of British officer's wives who made no secret of their contempt for Germans. Such knowledge might add to the burden Hans already bore over having a prodigal daughter. Sometimes there just were no ready answers.

"*Herr* Kichline, I am wondering, do you have need of another mill hand?"

He perked up. "Why, yes, I might. Do you know someone?"

"My nephew is coming from Germany. I'd like to bring him to my home."

"How old is he?"

"Seventeen, a *gut* age for hard work."

"Yes, by all means. When do you expect him?"

"*Vielen dank*. He is to come in a few weeks. Well, then, I must get to work. We are readying for spring, *ja?*"

"Yes, spring will soon be here."

He watched them walk toward the grist mill, smiling. Sometimes life could be hard, requiring a strong effort. Other times, the right things just seemed to fall into place.

♛

He was about to leave when William came to him near the sawmill entrance. "May I have a word, sir?"

"Yes, of course." Sensing this was going to be serious, Peter nodded toward the door. "Let's go outside."

A breeze had picked up, cooling the sun-splashed morning.

He looked intently at the young man whose shoulders had filled out since his arrival in Easton. "What's on your mind, son?"

William rolled his lips together, then he began. "Well, sir, I been thinkin' about that man who came to the house a whiles back, the one sayin' as how his son shouldn't be fightin' because they be Men-Men-"

"Mennonites."

"Yes, Menno-nites. He was sayin' his son is needed on the farm."

Peter folded his arms across his chest. "Yes, that's right."

"You see, sir, because of that Common Sense story I come to believe in what you be fightin' for." He lifted his deep brown eyes and looked straight at Peter. "I believe in freedom, sir, and I would like to join your 'Sociators."

He opened his mouth to say something, but William wasn't finished.

"Sir, I do beg your pardon. I have no right to ask anything of you, but I do have an idea if you don't consider me out of line."

"You can always come to me with your concerns. What is your idea?" He unfolded his arms, shifted his weight.

"This Menno-nite man is needin' help on the farm. His son is needin' to fight for what he believes in. I'd like to fight for what I believe in too, and I do think there be a way for me to serve." He inhaled then released his next words. "Sir, I would like to trade with his son."

Peter cocked his head, squinted. "Trade with his son?"

"Yes, sir. I would like to work in his son's place on the farm so's his son can fight for freedom. That way I sort of be fightin' for freedom too."

"I see."

"Still, sir, I know I be important to you here, you be needin' me as well, especially if you have to go and fight. I's sorry, but I don't have no remedy for such as that."

Peter smiled as he put his right hand on William's shoulder. "I think I do."

Frau Hamster was running down the hallway bearing a basin, in hot pursuit of Joe, her German pouring forth like floodwater. *Beeile dich! Schneller! Schneller!*

They both skidded toward him in the hallway as Peter raised his hands, taking inventory of the situation. Then he heard the deep groans of a woman in labor. His face paled, and the diminutive *hausälterin* seemed to read his mind. "*Nein! Es ist Frau Benner.*"

Peter let out a sharp breath, then asked if she needed the doctor.

"*Ich werde nach ihm schicken, wenn es sein muss.*" For now, the women had the situation well in hand, and she would send for the doctor just in case something went wrong.

"Put on your cloak, Joe, and come with me," Peter said.

The boy practically exhaled relief all over the floorboards. "*Ja*, sir!" He ran to the back, presumably to get his outer garment, and moments later, they fled from the house of screams.

Peter clapped the boy on the upper back. "That is no place for a man."

"*Ja*, sir!"

They moved quickly down Northampton Street to the Great Square where Dr. Ledlie lived and knocked on the door of the stone house. Footsteps sounded toward them on the other side, and a musty looking woman with a mole on her left cheek opened the door, sizing them up.

"Good day, Sheriff."

Should he bother to correct her? Did her getting his title right really matter? "Good day, Mrs. Marr. Is the doctor in?"

She straightened. "He's with a patient. Won't you come in?"

"Thank you, no. Please tell him my niece, Mrs. Benner, has gone into labor. My wife and housekeeper are with her and probably a friend." He thought of Elizabeth Traill, who was often in their company. "I just want him to be aware of the situation should he be needed."

"I will give him the information." She bowed and closed the door.

Wide-eyed, Joe looked up at him. Peter lifted his hands palms up, and smiled. "Let's go to my son's house. Perhaps Mrs. Kichline can keep you company for the time being."

"I would be delighted," Sarah said when they appeared at the door moments later. She smiled at Joe, then at her father-in-law as she stepped aside for them to enter. "Your coming is timely. Peter has some very good news."

"Oh?"

"He's just bought some land to the west of Easton, near your tract."

"How splendid!"

He ventured back to his own home where he encountered Catherine. For some reason, he thought he should speak quietly. "Is everything alright?"

"Yes, husband, Phoebe is doing well." She smiled, her face glistening.

He dipped his chin. "Are you alright?"

"Oh, yes. Elizabeth is here, and Susannah is fetching water and cloths."

"Don't overdo."

"I won't."

"I stopped by Dr. Ledlie's to let him know Phoebe is in labor. Would you mind very much if I paid a visit to *Herr* Drunkenmiller in Lower Saucon? I could be back by early evening. Of course, if I'm needed here ..."

She cupped his chin with her hand. "Go, my dear. We're fine."

He reached up and kissed her hand.

Covering the lengthy distance to the Drunkenmiller's farm with William, he marveled over Andrew's commitment. Regularly, this young man walked more than a dozen miles from Lower Saucon over rough terrain to drill with the Associators. Peter had the luxury of Abelard, his chestnut gelding, and William one of the other Kichline horses, but Andrew had had barely functioning shoes when he first started appearing on the field. Lately, Peter noticed the footgear had become more worthy of its owner and wondered whether the father had had any changes of heart. When he stopped at a local tavern to refresh himself and his horse, Peter got an answer from Yost Driesbach, a member of the Committee of Observation from these parts. The robust German placed both his hands on the table. "*Ja*, I know of Drunkenmiller. He's been making his displeasure known about his son."

Peter nodded. "Has he been antagonistic?" William sat with them, barely touching his drink.

Driesbach frowned. "*Nein*. Not antagonistic, more—disappointed."

"What's the general consensus among the Mennonites and Moravians here?"

He grinned, then coughed. "You didn't expect them to sign up, did you?"

"No, my friend, I most certainly did not." He leaned back, stretching his legs.

"Mostly they just want to stay out of our way and would like us to do the same."

Peter gazed out the window, watching the horses eating hay. He believed he bore good news for Drunkenmiller and his family. He just wasn't so sure the head of the house would agree.

Frau Drunkenmiller looked as if she'd seen a wild boar at the sight of him and William. "*Wie kann ich Ihnen helfen?*"

He smiled, hoping to douse her anxiety. "I would like to speak with your husband."

She pointed to the barn. Drunkenmiller happened to be coming out of the building, and when he saw Peter, the farmer's jaw clenched. He looked from him to William. "*Mein Junge ist nicht hier.*"

"Actually, I'm here to talk with you about something, *Herr* Drunkenmiller." When the man grunted, he introduced William.

"*Ist das dein Sklave?*"

Peter cringed, deciding to get straight to the point. "William works in my saw mill, and he believes strongly in our need to break away from Great Britain. Since he cannot fight just yet, he would like to replace Andrew for as long as your son serves in the militia."

Drunkenmiller's wooly eyebrows lifted. He stared at William, who met the stern gaze, then looked at the ground where he stood on a patch of melting, grainy snow. "*Ich kann nicht bezahlen.*"

Peter had figured as much. "I will reimburse him myself." He let the farmer dip deep into his thoughts, then spoke. "Do we have a deal?"

"*Ich möchte nicht, dass du denkst, ich stimme deiner Sache zu.*"

Peter nodded. "I understand you're in no way accepting our Cause."

At last the farmer jutted out not only his chin, but his right hand. They had a deal. According to the spoken terms, William would move to Lower Saucon within two weeks, and Andrew would leave for Easton. William would stay in quarters located in the barn, which compared to the family's tiny log cabin, was not such a bad deal, as he mentioned to Peter on the way back. Andrew would stay in William's home at the saw mill.

"William, when your service to Drunkenmiller ends, you and I will discuss your freedom."

The young man's expression lit up, a flame to dry kindling. "For real, sir?"

"For real."

♛

They reached the village of Easton at dusk to the sound of cowbells and clopping horses' hooves. He considered treating William to a meal at Shannon's Tavern since the ladies of his house had been preoccupied with bringing a precious life into the world. As soon as he stabled the horses, though, he wanted to check the situation at home.

"Did you have a good trip?" Conrad Fartenius asked as he accepted Aberlard's reins.

"Yes, I believe things went well," he told the proprietor, who doubled as an Associator. "Have you heard any news about Mrs. Benner?"

"*Nein*. I hope all is well."

He did too. When he and William entered the candlelit hallway, a soft glow and silence permeated the home. Susannah appeared from the back bearing an armful of linens.

"Hello, Papa," she smile-whispered. "Phoebe is asleep. So is the baby."

He restrained his mirth. "They are both well, then?"

"Yes. She didn't need Dr. Ledlie, but he stopped by a little while ago." She seemed to read his mind. "Mother Catherine is sleeping as well."

"William and I will just slip over to Shannon's for a bite."

"I could fix something for you." She appeared eager to help, but her eyes belied her own fatigue.

"No, you rest too, *Liebling*." He turned to go, then abruptly turned around. "Boy or girl?"

"A boy."

"Is Hanlon here yet?"

"No, Papa. We had no way of getting to him."

"As soon as William and I have had a meal, I'll go across the river to find him."

"But you just got back from a journey."

"Yes, my dear, but he needs to know his wife has just delivered a child."

Chapter Seven

Ethan stood next to his mother at the kitchen table. "Uh, Mom, what is that?"

"What is what?" Her head was bent over an essay, her pen poised to make some sort of comment, but what could she possibly say to this student?

"What you're eating." When he got no response, Ethan waved his hand in front of her eyes. "Mom!"

She looked up, removing her reading glasses. "Oh, hello, Ethan. What did you say?"

"Mom, you are zoning out big time here."

"I'm correcting tests." She stared at the soft flame of a pumpkin-scented candle. She knew she was rushing the season when the temperature hadn't dipped below sixty-five at night yet, but she loved autumn and wanted to introduce its earthy scents to her new home.

"So, what are you eating?"

"Uh, let's see, blueberry Greek yogurt, red beets, and anchovies."

He wrinkled his nose. "Man! How can you eat that stuff?"

When Ethan started to walk away, she put her hand on the small of his back. "Stick around. I could use your help with something."

"What?"

"You know what Jamestown and Plymouth were, don't you?" She happened to notice his jeans were at the high water mark. Hadn't she just bought them for the start of school?

"Well, yeah, sort of."

She lifted her arms, stretching, then moved her stiff neck from side to side. "Tell me what you know. I'm just curious."

"Well, okay." He shifted his weight from one foot to the other. "Isn't Plymouth about Plymouth Rock and the *Mayflower* and the Pilgrims, the first Thanksgiving and all?"

"Yes, you're right." Her smile reached all the way inside--her son had a basic grasp of American history. "What about Jamestown?"

"Um, I think those people actually went there earlier than the Pilgrims, but I'm not sure."

"Correct. Now, do you know where Jamestown is?"

He scrunched up his face. "Virginia?"

"Right! Do you know anything about what makes the two colonization efforts different?"

This was the crux of the question she'd put to her students. She'd required a paragraph from them but would settle for an incomplete sentence from her middle-schooler.

"I'm not really sure about Jamestown, but the Pilgrims came to America for religious freedom. Did the Jamestown people want that too?"

"They were devoutly Christian overall, but the Jamestown settlement was more of an official expedition of the English government. Did you know there was a colonization effort even before theirs?"

"I think you may have read me a story about it when I was a kid."

She struggled not to laugh. When he was a kid? He was still a kid, though maybe not such a little one anymore. In another year or two, Ethan would be nearly as tall as her. "In 1587 a group of English people crossed the ocean to what we know today as the Outer Banks of North Carolina. They wanted to establish the first English colony in the Americas, but something went wrong, and no one really knows exactly what."

His face brightened. "I know! They were lost colonists, right? Some people think they died, and others think they went to live with the Indians."

"Right on all counts."

He leaned his body against the table and scratched one of Toby's ears with his sock foot. "So, uh, Mom, why are you asking me all this stuff?"

"The questions are from a test I just gave to my students."

"How did they do?"

She drummed on the pile with the back of her fingertips. "Mostly well. Except for one student."

"What happened?"

"He gave some crazy answers." She picked up the test paper and her glasses. "'The Pilgrims came to Massachusetts in 1620 wearing strange hats and funny clothes, mostly black because they disliked colors and were always sad about something. People in England hated them, so they came here to torment the Native Americans.'"

Ethan's eyes popped. "Woah! What kind of grade is he getting?"

"Not a good one." And there was the rub. Except for multiple choice answers, Marty Lee had written flippant responses with just enough truth to make her struggle over whether or not to pass him. She knew he was baiting her, all because she'd inadvertently called attention to his ethnicity, so she could forge a connection with him. They were connected alright, but not in any positive way. This student was a millstone around her neck.

Ethan interrupted her thoughts. "Do you mind if I get some ice cream? I ate all my dinner, even those lima beans." He stuck out his tongue.

"Yes, of course. Grab a fudge bar for me, too." She muttered, "I think I want some of those leftover lima beans too."

Toby headed for the family room as if he didn't want to be anywhere near Erin when she mixed her latest concoction.

"Am I calling at a bad time?"

"Not at all." She was glad to hear Connie's voice while checking her lecture notes one last time.

"Are you getting settled?"

"Yes, I am. The last box went out with yesterday's recycling. I just love the house." She glanced out the office window to the Quad where students walked along the pristine walkways, mostly in the Farinon Center's direction. She didn't tell her friend she wasn't faring as well as she'd hoped with her teaching job.

"Do you think you might have some time to take on an extra project?"

"I guess that depends on the project."

"I think you'll like this one," Connie said. "At a meeting last night, the board decided to ask if you'd consider writing an article about Colonel Kichline for the journal of the Northampton County Historical and Genealogical Society."

She felt as if she'd just swallowed a cold, creamy spoonful of moose tracks ice cream. "Oh, I would! Tell me more."

"I think the last time there was any kind of presentation about him was an address to the Society almost a hundred years ago. You've brought him back to our attention, and we think an article about his life overall would be just the ticket. This doesn't give you a lot of space to explore any one aspect of his life, but more of an overview. Of course, there would be some remuneration, though not a lot."

She'd be happy to write such a story about her ancestor for free, although she didn't say so. "How long of an article?"

"Seven to ten pages in the journal. This would be the cover story for the winter/spring edition, so we'd need the article by the end of November. Does that work for you?"

"Oh, yes! I'm going to love writing this."

"You'll do a great job. Thanks so much."

"Thank you, Connie." She smiled. "Oh, and thank you so much for the basket you left on moving day."

"Now, how did you find out?"

"A little birdie told me?"

Herman came by her office a few days later bearing what appeared to be a test, which she recognized immediately. The tuna sandwich she'd had for lunch started swimming in her stomach acid. "I know why you're here."

He lowered himself into the chair opposite her desk. "Marty came to me complaining about his grade."

She squared her shoulders. "I figured he would."

"I read his answers and believe you graded him unfairly."

Why was he smirking? "Unfairly?"

"Yes." He crossed his right leg over his left. "You were far too generous."

She tried to keep her sigh from blowing across her desk into his face. "How am I supposed to handle him? I've had challenging students before, but never like this. This kid is irrational."

"I would tend to agree." He tapped the paper with his forefinger. "No one would fault you for this grade."

"Did you tell him?"

"I assured him if he continued to hand in work like this, he would be giving you no choice but to barely pass him, if at all."

The tuna came to rest in her settling stomach. "What happens now?"

"I've never had a problem like this one either." He raised his hands. "You are not an unreasonable person, quite the contrary. I'd suggest just steering clear of him as much as you can, and if he gets aggressive in any way, come to me right away. We could take disciplinary action."

"Thank you, Herman." After a long moment she said, "By the way, I have some good news to share."

"Wonderful! Tell me your good news."

"I've been asked to write an article about my ancestor, Colonel Peter Kichline, for the journal of the Northampton County Historical and Genealogical Society."

"Congratulations, Erin. I'm sure you'll enjoy writing such a piece." He pinched his lips together. "You know, writing for the local historical society is all well and good, but your future would be better served writing for academic journals. Our department has a proud tradition of publishing in the best ones."

He obviously thought he was encouraging her, so why was that darned tuna doing more laps?

She was looking forward to Ethan's soccer game after school on Friday, thankful her office hours would be over before she needed to pick up her dad. If no one showed up by one forty-five, she would just leave fifteen minutes early, figuring no one would mind. To pass the time, she reviewed and revised her notes for next week's classes while eating a pickled egg and washing it down with orange soda. She reached for a book a grad school professor had given her about Anne Hutchinson, who happened to be his ancestor. Actually, she'd always "seen" the family resemblance. Her professor was somewhat iconoclastic, though not totally outside orthodoxy, which made for entertaining class discussions. *I wonder how my students see me? Am I making any kind of positive impact on their lives?*

A figure appeared in her doorway, and she looked up.

"Hello, Dr. Miles."

Erin put the book on her desk. "Well, hello, Mia. Come in. Have a seat."

"Thank you." She put her book bag on the floor next to her and smiled shyly at Erin. "I hope I'm not bothering you or anything."

"Not at all. I'm glad you stopped by. I'll bet you're pleased with your test grade. You wrote one of the strongest essays out of all my students."

She flushed slightly. "Thanks. I really like history, I mean I didn't always, you know, like history, but I do now." She looked into Erin's face. "You're a really good teacher."

Boy, did Erin need to hear those words. She almost said, "I wish everyone thought so."

"I don't actually need anything, but I, I thought if you weren't busy, I might like to talk to you, a little." She started picking the remains of yellow polish from her nails.

"Of course. What's on your mind?" She leaned back into the leather chair, ready to listen.

"You went to school here, didn't you?"

"Yes, I did—back in the dark ages." She gave a small laugh. "More like the nineties."

"What was Lafayette like then?"

Erin wasn't sure what was on Mia's mind and decided to try and let the girl's reasons for coming unfold without too much prompting. "Well, in some ways the school was the same, academically competitive, a place where professors were always there for the students …" She hesitated, but just for a moment. "A place where students studied hard and tended to party hard."

Mia's light blue eyes seemed to awaken. "It's still the same way." She swallowed, looked down. "I don't always feel like I, like I fit in with the other kids."

"How so?"

"Well, did you ever have roommate problems?"

"I think a lot of people do, and, yes, I did."

"What happened?"

"Let's just say we had different ideas about who should be sharing our room and when."

Mia nodded. "What did you do?"

"I felt really awkward saying anything to her, but I needed to, or spend an inordinate amount of time sitting outside our door waiting to go in, or hanging out at the library." Erin had a mental picture of her former roommate, a beautiful young woman from Eastern Europe, a flame to many campus moths.

"What did she say, or do?"

"We reached an agreement, and the rest of the semester went more smoothly. We ended up switching roommates for the next semester."

Mia picked a last trace of polish from her left thumb. "I don't mind having a good time—in fact, I'm pretty fun-loving, but there are some things I dislike."

She waited for her to fill in the blanks. When she didn't, Erin prompted her. "What types of things?"

She looked up again. "There's this sort of game kids play on campus. I'm embarrassed to even say the name." The eyes were focused on her left pinky now. "There are signs around, though, so maybe you've seen them."

Erin closed her eyes and sighed. Yes, she'd seen them, a far cry from the pub night signs of her student days featuring a cooling tower and the inscription, "Come on down and react with us!" She'd actually cringed when a few days ago, she'd seen an ad on a Farinon bulletin board for "Condom Bingo."

"Sometimes," Mia continued, "I don't know if I really belong here. Did you know a student nearly died last weekend after he got drunk and fell down a flight of stairs?"

"Yes, I heard. Thank God he survived." She paused. "Have you been able to make any friends, people who share your interests and values?"

Mia shrugged her shoulders. "I'm going to a campus ministry group, but even there, I don't know. I just feel like most of them believe 'anything goes,' and my convictions are way too narrow to them. I feel like that with most of my professors too, like everything is so relative in life when I happen to think there are some things we're supposed to believe in. Oh, and about politics ..." She closed her eyes and shook her head. "Sometimes I think I'm the only Republican on the entire campus. Believe me, I learned not to open my mouth when people are discussing politics." She looked at Erin, a plea filling her expression. "Am I making any sense? I don't want to be offensive or anything. I just sensed, well, thought maybe you might understand."

Her heart went out to this girl, maybe because if she were completely honest with herself, Erin was having some of the same struggles.

Tony Pelleriti's face reflected the sun's warmth. "What great weather we're having. I just love being outside like this."

"Lately the temperatures have been more like summer than autumn," Erin said. "I'm still waiting to unpack my fall and winter clothes."

"Where's Ethan?"

Erin shaded her eyes with her flattened right hand over her eyebrows, scanning the soccer players on the school's field. Then she pointed. "There he is, Dad. Number twelve."

Tony lifted his chin and moved his head back and forth. Then he called out over the voices of the boys and spectators, "Oh, yeah, I see him now. What a fine-looking boy he is. I see a lot of Jim in him."

Erin turned her wedding band on her finger. "I do too."

"Thanks for bringing me today. I've never seen him play before."

No, and he had never seen her either, not when she was on the tennis team, nor in school plays nor … Choosing not to go there, she focused on the present, on the joy of belonging. So many times in Lansdale, sitting in the bleachers with other parents and grandparents, she'd felt like an outsider although she'd lived there most of her adult life. Easton was home. These were her people. Out of the blue, her heart suddenly thudded in her chest. Her ears rang and not with the sound of excited boys about to begin a soccer game. *Is that Alana? With my mother? What is Alana doing here with my mother?* Who knew what would happen when these two battleships collided?

Chapter Eight

After a full day of drilling his men, he was restless, flipping and flopping like shad on their annual trek up the Delaware. Catherine could sleep through a cannon's roar, so he was grateful his moving about hadn't wakened her. He prayed through the Twenty-Third and One-Hundredth Psalms several times, hoping they would lull him. Although he received in return a semblance of peace, sleep eluded him. He needed to get up, to stretch his limbs, to breathe some fresh air. He needed the rivers. He rose and dressed quickly, leaving through the front door as noiselessly as possible.

The houses and businesses along Northampton Street reposed in pockets of slumber. A light wind filtered through spring's first leaves, and in the distance, a horse whinnied as he walked toward the forks of the Delaware. Fresh air and the feeling of his legs moving underneath him brought a measure of serenity. When he reached the bluff just upstream from the Lehigh and the Ferry House, Peter found a level patch of ground and lowered himself to a sitting position. In the darkness, he could hear, though not see, the Delaware moving downstream, swollen from rain and recently melted snow. There was something altogether soothing about being enveloped in the creamy darkness with a breeze on his face.

He methodically sorted through the matters weighing on his mind, beginning with the letter from his brother Charles in Bedminster. Although Peter had known their younger brother, Andrew, had also been training men for war for over a year, Charles had sent further news. Since late last year, Andrew had been serving as a First Lieutenant in the Second Pennsylvania Battalion, Continental Line, which had engaged the British in the Battle of Quebec. Andrew, Charles was pleased to inform Peter, had survived the conflict, despite the loss of their commanding general and the severe wounding of another. Where Andrew was just now, however, remained something of a mystery, although Charles suspected he was somewhere around Albany. His brother's concluding sentences had stayed with Peter:

> *You and Andrew are good men in what I believe to be a good cause. As I am the gray-haired father of six children ten years of age and under, with another on the way, I am reluctant to march to the drilling grounds like the brothers I so admire. Rest assured, however, my commitment to the Cause is firm. If I must take up arms, I can be counted upon.*

He didn't begrudge Charles his decision, but Peter was committed from his toes to his own graying hair. The main thing bothering him now was the shadow of doubt being cast upon his motives. The day before, Robert Traill had taken him aside after Peter returned from drilling.

"What I am about to ask you is only because I want to accurately answer any questions. You must never for once think I mistrust you." He let out a puff of air, shook his head. "I find this most distasteful even to put such a thing into words, but did you recently buy property to the west of town?"

He narrowed his eyes. "No."

Traill cocked his head, twisting his face. "Really?"

"Really."

"That's strange. There's a deed recorded in your name."

Peter's spirit lightened, a little. "Peter Jr. bought several acres."

"Why, yes, yes, of course!" Then a shadow eclipsed his brightness. "Oh, my friend, the depths some people will stoop to."

"Don't tell me—you've heard I'm being bribed by the Assembly with an offer of land to curry favor toward the current, majority position."

Traill's jaw slipped a notch. "You've heard then."

"Yes, I've heard."

"Who started this damnable lie?"

"John Musch. As far as I can tell, he and some of his cohorts are angry with what they believe is a too-slow pace toward independence."

"So, the only reason you would be dragging your feet as it were is because you've been paid to slow the process down?"

"Yes, Robert, I do believe you have the gist of the matter."

"What should we do in response?"

"To be honest, I'm not sure. Fortunately, I have my good reputation to rest upon. Perhaps this will be enough."

As he sat on the riverbank, Peter recalled Traill's furrowed brow. Maybe he would have to fight the rumor after all, but for now, he needed to focus on preparing his men for a war he believed was inevitable. Besides, he wasn't the only man from the Committee of Observation who'd come under personal attack. Just two days ago at Meyer Hart's store, he'd overheard someone refer to Lewis Gordon as a "Scotch bugger." Factions had been lining up, one preparing for battle with Great Britain—men like his Associators and the women who also supported the Cause. Another, which included Musch, alleged the Associators and Committee weren't going far enough or fast enough. Then there were the Moravians and Mennonites who didn't want to fight at all, and some of Scotch-Irish descent who felt a certain kinship toward the British and were insisting on a more "measured" response.

Peter sat by himself with clear-headed faith in his own motives and actions to bring about the best result for everyone involved, until the sun began rising beyond the New Jersey hills. One burr remained in his side, the possibility of having to march off to war so closely to the time of Catherine's delivery. Since he had no control over the timing, however, he would need to place this firmly in God's hands or cause himself unnecessary grief.

He needed to get back home where his good wife would be wondering where he was. Goodness knew, he didn't want to cause her any more anxiety. He rose from the dew-splattered ground and shook the chill off by clapping his hands and arms against his chest a few times. A brisk walk up Northampton Street would warm him. He cast one last look across the shimmering waters before heading home.

Later that morning as he walked past the courthouse, he spotted an old friend. "Good day, Mr. Gress."

The church elder stood before Peter, his jaw firmly set. "*Guten Morgen.* Do you have a moment? There's something I must say to you."

Peter braced himself. Gress was usually the soul of amiability. "I always have time for you."

"I have given this much thought. I know I am growing *alt*, but my spirit and convictions are as strong as ever they were in my youth." He paused. "Colonel Kichline, I would like to join your Associators. Do you have room for such as I?"

Peter examined his friend's vulnerable expression, his own faith in humanity suddenly restored. He grasped Gress's hand. "Yes, my friend. Oh, yes."

"Honestly, Peter, I believe you're the right person for this job, especially since you're a member of the Assembly."

He'd tried to make himself smaller, to not be noticed among the informal gathering of committee members, but of course, this was impossible for the tallest man in Easton. He nodded his assent to Lewis Gordon, a half-hearted gesture at best. This was exactly the kind of thing he didn't miss about being the Sheriff of Northampton County. Why couldn't they have called upon Henry Fullert? Then again, he wasn't Lt. Colonel of the First Battalion of Associators, some of whom had gotten out of line. Way out of line.

He used to enjoy his treks to Hanover Township back in the days before his old friend Wilhelm Konk had told Peter he was no longer welcome. The devout Moravian had no use for anyone who would break away from Great Britain after pledging allegiance as a newly-arrived immigrant from a country burning with dissent.

"Beautiful day, isn't it, Peter?"

"I'm always grateful for the annual renewing of nature." He smiled at his portly companion. "As I am grateful for your presence on this odious visit."

"I could tell this wasn't something you relished doing." Robert Traill shook his head. "A nasty business, this. I don't see how Romisch didn't think he'd get caught."

"Such is our hubris. Our sins always have a way of finding us out."

He felt the up and down rhythm of his good horse underneath him, and he filled his lungs with the intoxicating smells of nascent foliage and flowers. He was going to enjoy at least this aspect of their journey, if nothing else.

Romisch refused to open his door more than a crack, just enough to hurl his foul words in their direction. "I have nothing more to say to you, gentlemen." He spat the last word.

"Oh, but the Committee has a good deal to say to you, Mr. Romisch," Traill said.

Peter needed to let the intransigent fellow know this was not a request. "You need to come with us to Easton. There are charges against you."

Romisch opened the door a bit wider and sent forth a bitter laugh. "For what?"

"You know exactly what," Peter said.

"Perhaps you should tell me."

"Very well, I will spell out the matter for you. You took one of the Associators' books in order to recruit men to join the militia, to fight for our rights and freedoms. This was an honorable and good thing to do. However, Mr. Romisch, you saw this as an opportunity to enrich yourself. You not only turned in your expenses to the Committee, but you went a step further, an illegal step further. You told the Assembly you weren't being paid by Northampton County, so they reimbursed you as well. Now do you see the problem?"

He found talking through a door infuriating. What angered Peter more was how a dishonest, fellow Associator was putting his own interests ahead of the Cause. He resisted the urge to push open the door and give the n'er-do-well a solid thrashing.

Again, the strident laugh, accompanied by a sing-song voice. "Come now, Colonel Kichline. Haven't you put your own hand to your Assembly?"

Peter's right hand shot forward, backed by his every intention to yank Romisch from his cabin and tan his hide. Only his friend's forceful tug kept him from putting his emotions where his fist was. He took a handful of deep breaths, telling himself he needed to rise above such rabble. He gave the miscreant one more opportunity to cooperate.

"Are you or are you not coming with us, Romisch?"

The voice behind the door launched a volley in German. "*Herr Kichline, Ich scheiße auf Sie.*"

Peter felt the blood drain from his face, then just as quickly rush back. Gathering what was left of his self-control, he motioned to his friend. "Let's get out of here, Mr. Traill."

As they mounted their horses, Traill scrunched up his face. "What did he say?"

"Believe me, you don't want to know."

He sat across from Lewis Gordon in his home office, its familiarity a comfort in such stressful times when men like Romisch and Musch endangered the move toward independence. After relaying everything to his longtime associate, including the part about the last verbal salvo, Gordon looked up, confused.

"What did he say in German?"

"The message was crude and hateful."

Gordon looked older than his years as he gazed out the window. "Well, then, I'm in very good company, Peter. As I'm sure you've heard, someone in Easton recently referred to me as 'the Scotch bugger.'"

A moment hung between them before their eyes met and, filling with mirth, they had themselves a very good laugh.

Chapter Nine

She could get used to being part of a regular family gathering in Easton. She smiled as Ethan's laughter mixed with Paul's from the bottom of an impromptu dog pile with the cousins, everyone giddy from watching Zoe open birthday presents and from eating triple chocolate cake. She was especially glad to see her son and—was he her boyfriend?—getting along well. Her heart swelling, Erin wandered back upstairs to the dining room where Audrey sat before an untouched piece of dessert while conversation swirled around her.

She leaned close to Audrey's ear. "Don't you want your cake, Mom?"

"Well, Erin, I'm not used to eating cake without having coffee."

"I'll get you a cup. Cream and sugar?"

"No sugar, a little cream."

Erin went to the kitchen where Alana filled a tea kettle with water, and Neal set up an array of coffee pods.

"Do you need anything, Aunt Erin?" Alana asked.

"I'm fine. Grammy just needs some coffee."

"Coming right up!" Neal said. He popped a small container of medium roast in the machine and pushed the "on" button.

Her niece turned the burner on under the tea kettle and turned to Erin, who noticed the sudden downturn of her expression. "I owe you an apology."

She cocked her head. "Whatever for?"

Alana lowered her voice. "For what happened at the soccer game. I put you in a bad spot."

Erin started to say something, but her niece closed her eyes and shook her head. "I had no idea Pop Pop would be there too, otherwise I never would have brought her." She said breathlessly, "I'd gone to visit her, and I happened to mention Charlie and Ethan were playing soccer, so I had to be going, and then I thought, 'Why not ask her to come?' She seemed a little housebound, and when I suggested she come to the games, she jumped at the chance." Alana exhaled. "When I saw you sitting in the stands with Pop Pop, my heart sank to my feet."

Erin touched her niece's slender shoulder. "I think you did something very nice for Grammy, and you handled the situation really well." She dipped her chin, grinning. "If you could've seen yourself!"

She was glad to have eked a chuckle out of Alana. "I never moved so fast in my life! I just steered her away from where you and Pop Pop were to the field where Charlie was playing."

"I did my best to distract him while you made a clean getaway."

Alana's laughter was in full sail. "What a close call!" She went to the stove and turned off the whistling tea kettle, becoming quiet again. "Aunt Erin, you may not want to answer this but if you can, why won't Grammy Audrey talk to Pop Pop?"

She lifted her hands. "I think old hurts have yielded a garden of bitterness."

"Somehow I don't think Pop Pop feels the same way."

"I'm not sure. He does ask me how she's doing whenever I talk to him, though."

"Do you think maybe someday they'll talk again?"

She half smiled. "Well, I've always believed in miracles."

Ethan leaned against her desk, casting a shadow on her laptop. "Mom, you know I feel like a leopard."

Here we go again. She looked up, removing her reading glasses. "You feel like a leopard?"

"Yeah, you know those people in the Bible everyone avoided."

Erin closed her eyes and took a deep breath to avoid laughing out loud. "I think you mean 'leper.'"

"Yeah, a leper. Anyway, that's what I feel like."

"I'm afraid I missed the reason why." She tried pulling her mindset out of the eighteenth century and into the present to focus on her son, whose pants were too short, again. Actually, she knew why Ethan felt like he did.

This was one of the first big hurdles she'd faced as a single mother, leaving her feeling like a thirty-year-old car with a dead battery.

"I'm the only kid in the entire school who doesn't have a cell phone!"

Every time he'd asked over the last two weeks, she'd conjured up a mental image of Ethan turning into one of those teenage zombies with their eyes glued to a screen. She wished she could ask Jim what he thought. There was no way Erin would go along with an "everyone does it" mentality—that was parenting 101. She wondered, though, if there might be legitimate reasons for a sixth grader to have the responsibility for something as expensive and potentially volatile as a phone. She prayed for guidance to handle the situation right.

"Do you want a phone just because everyone else has one?"

His eyes sparked with what appeared to be a renewed sense of potentially getting what he wanted. "I do feel like I'm not very cool without a phone, but there are other reasons, good ones."

She waited for at least one. And waited while his face reddened. "Suppose you come up with a list, then we'll discuss this some more."

First, he frowned, then he brightened. "Okay, Mom."

She felt her jaw and upper body relax when Ethan left the room, figuring she'd need to be doing some research of her own. For now, however, she returned to a document about Peter Kichline's service as Northampton County sheriff. *I wonder if there are specific records somewhere about the cases he handled. Maybe I should email Connie, and Sandy Dunlap at the Marx Room.* She opened up her email browser and started composing a message when her cell phone rang.

"Hello, this is Erin."

"Hello, Erin. This is Stan Grube, the pastor at First Church."

She recognized his resonant voice. "Well, hello, Pastor Stan."

"I hope I'm not calling too late."

"Not at all."

"I wonder if you might have some time this week for me to stop by. I always try to visit newcomers, to get to know them and see how we might be of service."

"Sure. Let me check my schedule." She called up her online calendar and found Thursday evening open. "Is Thursday alright with you?"

"Sure. I could be there about six."

She and Ethan ate around five-thirty since he was "starved" after school and soccer practice. "Six is fine."

Maybe he would know something about kids and cell phones.

They sat in the living room across from each other on the leather sofas she and Jim had bought the year before Ethan was born. Between them was a plate of pumpkin cupcakes left over from Saturday's DAR meeting, along with a pot of green tea.

As she poured, Erin made a confession. "I must admit I've already eaten one, so don't let my hesitation stop you." What she didn't tell him was how she'd smeared her cupcake with a generous helping of horseradish, causing her dog and boy to flee to the back yard.

"I don't need to be invited twice." He reached for a cupcake. "This is one of the perks of my job."

"How long have you been at First Church?"

He chewed, swallowed, drank some tea. "Twelve years this fall."

Erin nodded. She guessed him to be about ten years older than herself, a guy who either worked out or ran on a regular basis but looked more scholarly than athletic with his short brown hair and tortoise shell glasses."Are you from the Easton area?"

"More or less." He wiped some crumbs from his chin just as Ethan came into the room.

"Ethan, you know Pastor Stan from church."

"Hi."

"Why, hello, Ethan. You have a very nice home." He reached out and shook the boy's hand.

"Thanks."

"How do you like Easton?"

"I like Easton a lot."

"I'm glad to hear it."

"Uh, Mom, could I have one of those?" He pointed to the plate of cupcakes.

"Sure."

He took a treat minus a plate or napkin. "I, um, I'm glad you came over."

"I am, too, Ethan." When the boy left, the pastor finished the cupcake and put the plate on the coffee table next to a burning candle. "I'm actually from Catasauqua. After high school I went to Asbury, then stayed there for seminary."

She frowned. "Asbury?"

"The schools are in Wilmore, Kentucky, just outside of Lexington. Horse country."

"Blue grass and all that?"

"Yes, with a strong hint of Mayberry thrown in for good measure."

"So, you weren't raised in this denomination?"

He shook his head. "No, more like a holiness Methodist. I kind of stumbled upon First Church. My wife and I were at a large congregation in Akron, Ohio, where I was an associate pastor. My mother heard about the opening at First UCC and asked if I'd be interested."

"I guess the session, or whatever it's called—"

"Consistory."

"—didn't mind about your not being part of their denomination."

"No, not really. Each congregation is run independently. The people have grown used to my particular holiness flavor, or at least they tolerate me." He smiled, resting against the sofa, a man comfortable in his own skin. "So, tell me, Erin, how are you getting along in Easton? You're from here, right?"

"Yes. I moved away after graduating from Lafayette. I met my husband at Villanova, and we settled in Lansdale where his family has a meat packing business." There was an obvious elephant in the room. Erin decided not to ignore the creature. "Jim died a year ago last May."

"I'm guessing his death was something of a surprise?"

"We found out a couple months before he died that he had liver cancer. There really wasn't much the doctors could do for him."

I'm saddened to hear this."

"Thank you." She looked away, toward a photo of them on their honeymoon. "I had twenty years with Jim, who was funny, talented, a great husband and father, a man of deep faith. Overall, I've been blessed. I just wish, of course, we could've had more time together."

"So, how did you come to be in Easton again?"

She told him the story of discovering her six times great-grandfather and his strong connection to Easton's founding, how she'd grown apart from her family over the years. She followed with her efforts at reconnection, along with a job offer from Lafayette, and the for sale sign at her aunt's former home.

Stan Grube jerked his head back in surprise. "This was your aunt's house?"

"Yes. This was my happy place as a little girl. When I saw a realtor out front, the pieces just started falling into place, right down to being able to rent my house in Lansdale."

"I can clearly trace God's movement in your life through all these events."

"So can I." Shadows gathered in the corners of her emotions. "There's something I just don't understand, though, Pastor Stan."

He put his hands on his lap and bent forward. "What is it?"

She sighed. "I thought this would be a kind of golden time for me, you know, everything would just sort of …" She spread her hands. "… work out, you know?"

"They haven't?"

She frowned. "Yes, overall, kind of. I mean, I really do feel like I belong here, but, well, my job isn't working out the way I hoped." She paused. "I really loved Lafayette when I went there, and somehow I thought the magic would still be there."

"And it's not?"

"I'm honored to be teaching there, believe me, but things have changed, or maybe I've changed." She laughed. "Maybe a little of both." Erin told him about the recalcitrant student and the political correctness, leaving out the rampant dissipation of some students.

"I think a lot of colleges are that way these days." He paused. "And how are things with your family?"

"Mostly good, although I'm still learning to relate to my divorced parents as an adult." She hesitated, then decided to speak more of her mind. "There's another thing. I just assumed Ethan and I would be attending First Church since my ancestor helped with the building, and generations of my family have gone there." She felt awkward. "I love being there, and the people have been so welcoming and kind, just like a family."

"But?"

"I feel funny telling you, but Ethan and I are used to a bigger church and Sunday school."

If he was at all offended, he didn't betray himself. "Our church is quite small and not a little on the elderly side. Have you looked elsewhere?"

She was surprised, and relieved. "My, uh, friend, has taken us to First Presbyterian in Bethlehem a few times."

"Now, there's a big, vibrant church for you," he said. "Of course, they've had their issues in recent years."

"Yes. And then I'm also adjusting to belonging to a different DAR chapter. The women are really nice, but the group is a lot smaller and older than the one I was in before." She raised her hands. "Honestly, is there ever any satisfying me?"

"Yes, Erin, I think so."

She was on a roll. "I did what I thought God wanted me to do, to move back here, teach at Lafayette, go to First Church, get to know my family better, and everything fell into place so I could. But now … well, I just didn't think life would be quite this complicated."

"I wouldn't let myself get discouraged, Erin, or second-guess myself." He leaned his elbows on his knees. "I have a sense God is working in one of those mysterious ways he's known for, and this is all going to come out right in the end."

She was sitting on the porch with Paul after the last of the Trick or Treaters had left, a veritable army of witches, wizards, Things One and Things Two, slashers, Harry Potters and Hermoines. Candles sputtered as they melted down in jack o' lanterns flanking the sides of the porch stairs.

"How many pieces do you think you gave out?" Paul asked.

Toby looked up, and Erin scratched his right ear. "Close to two hundred."

"I thought we were in the midst of a feeding frenzy."

Ethan burst onto the porch. "I got three hundred pieces Mom!"

She was both pleased and alarmed. "Don't eat them all tonight." Her cell phone rang, and she was happy to hear her mother-in-law on the other end.

"Trick or treat," Pat said brightly. "I thought I'd call after the kids stopped coming. Are you free?"

"Yes. I'm just sitting on the porch with Toby, Ethan, and Paul. We had quite a crowd. And you?"

"About the same—fifty or so. Now Al and I want to treat you and Ethan."

"Treat us? How do you mean?"

"How would you like to spend Thanksgiving with us in Disney World?"

Thanksgiving? She'd barely thought about the holiday. "Wow," she managed to say. "That's really kind of you." Overcoming her hesitation, she turned to Ethan. "How would you like to spend Thanksgiving at Disney World with Grammy Pat and Grandpa Al?"

His eyes popped. He started dancing around the porch, thundering against the floorboards. Erin might not have been overjoyed about going to a theme park, preferring historic sites and national parks, but she felt happy for Ethan, He needed infusions of joy in this time of transition. When she hung up, she turned sheepishly to Paul. "I guess you know where we're going next month."

His eyes twinkled. "What you don't know is I'm going to be in Orlando over Thanksgiving as well."

Chapter Ten

Late May, 1776

He surveyed his men at the parade ground. In his opinion, they were now battle-ready, if not battle-tested, and who knew when they would be called upon to put their skills to the ultimate test. At the end of the day's drilling, he turned to his subordinate. "Captain Sidman, will you please call the men to order? I'd like to have a word."

"Yes, sir." The officer cupped his hands around his mouth and called out, "Attention!" When the men didn't immediately line up, he raised his voice. "Attention!"

Peter watched the collection of farmers, tradesmen, and shopkeepers in their homespun outfits and rudimentary footwear fall into formation. Ziba Wiggins had arrived in his finest suit of clothes, which included a slightly threadbare waistcoat. The Royal Fusiliers they were not. As he sensed the approach of actual combat, he believed that when these stout German pioneers came cheek to jowl with the King's finest, they wouldn't flinch. "Attention!" Sidman's ruddy face was in full bloom as the militia finally came to order. Not knowing German, he spoke to them slowly. "The-colonel-would-like-a-word." He turned to Peter, who stepped forward.

"Thank you, Captain Sidman." He addressed his soldiers in their native tongue. "Men, we've come a long distance together these last months. As a result, some of Pennsylvania's best sharpshooters are standing before me right now." He allowed himself the luxury of a half smile, enjoying the sight of his men raising their chins. "I have some further news to share with you about British troop movements." A hawk swooped high above the parade ground, cawing over unseen prey. "As you know, back in March, General William Howe began evacuating his troops from Boston, and our good General Washington responded by sending his forces to New York.

"Many believe this is where we will engage the British next. I don't know what all of this portends for Northampton County's Associators. I do believe, however, the time will soon come when we'll be called to action. I urge you to prepare yourselves and your families as best you can."

When chattering began to break out, Peter signaled silence, and they quickly complied. "Now then, men, we don't know exactly what General Howe's next move will be, but …"

"And what is our Congress going to do about it? What will it take for them to finally break away from the English tyrant?"

The defiant comment was a kite stuck in the trees, flapping loudly. Every head had turned toward the belligerent voice, gasps breaking out like measles.

Sidman stepped forward, his face flushing, forgetting to speak distinctly. "Have the decency not to interrupt the colonel! Whoever shouted out is to come see me after our dismissal." He glared at them. They may not have understood his words, but they caught their meaning.

Peter squared his shoulders, widened his stance. "I think there is a strong possibility of the British establishing a new position in New York. If this is the case, we will most likely engage them near or around the city at a time," he paused for effect, "to be determined by our Congress and General Washington. I will, of course, keep you informed as I receive information and orders from the General. Until then, I encourage you to go about your business at home, and we will continue meeting weekly. That is all." He nodded toward Sidman.

"You are dismissed!" A few moments later, he approached Peter. His face reflected anger at the defiant soldier, as well as curiosity. "Do you think we'll actually engage the British without declaring our independence?"

"There is precedent."

The young officer gazed into the distance. "Lexington and Concord. Bunker Hill."

"A formal declaration may, of course, be forthcoming." He pursed his lips. "We are living in exciting, though unsettled, times, Captain."

Angry shouts from a copse of fir trees drew their attention. Andrew Drunkenmiller ran toward them. "There's a fight, sir!"

Peter strode in the direction of the scuffle, Sidman and Drunkenmiller on his heels. When he arrived, the men who'd formed a circle around the combatants stepped aside to reveal two men rolling on the ground, dirt and bits of grass clinging to their clothes, hair, and faces. Peter stepped in and grabbing the men, yanked them upward as a rush of energy surged through his body. "Stand to your feet, soldiers!" The men snarled like pack dogs as he pushed them apart. "What is the meaning of this?" Neither said anything. "What happened here?"

The smaller of the two men pointed at his opponent. "*Dieser Schurke sagte einige hasserfullte Dinge.*"

"What hateful things did he say?"

The man lowered his voice. "He, he accused you of being bribed by the Assembly."

His instincts were to level the lowlife with one fist to his rotten face. The malicious rumor had taken on a life of its own, a living beast circling him, his family, and the Cause, seeking how to inflict damage. Didn't those who spread the lie realize they weren't helping to bring about independence? He balled his hands into fists and took a cavernous breath to steady himself. "Mr. Schmutz, I hereby discharge you from the Associators." He grabbed the fellow's waistcoat, drawing him nose-to-nose. "And don't let me ever see your sorry face out here again." He pushed the young man hard, causing him to windmill to keep his balance. Then, grabbing his hat from the ground, Schmutz disappeared into the trees.

There seemed to be no end to conflict, but he especially resented how the ugly rumors had penetrated his family life. One morning, he found *Frau* Hamster pounding bread dough with fists the most hardened of his men would be reluctant to engage with. Susannah stood to the side, along with Joe, looking equally upset but as if the housekeeper were plenty angry enough for all of them.

"*Was ist falsch?*" he asked the old woman.

She raised her countenance, snarling. "*Schweine! Sie sind alle Schweine!*"

Why was she calling everyone pigs? He asked his daughter, "What is she talking about?"

Susannah took him by the elbow and led him into the hallway. "That horrible *Frau* Musch was at Mr. Hart's store today when we were there. She started taunting us about how we can buy anything we want because the Assembly has bought you." Her cheeks colored. "I'm sorry, Papa. I hate repeating those words."

His jugular vein pulsed. This nonsense had gone way too far. Something had to be done.

"Catherine, I need you to do something for yourself and for our baby."

"What, dear husband?" She looked up from the chair in their bedroom, dark circles under her eyes.

"Until I can get this odious matter settled, I would like you to leave Easton for a while."

She tipped her head to the side as a breeze caught the curtain at an open window. "Whatever for?"

"I see how this nonsense has affected *Frau* Hamster, Susannah, and Joe. Why, she's ready to pound the kitchen to the floorboards." He cracked a smile and was glad when his wife gave a small laugh. "They can handle the tension, but you need peace and rest."

"What do you propose?"

Sensing she wasn't going to put up a fight, he felt some of his own tension slip away. He outlined his plan for a visit to Phoebe and William in Greenwich for a couple of weeks, then watched her face for a reaction.

"I appreciate your concern for me, Peter, but what about Elizabeth?"

"Take her with you." He knelt before his wife feeling like a young suitor. "The rest of us can take care of ourselves, and if you were not with child, you would be right there fighting for my honor like the rest of the family. But right now, you must think of our little one, yourself and our unborn child."

"Thank you, dear husband. I will go." She raised his chin and gazed into his eyes. "You are the most honorable man I've ever known. If you ever doubt why this is happening, I urge you to read stories of men like Joseph and Nehemiah who were also unjustly accused. Stand in their shadows, darling."

Ziba Wiggins greeted him with a strong handshake. "I'm mighty glad to see you, Colonel Kichline."

Peter noticed his friend had lost a tooth, giving him the peculiar aspect of an old toddler. He knew by the greeting Wiggins wasn't buying any of Musch's twaddle. "How are you, Mr. Wiggins?"

"Faring well." He moved closer. "And you?"

"I'm going to be just fine, thank you." He wondered what kind of welcome he'd receive at the Committee of Observation meeting. "Well, then, I must be going inside."

"Good luck to you!"

Peter entered the courthouse teaming with present and to-be-elected members of the General Committee of Northampton County, feeling the brew of heat, excitement, and tension. Robert Traill came up to him. "Good day, my friend!" Peter shook his hand. "May the day be a good one for you."

"Thank you for making room for my petition, especially when new committee members are being elected."

"We can do no less to clear your good name," Traill said. "How is Catherine?"

"She and Elizabeth are doing well and enjoying their visit with the Hanlons."

"I'm glad, although my Elizabeth misses her greatly."

"They'll be back in about a week."

"I'll give my lady the good news." He leaned back, the buttons on his waistcoat straining against the cloth. "I would like to let you know of a recent development. Lewis Gordon hasn't been well the past few weeks, and has in fact, missed a number of meetings."

"I noticed he was exhibiting some pallor. What's wrong?"

"He won't say, but for now, we need to replace him."

Peter anticipated what was coming next and said with a smile. "Levers?"

His friend closed his eyes and nodded. What remained unsaid was their common estimation of Robert Levers, an energetic patriot with flawless loyalty to the Cause, along with a touch of self-promotion. Peter wondered where Levers stood on the matter of Musch's rumor mongering, hoping he would prove as faithful to him as Gordon would have been.

A voice boomed from the front of the courthouse. "Gentlemen!" Levers waved his arms over his head. "Gentlemen, if you would please. Let us begin."

Peter sat for an hour and a half, sweat trickling down his back and seeping through his linen shirt while men from more than two dozen townships were elected as members of the General Committee. Although Robert Levers was now chairing the Committee of Observation, he was also going to do double duty representing Hamilton Township. The men adjourned for fifteen minutes following the voting while Ziba Wiggins and Pastor Rodenheimer counted the ballots. Then Levers announced the results. The room suddenly seemed larger to Peter as those who had lost evidently saw no reason to remain in the overly-warm courthouse listening to a bacchanal of pigs and goats outside.

A motion was then made to appoint and seat Robert Levers in the chair vacated by Lewis Gordon. When it passed, the new leader lost no time getting down to the committee's business. Even though he seemed to have one volume, loud, much of what he was saying began lulling Peter into a premature nap.

"We have been called together in consequence of a letter from the Committee of Inspection and Observation of the City and Liberties of Philadelphia dated the twenty-first of May, Instant, delivered the twenty-sixth, Instant, to Mr. Lewis Gordon, Chairman, who is indisposed, but Mr. Frederick Ruhl and Mr. Christopher Ludwig, two of the members of the said Committee of Inspection ..."

Traill elbowed his friend. "Peter, your turn is coming to speak."

He moved his body from an involuntary slouch to a full sitting position, opened his eyes wider a couple of times, and swept cobwebs from the crooks of his mind. His throat felt approximately like old parchment, and he swallowed several times. Five minutes later, Levers made the announcement.

"Our good friend, Colonel Kichline, has requested to bring before this committee some pressing business. Colonel, would you like to come to the front of the room?"

Peter stood and walked past the committeemen to the appointed place. "Thank you, Mr. Levers."

Levers gave an elaborate bow, placing his right arm across his chest. "It is our pleasure."

"As I believe most of you are aware, a report has gone abroad about alleged dishonest dealings on my part." He had their full attention. "Mr. John Musch has been circulating a story about my accepting many hundreds of acres of land from the Assembly in exchange for my overall support of the current majority position. This, of course, is a blatant lie." Feeling his blood pulse, he told himself, *Slow down. Take your time. Stay above this.* "I remain as devoted as ever I have been to the Patriot Cause for which I have already toiled in earnest, often to the detriment of my home life and my businesses. I would never do such a thing as Mr. Musch is accusing me. My good son, Peter Jr., recently purchased some land to the west of Easton, and when Mr. Musch was informed of this and given the benefit of the doubt over a possible misunderstanding, he insisted my son's activity had nothing to do with his own accusation."

He took a deep breath. "As you can imagine, this slanderous charge has not only injured my own good reputation throughout the county, but the heart of our very Cause. Even some of our Associators haven't known what to believe. Our subscriptions are down by ten percent, and I fear if this story continues unchecked, the results would be most damaging to our quest for independence. Since the courts are now shut up, I ask you to bring Mr. Musch before the committee at your earliest convenience so he can give his reasons for spreading such slander about me."

His heart thudded, his ears rang.

Levers spoke. "I put Colonel Kichline's request to a vote. All in favor of bringing Mr. Musch before the Committee, say 'aye.'"

"Aye!"

"All against, say 'nay.'"

Silence.

"The ayes have it. We will ask Sheriff Fullert to bring Mr. Musch to the next committee meeting." He looked at Peter. "This is the very least we can do to clear your good name."

Chapter Eleven

She parked in the lot closest to the history building along Sullivan Road and had just reached across the front seat for her tote bag when she saw him. She wondered whether to restart the car and drive away, but stood her ground, getting out and locking the door remotely. Marty Lee was just a few yards away, wearing his backpack, probably walking to a class from his dorm. His lips formed a straight line until a slight rise on the left side turned his expression into a piercing sneer. Before she could turn away, he pulled a large Swiss Army-type knife from his right pocket and glanced evocatively at her driver-side front tire. Then he put the penknife back, turned, and walked away.

Erin felt as if she'd had one too many cups of coffee as she gathered her scattered wits. Then she felt the same sort of anger she'd known when years ago she'd seen a woman kick a puppy. She took her indignation straight to Herman Weinrich's office, relieved to find him alone.

"Good morning, Erin! And how is my favorite former student today?"

"Angry. Upset. Fuming."

"Whoa, there." He raised the palms of his hands. "Close the door and have a seat."

She tried not to slam the door or hurl the contents of his book-strewn chair clear across the room. "I've had it, Herman!"

"Let me guess—Marty Lee?"

"Yes, Marty Lee."

He tented his big hands. "Sit down, and tell me everything."

"I can't sit." But she did tell him everything. "You know, this kid is no longer just a nuisance; he's a menace. Now that he knows my car, I don't feel safe. What if he follows me to my house or threatens my son? Safety incidents are to be reported to your department head, and Herman, I'm reporting this to you." In case he didn't know she meant business, she moved her head forward and gazed at him.

Weinreich picked up his desk phone and tapped a few numbers. "Yes, good morning. This is Herman Weinreich, chair of … yes, good morning, Officer Beatty. Can you come to my office? Yes, there's been an incident. Right away if you would please." He nodded. "I'll be here." He hung up the phone. "He'll come in a few minutes."

Erin told the campus security official everything, from the start of the semester to the present distress. "You know," she added for good measure, "there are a lot of unstable people out there doing terrible things, like driving vans into crowds of people and shooting up concerts, not to mention schools. Who knows if Marty Lee is one of them?"

The officer stood across from her, a middle-aged man with a short, stocky frame and an oversized head. "I hear you, Doctor Miles. I'll look into this immediately." He wrote down her cell number. "In the meantime, if you have any concern at all, call 911."

In spite of her trembling body, her voice was unwavering. "Don't worry—I will."

The phone call from Paul shone brightly against the shadows formed by Marty Lee's conduct. "How's the article coming along?" he asked.

"Quite well. I'm having a great time doing the research. Now that I'm in Easton, I have constant access to the archives in town." She strained to hear Paul's response in the downstairs hallway of Ramer History House during a change of classes. "What did you say?"

"You're about to learn a whole lot more. I was at the historical society's library digging around and discovered Lafayette has an original copy of the Committee of Observation and Safety's minutes in their special collections."

She nearly dropped everything. "Oh, how wonderful!"

"I know. I called Donna Metz, the head archivist, and asked if we could see them. She said she'd have them ready by one o'clock."

"How do you manage these things?" She headed upstairs, flowing with the human tide.

He laughed. "Let's just say they owe me one."

"I'll meet you in front of the library at one."

He was waiting on the top step and broke into a full smile when Erin appeared. "Well, hello," she said. "Fancy meeting you here." She had decided not to say anything about Marty just yet, not wanting the unpleasantness to steal joy from finding new documents about her Grandfather Peter or having Paul on campus. "So, what's the deal with 'they owe you one'?" A student ran past Erin, bumping into her and calling "Sorry" as he rushed toward the entrance.

Paul frowned at the guy's retreating back. "I got a call this morning from Hal Bonyard in the development office. He's scheduled to give a presentation in New York this weekend about Lafayette's part in downtown Easton's renaissance, but he has bronchitis and can barely speak. He asked if I would go in his place."

"Oh, how nice for you, but of course, not for Hal."

"I don't know what's on your plate, but would you, or you and Ethan, care to go with me? We could spend the weekend there or just overnight." He paused. "Hal has a room reserved, and I will be happy to get one for you."

She appreciated his discretion. "Oh, Paul, I wish I could, but I'm planning to attend a Valley Forge DAR meeting on Saturday after dropping Ethan off at his best friend's for a sleep over. His grandparents are going to bring him back to Easton Sunday afternoon."

He touched her shoulder. "I wasn't expecting you to drop everything for a spur-of-the-moment thing. Besides, we'll see each other in Orlando over Thanksgiving."

"Yes, we will." She smiled.

"Shall we?" He swept his arm toward the entrance. "I told my parents and my sister you're going to Disney with your family. They would like to meet you." He paused. "If you like."

This day was throwing out surprises like a fast-pitch machine, barely giving her time to get a good grip. She had a sudden craving for Apple Jacks and seaweed crisps. "Uh, yes, I'd enjoy meeting your family." She wondered whether he'd present her as a friend or a girlfriend. Which one was she anyway? She liked Paul—a lot. As she got to know him better, though, she sometimes experienced fresh waves of grieving over Jim and what they had known together. The emotions left her feeling as if she were living in a bank of London fog. Although the sun often penetrated, she still didn't quite know where she was heading. She glanced down at her wedding ring. As her dad liked to say, "One day at a time."

He held the door open for her, and they entered the brightly-lit library, then walked up a flight of stairs to the right. Everything about Skillman was august, but the second floor even more so. Erin smiled to herself when she remembered Hatfield College's counterpart before a major renovation five years earlier. Dean Sanders had referred to the library as "an abomination of desolation." Off to the side of an upscale lobby with a marble bust of the Marquis, they entered a side door to a room featuring a few long tables, and a reception desk on the left.

"Paul! How are you?" A woman of indeterminate age greeted them with handshakes.

"I'm well, thanks. Donna, this is my, uh, friend, Erin Miles. Erin, Donna Metz."

"Hi, Erin. If you'll follow me, I have everything ready to show you." She stepped from behind a low-hanging door into the main area and led them to a table at the center of the room. Looking like she'd stepped out of a Talbots' catalog, Donna put on a pair of white cotton gloves and removed a thick sheaf of papers from a special box. "These are the original minutes of the Committee of Observation and Safety."

"Wow," was all Erin could manage.

"Paul told me about your ancestor. Peter Kichline's name is all over these documents."

She moved closer to the top paper and read aloud, "Minutes of the Committee of Observation of Northampton County, December ... December 21st, 1774 to August 14, 1777." She looked up at Paul and Donna. "The handwriting is quite nice but difficult to understand."

"Not to mention faded," said Donna.

"Who took the notes?"

"Robert Traill served as clerk of the first and second Committees, before and during the Revolution. He was also the third lawyer of the bar of Northampton County and the grandfather of Lafayette's esteemed professor, Dr. Traill Green." She pointed to the first page. "Your ancestor's name appears right off the bat. Here, put these on, and have a seat."

Erin slipped on the gloves and sat down. Adjusting her glasses, she read the first paragraph, slowly. "Agreeable to Notice for that purpose given to the Freeholders and Freemen of the County of Northampton qualified to, to Vote for Representatives in the Leg-is-la-ture, a very respectable number of them met at the Courthouse in Easton in the said County on the 21st day of December Anno 1774 when George Taylor, Peter Kachlein …" She looked up. "There he is!" Paul smiled at her as he stood with his arms folded. "Okay, so, 'and Henry Kooken Es …'"

"Esquires," Donna said. "Esquires were nominated Judges of the Election, for a committee of Observation and Inspection conformable to the Eleventh Article of the Association of the Continental Congress and recommended by the General Assembly of the Province." She could barely contain her grin. "I know, I sound like a Wikipedia article."

Erin smiled, then her face suddenly fell. "I'm afraid I don't have much time to try and make this out today. Donna, could I come back another time?"

The archivist exchanged a knowing look with Paul. "Feel free to come back any time, Erin, but I know wading through antiquated writing could send anyone heading for the medicine cabinet. Therefore, I have something for you." She reached for a manila envelope. "This is for you. Back in the 1930s, someone had the wherewithal to go through these minutes and transcribe them using a typewriter. I've made a copy for you."

"Wow! And today isn't even my birthday."

After lingering twenty more minutes, looking for references to her Grandfather Peter and finding several, Erin stood. "I can't thank you enough, Donna. This isn't just helpful for my article, but a personal treasure as well."

"My pleasure. I'm so pleased to know his legacy is being showcased again. He was an amazing individual."

She shook Donna's hand and left with Paul, clutching the envelope to her breast. Outside she let out a happy sigh. "This is all so wonderful, Paul—all these discoveries. I feel like I'm getting to know my ancestor even better."

"You are."

"You know, I've been wondering, do you have any idea where he lived in Easton?"

Paul frowned. "I've given the matter a lot of thought but haven't come up with anything decisive."

"How strange. I mean, he was one of Easton's leading citizens."

"You're right. His name is on a number of land deeds, and we know he had a tavern before he became sheriff the first time and the place was on Northampton Street. I do have my suspicions."

Erin gave a start when she looked at a wall clock. "Oh! I need to be going. Can we continue this conversation later?"

"Most definitely."

She slipped away from her in-laws' house after dinner and drove three miles to the cemetery, parking the car along the neatly-edged road. She walked carefully across three rows of graves before locating one with lighter-colored grass. Erin got on her knees and dug a hole just to the side of Jim's plot so she could plant a medium-sized container of mums. "I know you always liked crimson mums," she said. She hit a rock and made incisions along the outside with her small spade so she could extract the stone. "Things are going pretty well for Ethan and me. He's making some new friends and loving Easton. I'm enjoying my life there, too, Jim, although things aren't going the way I thought they would." She sat back on her knees. "I think life is just that way sometimes, though."

She remained steady throughout the planting of the flower, but when she finished, tears started flowing. "I miss you so much." Her next words caught on a quiet sob. "I wish you were here. Sometimes I feel like a leg or an arm is missing because you're gone." When the emotion subsided, she blew her nose, gathered her things, and left.

She'd been looking forward to this moment at home after returning from an overnight with her in-laws and a Valley Forge DAR meeting where the members greeted her like a visiting dignitary.

"Oh, we've missed you, Erin! How goes the new house, the new job, and the new chapter?" Sydney Stordahl had asked after an epic hug.

"Things are going pretty well."

Sydney cocked her head. "Do I detect a note of caution?"

She held her thumb and forefinger an inch apart. "Just a little one. I love being in Easton, and Ethan is adjusting well. The George Taylor Chapter has welcomed me, but it's so much smaller than this." She thought back to the meeting in which one of the members asked if her mother was a DAR. When Erin had said she wasn't, the lady urged her to invite Audrey to come. She felt guilty about not wanting her mom to share this part of her life. Easton was fresh and new for Erin, and she wasn't sure how to figure her family into the equation, especially her parents, who weren't on the same page as her. Maybe she wasn't really being snooty, though. Maybe bringing her mom to a meeting was just a little too much like having a parent go along on a date.

"Each chapter has its own personality, and bigger isn't always better. I mean, there can be greater opportunities to lead in a smaller one." Sydney grinned. "You know I always had you pegged for leadership here."

Rather than going into details about school and her church, Erin chose a different tack. "What really excites me just now is an article about Peter Kichline I'm writing for the Northampton County Historical and Genealogical Society."

"How nice for you! I'll bet you're finding a lot of great information up there." Erin nodded. "As for the rest, God and time have a way of smoothing things out."

Back home in Easton, she was sitting under her favorite throw on a family room couch with a fire going and Toby next to her. Ethan was at his best friend Jake's house, and Al and Pat Miles would bring him back to Easton after church. She placed a cup of green tea and a brownie with cottage cheese and olives on the side table, then reached for the packet Donna Metz had given her. Clearly, the transcribed Committee of Observation document had been created on an almost antique typewriter given the uneven, boxy quality of the letters. She would have waded through mud, however, to read this account of Revolutionary War-era Easton and her many times great-grandfather's role.

Donna had been right; his name was everywhere. He'd been present at every committee meeting and was a key player in Northampton County's military preparations through the summer of 1776. Then, he literally disappeared into the ranks he'd led to the defense of New York in August. She marveled at his dedication, his energy. She was as filled with warmth and affection toward him as if she'd sat on his knee as a child and listened to his stories as she'd done with her Grandfather Ott.

There'd been problems as well in those quaking days when the ground of British rule shook underneath them. One fellow refused to surrender his guns in spite of the militia's dire need for them. Another used his position to earn a fast buck. Dr. Ledlie's housekeeper had been referred to as a troublesome whore, and what was this? Even her ancestor had been caught up in the whirlpool of accusations. *How can he have? He was so well-regarded!* She read an entry from July 9, 1776, the day after Peter Kichline had led his troops to the courthouse for a reading of the newly-minted Declaration of Independence.

> Upon the complaint of Peter Kachlein Esq. Lieut. Colonel of the first Battalion of Associators in the County representing that a certain John Musch of the town of Easton had falsely and maliciously calumniated and slandered him by circulating a report that the said Peter Kachlein was proffered the quantity of two thousand Acres of land as a Bribe or Reward to use his best influence and Interest to keep up and support the Assembly of this Province and the said Peter Kachlein farther represented that the Courts of Law being now shut up he could find no redress or remedy from them; he therefore prayed this Committee to take the same into consideration. Whereupon it is resolved that the parties and their Evidences be heard immediately …"

Erin sipped her tea and took a bite of the brownie, reflecting on this surprise twist in her beloved ancestor's story. *No wonder he was upset at this mushy guy, or whatever his name was! How dare he accuse Grandfather Peter of such a thing.* "Can you believe him, Toby? After all Peter Kichline was doing for the town and the county, this idiot had to go and spread lies about him. I wonder why." Her imagination stirred the contents of her thoughts. "Maybe when Grandfather Peter was the sheriff, he arrested Musch, or Musch was just plain jealous, or who knows what makes people be so offensive."

She suddenly shot up from the sofa, knocking the plate, the brownie, and the throw onto the floor. Toby lifted his head and stared. "Grandfather Peter, you had your Musch, and I have my Lee! In Easton. You went to the authorities, and I went to mine. How much our stories are alike! How uncanny." Erin thought about the phone call from campus security early Saturday morning while she was in Lansdale.

"Dr. Miles, I just want you to know we went to Marty Lee's room and found a good bit of meth. The kid's been kite-high since the beginning of the semester. He's been arrested for illegal possession, and the college is in the process of suspending him, effective immediately."

Determined to know what had happened to her ancestor, Erin gathered the mess from the floor and read on.

She wasn't exactly afraid when she went to bed. Marty Lee was likely in police custody or back home, but she wasn't taking chances. Before going upstairs, she locked the door to the garage, as well as the lower lock on the back, side door.

She awakened to a seven o'clock alarm Sunday morning and after stretching, threw on yesterday's jeans and a polartec sweatshirt to take Toby out. Deciding to go through the garage, she left her cell phone on the kitchen counter since this was only going to be a quick walk to the end of the block. Back at the house five minutes later, Erin punched in the code to open the garage door, then discovered the door leading into the kitchen was locked.

"Oh, brother! I forgot I locked the bottom part of the door last night. Let's go around back, Toby."

To her dismay, the same thing had happened there. In securing her domicile for the night, she'd managed to lock herself out—without having the benefit of her cell phone.

"What a dunderhead!" She felt utterly alone. Paul was out of town. She couldn't call her dad, mom, Alana, or Allen because she had no phone. She obviously needed a locksmith, and how much did they cost anyway? She decided to walk to Connie's house, where her friend welcomed her and Toby, fed her tea and toast and called a locksmith.

When she was safely back in her own house an hour and one hundred and fifty dollars later, her house phone was ringing. "Yes, hello?"

"Hello, Erin, this is Bobbi Emrick. My husband and I rent your house in Lansdale."

"Oh, yes, hello, Bobbi. How are you?"

"I'm fine, thanks. We just love your home. I hate to bother you. I know your father-in-law is managing the rental, but he's away on a retreat, and this can't wait."

Her gut seized. "What happened?"

"A bathroom pipe broke, and water came through the kitchen ceiling."

She imagined water spilling like the Niagara River into her kitchen. "How bad is the damage?"

"I'd say not awful, but still a mess. Steve managed to shut off the water before any more could flow into the kitchen."

"Thank God."

"Who should I call for help?"

"Just give me a second here." Erin reached into a cabinet for an address book, knowing Jim had kept emergency numbers written inside the cover. She found the name of a plumber and a painter and repeated the information for Bobbi. "You can give the bills to my father-in-law, and we'll go from there. Let me know what happens, okay?"

"Absolutely."

Erin hung up the receiver and looked down at Toby. "There's something I just don't understand, old boy. Didn't I do the right thing by moving up here? But then, why is my life so unsettled?"

Chapter Twelve

He'd agreed to allow Jacob to drill with his Associators, but the sight of him on the field of mock battle rattled Peter. Hans Schmidt's nephew Rudolph had indentured himself to the colonel and begun working at the mills, along with Schmidt's oldest son. Peter Horeback had completed his own service to Peter and joined the militia. Looking in his son's direction, he wondered, *Who will stay with Catherine, Elizabeth, and Susannah if—when—I'm called off to war, if Jacob goes too? Is Andrew's presence enough?*

Peter felt someone looking at him and turned just to the left to see Captain Sidman fixing his eyes steadily on him. "If I may say so, he's a good son, colonel, one of our best recruits."

"Thank you, Captain. I just wish he could be content at home."

Sidman's face broke into a lop-sided grin. "After all, sir, he can't help being who he is."

He wasn't sure she should be hearing any of this. Wasn't her condition delicate? Shouldn't she be as calm as possible? Of course, Catherine was a strong woman, not to say determined.

She dropped her knitting onto her growing waist. "Peter, dear, you mustn't worry so much about me or the baby. We won't fall apart." She grinned. "Besides, none of this is exactly a secret in the village."

Robert Traill coughed behind his hand, and Peter saw he wasn't clearing his throat—mirth was written all over his face. "Who did they send?" he asked, grateful not to be on such odious duty anymore. He did, however, miss being the first to know what was going on.

"Traxler from Macungie Township."

Peter nodded, the eight-day clock keeping time with his thoughts. "Let me fully understand this. Josiah Strong, who served as a Committeeman last year, raised up a rifle company for the Continentals."

Traill nodded. "Yes, then Strong collected money from his township to defray his expenses."

"But he didn't stop there," Catherine said.

Both men looked in her direction. "You're right, Mrs. Kichline, he did not. Afterwards he appealed to the Congress as well for the same expenditures and received the moneys."

Peter felt not only the heat of the June day but of anger toward men who would put their own interests ahead of their community's welfare. "When was this first discovered?"

"Apparently John Eich from his township overheard Strong boasting to someone in a tavern about the deception ..."

"Not to mention outright thievery," Catherine said.

Peter snorted. "This has had a bad effect on morale. Some men have turned away from signing up in his district because of the belief certain people are in this merely for themselves."

"Quite right. So, Eich reported the thefts to the Committee of Observation, and we took the matter from there." Traill shook his head. "This is where things get really odd, though." He looked over at Catherine, who remained silent. "We, that is the Committee, called Eich to appear before us to provide testimony in this matter, but he refused. We sent Traxler again, assuring him he wouldn't be forced if he came peaceably, but still he wouldn't come."

Catherine frowned. "There seems to be a lot of that going around. Why wouldn't he come? He was only supposed to provide testimony against Mr. Strong."

"Yes, well, we initially thought so as well. Then Mr. Levers began digging deeper and discovered Eich had been receiving a cut of Strong's extra monies in exchange for not telling anyone what he knew. Eventually, however, Strong refused to go along with the blackmail, and came clean before the Committee, but Eich remained intransigent. We finally sent Traxler and another fellow, only to find Eich had barricaded himself inside his house. He told Traxler he would come to the Committee on the appointed day, but he never showed. Once again, a summons was issued and unheeded. Finally, Traxler took a company of men with him to force Eich to come to Easton. At this time, Eich appeared at a window and said he had a gun in his hand. Traxler told him to put down the weapon and open the front door, but Eich said he wouldn't, he was in such a passion he couldn't be sure what he might do."

Peter's muscles stiffened. He'd been in similar situations as sheriff.

"Traxler signaled to one of his men to unlatch the front door while Traxler kept talking to Eich. When he'd gained admittance, two other men entered the house and overcame Eich before the man knew what was happening."

"Nice work," Peter said. He gazed at Catherine, her attention rapt, still wishing she wasn't hearing any of this. He didn't want her overcome with worry about what might happen to their family if Musch went off half-cocked.

"Traxler found Eich's gun primed and loaded with swan shot and powder. They brought him to Easton where, as you probably know by now, Eich was told unless he paid back the bribe and recanted his actions against the Committee, his name would be published in the English and German newspapers as an enemy of his country."

"What did Mr. Eich do?" Catherine asked.

"He recanted and is in the process of returning the bribe. Likewise, Strong paid back the money he took from the Congress." Traill stretched out his thick legs and took a deep draught of the cider Frau Hamster had served. "Then there's the case of some other Macungie men who refused to give up their arms ..."

Peter was as close to Robert Traill as he was to his own brothers, but at this particular moment he wasn't enjoying the man's company at all. Catherine, seven months along, didn't need this kind of news. He shot a look at his friend and pressed his lips together.

"Ah, yes, well, duty calls." Traill rose. "I really should be shoving along."

He didn't want her going out in the heat, but Catherine had insisted she needed to see the light of day. Plus, she wanted some items from Meyer Hart's store.

"I can bring *Frau* Hamster, Peter, dear. I know you have more important things to do."

He bowed. "Nothing could be more important than tending to your needs."

He offered his right arm, and they left the house. She may have won the argument about not staying home, but he insisted they walk slowly, her normal limp more pronounced by her extra weight. After the usual greetings of passersby, including Pastor Rodenheimer, Peter helped her up the few steps to the store. Somehow, the place always had an edge of coolness, no matter the outside temperature, and he welcomed the chill for his wife's sake.

"Ah, *Frau* Kichline!" Hart lifted his hands and grinned. "How very good to see you." He turned to Peter, his eyes still on Catherine. "And you, colonel. You brighten my day."

"I say the same for you, *Herr* Hart," she said. "I could stand being inside no longer."

The proprietor nodded, closing his expressive eyes. "Ah, yes, I can imagine. The colonel does not want you exerting yourself."

"You know me well," Peter said.

He rubbed his hands together. "So, how may I be of service to you?"

"I am in need of sugar, salt, and coffee."

Peter's mouth hung open. "Why didn't you let *Frau* Hamster …"

"Sometimes a woman just needs to shop."

Hart placed his right index finger against the side of his nose. "This is true. Help yourself to a look while I gather your comestibles."

Peter saw, of all people, John Musch come through the door. A vein in his temple pulsed as he tried to block Catherine's view of the man and the hard look they exchanged. Suddenly, she dodged out from behind Peter and stood face-to-face with her husband's accuser.

"You should be ashamed of yourself, Mr. Musch." She waved a finger in his face as if he were a child. "Spreading rumors about my good husband. Endangering the sacred cause of our country, the one you say you love so much." When Musch opened his mouth, she gave him no berth. "You will stand here, and you will listen to me. You are a bad person, and I don't know how you live with yourself."

Musch turned on his heel and fled, Catherine's voice trailing after him.

July 2, 1776

Bedminster, PA

My dear brother,

I have desired to write to you since my return from the North, but many duties related to the Sacred Cause have prevented me. I apologize in advance for what will be a brief letter, but at least I will be able to relieve any anxiety you or your family may have had about me.

As you, know, last October I marched to New York under the command of Colonel Allen to take part in an expedition against Canada. In early May, we were within three miles of our destination when we were met with General Thomas, who had led the first expedition, as he was returning from Quebec. We helped cover General Arnold's retreat and were involved in several skirmishes with the British and Indians, not to mention the battle of Three Rivers in June. Our men suffered intense hardships, advancing, retreating, and marching through swamps and wilderness. We were the victims not only of nature, but of treacherous guides. We lacked sufficient food and clothing and were often lost, cut off from the main command. When we at last reached Ft. Ticonderoga, I was able to secure my discharge and have recently made my way home and into the bosom of my good family.

Just yesterday as Bucks County was reorganized for active service, I was selected Colonel of the Third Battalion, Militia. I am sorry to say I did not leave my enemies behind in New York, however. A complaint was made to the Committee of Safety to the effect that I used undue influence in getting myself elected colonel. Fortunately, the good men of the Committee immediately recognized this as a matter of personal jealousy. I tell you this unfortunate story in case you should get wind of the lies up your way.

A good name is always cleared eventually, and a good cause will always win the day. I count on these truths, and the God who set such things into motion upon creating our world. We are embarking on a noble pursuit of liberty from tyranny, and I pray you and yours are well as we strive towards a happy ending.

My beloved wife greets you. Mother and Father Koppelger are in good health, as are brother Charles and his Susanna.

Your devoted brother,

Andrew

Ziba Wiggins leaned closer to Peter at the courthouse entrance. "He isn't here, colonel." Peter glanced upward, thinking. Should he bother to sit through the committee meeting in case Musch showed? He certainly had other pressing matters to attend to.

"Who knows, he might just come after all. The pressure has been on for some time."

"Thank you, Mr. Wiggins. I do believe I'll go in—for a while."

"Sir." Wiggins stood just in front of Peter, blocking his way. "If you would, please. As injurious as Musch's rumor has been, I find as time goes on, fewer and fewer suspect you of all people of wrong doing. None of us Associators do."

Peter smiled. "I appreciate your show of support, my friend." He entered the courthouse which, unlike Meyer Hart's store, was not cool in the heat of summer. Finding the proceedings of the Committee's regular meeting already underway, he found a seat toward the back of the room, and catching the eyes of his former colleagues, nodded in their direction. When he made eye contact with Robert Traill, Peter's friend shrugged his shoulders. When was Musch going to abandon not only his vicious slander, but his abject disrespect for authority? He listened as Jesse Jones, serving in place of Lewis Gordon and Robert Levers, read one of several complaints.

"Peter Haas says that when Nicholas Klotz was called upon for his Arms, he said that his gun was taken away from him without his knowledge—but that since he was summoned, he had delivered up his musket—ordered that the said Klotz pay the said Haas and Moser for their expenses."

Robert Traill wrote down the information as Jones waited a moment before continuing. "Ludwig Meckel confesses that he had two guns, but that he had sold them to Casper Ebenberg of Whitehall Township. However, he agrees to deliver them up to the said collectors of arms by next Monday. Ordered that he also pay to the said Haas and Moser for their trouble and expense." He paused once again for Traill, then consulted his notes. "Leonard Miller confesses that he has a gun in his house, but says it belongs to his son who is now in the Continental Service and is willing to deliver it up to the said collectors, provided they give him a receipt for the same, mentioning the value thereof. Ordered that the said collectors give him a receipt accordingly, and that he also pay said Haas and Moser."

Peter shifted his weight in the too-small seat, thanking God for the privilege of leading men in the field, rather than quibbling over the tedious collection of guns. At times, he caught himself mentally wringing his hands over the riff-raff affairs of a county whose people were anything but unanimous in their support of the Cause. How would they be able to win battles against the formidable British when there was so much infighting? Shaking the dark shadows from his spirit, he knew where he stood, the power of his own resolve, and the Power guiding him. Ultimately, he would stand before his Creator and give an accounting for none but himself. He fully intended to be found faithful.

As the dealings unfurled, he waited for some pronouncement about his own case, which came as the red-haired Jones gathered the last of his papers.

"As I see Colonel Kichline among us, let me mention we continue to summon John Musch to appear before this committee to give an answer to his charges against our upstanding citizen. However, Mr. Musch has consistently refused to comply." He looked toward the back of the room. "Let me assure you, Colonel Kichline, this committee is doing everything in its power to bring your case against Musch forward. Our patience is not limitless. I believe this fellow has had ample opportunity to fulfill our simple request, and I give you my personal word he will appear, if not voluntarily, by force."

Andrew Drunkenmiller could barely hold a musket when he'd first joined the Associators. The young man had since learned to handle his firearm like the best of Peter's soldiers, but because of his youth, Drunkenmiller was serving as a drummer. The boy's face had drooped when he'd first learned of his assignment, but after realizing how important the job was to the entire company, he'd worked on his responsibilities with his customary intensity.

Peter, Andrew, and Jacob headed back to the village after their morning drills, batting at flies and bees drawn by their sweat. At the top of Hamilton Street, Jacob said, "Father, I'm going to take a dip in the Bushkill before getting to work."

"I'd like to do the same," Drunkenmiller said.

Peter waved across his face at a determined gnat. "I might just join you after checking in at home."

Jacob gave him a sideways grimace. "Mother Catherine might prefer you bathe first."

He guffawed. "And if she doesn't, *Frau* Hamster might turn me out."

The stocky frame of Robert Traill huffed toward them up Northampton Street, his face pink from heat and exertion. "Colonel Kichline! May I have a word?"

Peter stopped so his friend could catch up. Turning to his boys, he urged them to go on ahead of him. "What's happening my friend?"

"There is news." He reached Peter, mopped his face. "Lewis would like to see you right away—actually Lewis and Taylor. They're at Lewis's house right now."

Since they were alone, Peter addressed his friend informally. "As you can see, Robert, I'm attracting gnats and flies as strongly as the porcine contingent at the courthouse. Might I freshen up first?"

Traill covered his nose. "I suppose you have the right idea."

"Tell them I'll be there presently."

At home, Peter shed his clothes, handing them to Joe, who'd brought a basin of fresh water to the bedroom, then left in what seemed to be a particular hurry. Peter hadn't needed to ask his wife for privacy; she'd fled to the kitchen when he came through the front door. A basin bath might not be as refreshing as submersion in the Bushkill Creek, but he was refreshed and clean enough to make haste to his friend's home down the street.

"Please excuse my delay, gentlemen," he said, after giving his hat to *Frau* Neuss at the door and smoothing back his hair.

"Not to worry, my friend," Gordon said.

Lewis's ashen complexion weighed on Peter's spirit, as well as the deep wrinkles appearing around the lawyer's eyes and forehead. "How are you faring?"

Lewis sighed. "My infirmity comes and goes. Presently, I feel quite well, thank you. And how went the drilling today?"

"The men are coming along nicely." Peter leaned against the wall closest to an open window to catch whatever air might happen to stir.

George Taylor, who was sitting next to Traill across from Lewis's desk, spoke. He appeared as cool as if the temperature were in the fifties, rather than the high eighties. "We wanted to tell you some news apart from the general committee."

Peter wondered if the information might have something to do with Musch.

"A number of things have been happening at a quickening pace," Taylor said. "I will be going to Philadelphia shortly to a meeting of the Continental Congress representing Pennsylvania."

The skin on the back of Peter's neck prickled. "We may be heading toward a declaration, then?"

"Independence will surely be at the forefront of the meetings, but I must caution you. Not everyone is on the same page, not in Pennsylvania anyway, as you well know."

Chapter Thirteen

Erin hadn't quite figured out how to do holidays since becoming a widow. She had a vague memory of last Christmas, the first one since Jim's death, an experience something like trying to have a conversation while emerging from general anesthesia. She knew there had been a tree—but she hadn't put it up or done the trimming—and presents—which she hadn't bought. Some time right after New Year's, the tree had been taken down and placed in the middle part of the basement near Jim's boyhood toboggan. Erin suspected her in-laws and Melissa had played elf and Santa, something she'd ask them about when she had a chance. Her one goal had been to make the red letter days as pleasant for Ethan as she possibly could.

She wanted this year to be different, more like the ones she used to know in the house on College Hill when she was a girl—before the relational pipe bomb had detonated, scattering her family in different directions. Maybe she would even forego the usual artificial tree and buy a real one. Ethan would like that. Hope was taking her by the hand and leading her to a more level place. She didn't dare think too far ahead just now, however. One day at a time …

As she drove to her mother's apartment to take Audrey to the store, Erin shifted from thoughts of Christmas to more immediate ones about Thanksgiving. She was halfway across the "new bridge" when she recalled being at her brother's house in Bethlehem the previous year, or had she been there for a Christmas party? She shook her head over this form of amnesia. At any rate, she would not be with her side of the family this year on Thanksgiving. Taking Ethan to Disney World with her in-laws wouldn't bother her dad. Tony had never been too big on holidays as she was growing up, and time hadn't altered his opinion.

Her mother was totally different. Family needed to be together, traditions needed to be observed. Over the years, Erin had done her best to honor her mom's wishes, but she had also built in boundaries for herself, Jim, and Ethan. Thanksgiving was always spent with the Miles family, but Erin would visit her mom that Friday or Saturday. As for Christmas, she would go the day before, arranging her schedule in order to be at her church for the seven-thirty Christmas Eve service. She had never wanted any unpleasant family dynamics spilling onto her festivities. Inevitably, Audrey would bring up stories about Tony's abject Scrooginess. Erin had heard multiple times about the year when she was four, and her dad refused to get a tree or provide money for presents because "Jesus wasn't actually born on the 25th of December, and I'm not about to celebrate the fat man." Grammy Ott had supplied money for a tree and a few gifts.

Erin sighed, trying to expel the unpleasantness. *This is now.* She was reclaiming Easton for herself, to create the kind of faithful, fruitful life her Grandfather Peter and generations of her family had known along these hills and rivers. She couldn't help but wonder when all the craziness had started. Maybe with her great-grandmother's quirks and tragedies? Or had her parents been somehow off-beat? *At any rate, the buck stops here.*

She sat across from Audrey at a fast food restaurant her mother insisted on calling "Carolina Chicken." This was not a place Erin ever cared to dine at, but her mom loved coming here, and she wanted Audrey to be in a good mood when she shared her holiday news.

"So, Erin, what new family discoveries have you made?" Her mom dipped her fork into mashed potatoes slathered in brown gravy.

Erin ignored the drop of gravy slipping onto her mom's blouse knowing if she said anything, Audrey would either cry or become angry. "Actually, I've made some very good ones this past week. I found minutes of the Committee of Observation at Skillman Library, in the special collections area."

Audrey frowned. "What kind of committee?"

"Before the Declaration of Independence, Pennsylvania had begun to slip out from under royal rule. There was still a colonial assembly, but on the local level, counties and townships needed committees to carry out the laws. Grandfather Peter was a leading man in Northampton County's Committee of Observation."

"Peter Kichline was a pretty big noise around these parts." She shook her head. "I don't know why my mother never told me about him."

"I don't think she knew. Remember, she didn't even know her own grandmother's name."

"Well, people back then didn't have the time for such things. They were busy making a living and raising kids."

Erin wasn't sure she agreed with her mother's logic, but she thought there might be a grain of truth.

"So, how did you find out about this observation committee?"

"Paul told me. He knows so much about local history."

"This Paul seems interested in more than local history."

Erin gave a small laugh and looked down at the table.

"I like him, what little I've seen of him." Her mom paused. "Do you like him?"

"Yes, he's a very nice person, and a good friend."

"Where are his people from?"

This felt like a perfect way to introduce the subject of Thanksgiving. "They live in Orlando, near his sister and her family."

Audrey chewed a green bean, then swallowed. "Do you think there could be more?"

She shifted on the bench. "I don't know, Mom. I mean, I think so, maybe, but I don't know … Jim hasn't been gone very long."

"I understand. But Erin." She leaned across the table. "Grandfather Peter was married how many times?"

"Three."

"Because his first two wives died, right?"

"Right."

"Well, people do remarry, especially if they've had good relationships. I didn't because my husband didn't die. I didn't have a happy marriage, but if I had, and he had died, well, maybe I would have. Who knows?"

Erin decided to take the plunge. "Hey, Mom, are you going to Allen's again for Thanksgiving this year?"

"I always do. Will you be coming?"

"Uh, no, I actually have other plans."

"You have other plans."

The narrowing of her mother's eyes told her to proceed with caution. "Yes. You know, Jim and I always used to go to his parents' for Thanksgiving. Last year the holidays were hard for them, and they decided to do something different this year."

"Which is?" Her mother was judge and jury.

"They're taking Ethan and me to Disney World." She added an uplift to her voice on the last two words.

"Disney World?"

"Yes."

"What kind of place is Disney World for Thanksgiving?"

"A lot of people go there for holidays."

"Well, I'm not a lot of people. I think you should be with family. Besides, I never had money to take you to Disney World."

"I will be with family, Jim's family. But I'll be home for Christmas." She felt like she was throwing Audrey a bone.

"You better be."

♛

She was more relaxed since Marty Lee's expulsion. The bad apple had been plucked out of the barrel, and she could stand before her class without trembling so hard she had to consciously will her teeth not to chatter.

Herman popped into her office smiling. "So, how are you doing now?"

She looked away from her laptop and removed her reading glasses. "Really well, thanks."

"You survived an ordeal, and now things will go a lot more smoothly."

She hoped so. For all her relief, she still wasn't feeling the love. Maybe she just needed to give the healing process time. Fifteen minutes later, a knock sounded at the door, and she looked up to find Mia—jolted by the freshman's paleness.

"Mia, come in."

She hesitated. "Am I disturbing you?"

"No, I'm having office hours. Besides, you couldn't disturb me if you tried." The coed's smile was weak. She must've lost ten pounds, rather than acquiring the usual "freshman ten." "Please sit down."

Mia dropped her backpack on the floor next to the chair. When she didn't say anything, Erin spoke. "You seem tired."

"I haven't been sleeping too well." Before Erin could ask why, the young woman continued. "I came to apologize for the bad job I did on my essay about King Philip's War."

"There's no need to apologize. Clearly, though, this wasn't your usual quality of work."

"I haven't been able to concentrate very well in any of my classes."

Erin rested her arms on the top of her desk. "What's wrong, Mia?"

Tears flashflooded her eyes, and Erin rose to shut the door so the girl could have some privacy. Then she returned to her chair. "Take your time." She sat silently, praying for wisdom to know how to help.

A few minutes later, Mia reached for a tissue from a box on the desk and blew her nose delicately. "I'm sorry. I'm such a mess."

Her heart thudded against her chest, wondering what she was about to hear.

"I think you know I haven't exactly been comfortable here." Erin nodded. "I've tried really hard to fit in, to do things other kids consider important. I just, I don't know, I just feel different."

"Something happened."

Mia gave a sort of shudder. "A week ago, I was at a party with my roommate. I didn't really want to go, but I thought getting out of my room might help, so I went. A group of guys were getting smashed, and I just sort of sat on a couch sipping some wine. I didn't like the taste, but I thought holding the glass would make the others think I belonged, you know? Then this guy came over to me. He wasn't half-bad looking, but his breath reeked from drinking and … he … he sat really close to me, and I kept trying to inch away. Then he … he … put his hands where they didn't belong." Tears reappeared. "I didn't know what to do. I couldn't move any further away, so when he wouldn't stop after I asked him to, I smacked his face."

Erin struggled to maintain her professionalism. She felt like smacking the guy too.

"Then he, uh, started moving his body like he was going to get on top of me, and thankfully my roommate saw what was happening and grabbed me by the arm. She pulled me away from him, and we left in a hurry."

"Thank God she helped you."

Mia's face soured. "That's what I thought. On the way back to our dorm, she told me I needed to loosen up."

Erin held back an explosion of words.

"Since then, I haven't been sleeping well, and I haven't had much of an appetite. I'm just going through the motions, Dr. Miles. I came here because I thought, well, I thought maybe you would understand."

She did. Memories flickered onto her mental screen of a similar incident when she was a senior on a month-long trip abroad. While she was busy roaming museums, concert halls, and marketplaces, most of the guys were urinating in cups in the back of their tour bus after breaking out the beer before breakfast.

"You said Lafayette was like this when you went here, right?"

"This has been known as a party school for a long time. Don't get me wrong—students studied hard. You had to if you were going to survive. I think most colleges tend to have this sort of thing going on. When I was a student, I also had my family nearby." She had a sudden thought. "Where are you from, Mia?"

"South Dakota."

Erin's eyes enlarged. "South Dakota! You've come a long way."

"I wanted to see something different. I'd always heard about the great schools back east, and I wanted a good education. I liked the campus when my parents brought me to visit—like some preppy dream. This seemed exactly what I wanted. But now, I don't know. I'm just so homesick I could cry." She glanced at Erin and gave a laugh.

This is good. She still has a sense of humor.

"I'm seriously thinking of quitting—of just going home. Dr. Miles, I don't think I can take much more of this."

Erin wanted to say the right things, to help this distressed girl, but she was no counselor. What if she said the wrong thing? What if Mia tried to hurt herself? Still, she didn't strike Erin as the kind of girl who would, not with the faith Erin knew her to have.

"Are you going home for Thanksgiving?"

"No. Not until Christmas."

"Have you told your parents about any of this?"

Mia seemed to disappear between her shoulders. "I've told them I'm having trouble adjusting."

"I have an idea, but your parents would need to be brought on board. I think the best thing would be if you stuck out the rest of the semester, then if you still felt Lafayette wasn't the right place for you, you could transfer to a different school. That way, you'd have your first semester under your belt, and you wouldn't have to start from scratch somewhere else."

Mia seemed to be studying Erin's face, and a little color popped onto her cheeks.

"There are only about five weeks until the end of the semester. Even if you struggled the whole way through, I believe in the end you would come away from the experience feeling stronger."

She smiled, a little.

"Over Thanksgiving, I'm going with my family to Disney World, and I could use a house and dog sitter. I live just off campus. If you'd like, and your parents agree, would you consider staying at my home?" She added, "I'll pay you, of course."

"Oh, Dr. Miles! Really? I would love to. Then I could sort of collect myself and spend some time away from the dorm thinking about my options." She paused. "What kind of dog do you have?"

"A big, old, drooly basset hound."

"I love big, old, drooly basset hounds."

Erin glanced at her watch. "I have a class in five minutes. Can you come back in an hour, and we'll call your parents?"

"I'll be here. Thank you, Dr. Miles."

Erin rose. "This isn't exactly PC, but I know you and I share the same faith, so I'm going to leave you with this thought—Philippians 4:13."

Chapter Fourteen

He hailed Robert Levers, who was waiting for the stage. "Good morning. I see you're heading back to Philadelphia."

"Yes, my friend, I assure you my wife is beginning to feel like a widow these past weeks." His face looked pinched, as if slowing his pace caused physical pain.

"Even so, she tells my wife how proud she is of what you are doing to win our liberty."

"Thank you for saying so. I know you trod a similar path before taking over the county's military duties. I am always concerned for her and my children's welfare when I must be away. So, Colonel, are you pleased with your Associators?"

Naturally, Levers knew all of the county's business and much of the commonwealth's. Peter figured he wanted to go deeper than what he heard at meetings.

"My men are deeply committed to the Cause. They've already sacrificed so much."

"I'm glad to hear this. Given all the challenges we're facing, those numbers aren't bad at all." He was clearly getting wound up. "You know how things go in Pennsylvania. With our disparate religions and ethnicities, our leaders have been far too cautious." He shook his head, sighed. "Still, I am hopeful our just Cause shall prevail, especially after the Assembly removed restrictions for our delegates to the Continental Congress about discussing independence. Were you there for the vote?"

"I'm afraid not, but I was pleased to hear of this as well," Peter said. He wondered if he should say anything about Musch and decided not to. For better or worse, Levers did.

"Colonel, I want you to know you have my full support in the unfortunate matter you've been dealing with."

"Thank you."

"I believe Musch is the worst kind of miscreant. Because we aren't going at a fast enough pace toward liberty, in his expert estimation of course, we must, therefore, be under the undo influence of the Assembly. He may as well have pointed a finger toward myself." He straightened his shoulders and smiled. "Chin up, my friend! Most of the people in the county believe you, at least those with half a brain." He took a step closer to Peter, who didn't need the additional warmth in his personal space. "I feel in my bones, Colonel Kichline, this is the time of reckoning. This is the day when destiny takes a firm hand." He pressed his lips together and made a fist.

Peter kept his smile to himself. "And you will be in the thick of history being made."

"Yes, but my good man, while you remain in Easton training our men for war, you are making history as well. As a matter of fact …" Levers took him by the elbow and steered him away from what constituted a crowd in Easton's Centre Square. "I have the makings of an idea I'd like to share with you."

Peter allowed himself to be led off to the side of the courthouse facing toward the church. "What's on your mind, Mr. Levers?" He discreetly moved his arm to break free of the man's hand.

"I believe I will not be returning to Easton empty-handed." His dark eyes kindled. "If the provincial and colonial representatives do their jobs correctly, if they read this moment in the annals of time rightly, there will be a pronouncement of our independence from Great Britain."

The back of Peter's neck tingled. He'd been sensing the same destiny about to pour over the colonies, but he'd been reluctant to give voice to the belief because anything might happen in Philadelphia. There were no guarantees since there wasn't unanimity among the delegates about how, or even if, independence should be achieved. Since the appearance of the Common Sense pamphlet, however, the streams of liberty had been swelling. Levers was still speaking, and he focused on the earnest face of a man he'd come to know well these last few years.

"When Mr. Taylor and I return from Philadelphia with an announcement, I would ask you to bring your Associators to the courthouse in a show of fanfare and celebration."

He began imagining what such a scene would look like and decided to think more on this later. "You do me a great honor, Mr. Levers."

"Great honor is owed you," he said with a bow.

"Thank you."

The sound of carriage wheels and horses on cobblestones alerted them to the coach's arrival.

"Perhaps you could begin to think about this so we can be ready."

"I will be glad to."

His eyes shone. "No one should ever live to forget such a day."

He was itching to bring his men to General Washington's aid in the defense of New York, but he was also dreading to bring his men to General Washington's aid in the defense of New York. According to Dr. Ledlie, and no less an authority on childbirth than *Frau* Hamster, Catherine would be delivering her second baby right around the end of July or beginning of August. What if he wasn't there for her? For their baby? Already she was too unwieldy to leave the house, and the confinement had left her on this side of irritable, although Peter thought she controlled her impulses well. She often smiled at him, assuring her nervous husband she and the baby were doing just fine. Elizabeth's healthy birth had done much to diminish his fears, which had accumulated like barnacles in his spirit after losing his second wife and their premature infants. Anxiety, however, still had a way of pouncing on him.

He decided to call a family conference. "In the event I must leave before Catherine's time has come, I must know all of you will see to her every need as well as the baby's, and little Elizabeth's."

"*Jawohl.*" *Frau* Hamster's eyes were fierce.

"Yes, *wohl*!" Joe said.

Andrew spoke up. "I'll do everything I can."

Jacob echoed his brother. "That goes for me as well." Peter appreciated his son's own form of sacrifice. He knew Jacob would much prefer being with the Associators in the thick of battle than looking after his stepmother.

"My dear husband, you would definitely be missed if you must go before my time comes," Catherine said. "However, I am surrounded by capable people. Phoebe will return to help me, and Elizabeth Traill will be by my side." She smoothed the back of his oldest daughter's blonde head. "Susannah is a capable young woman, and Dr. Ledlie is right around the corner. You have nothing to worry about."

"Yes, Papa," Susannah said. "We hardly need you at all!" Her eyes flew open wider, and she popped her hand against her mouth. "I didn't mean to say those words exactly. Of course we need you. And we want you. I just meant …"

He put his forefinger to his lips, as if she were a little girl again. "I know what you meant, *Liebling*." Why was he feeling such a strange combination of freedom and superfluousness?

He had just finished the evening meal when someone pounded on the front door. His scalp tingling, he rose from the table and headed down the hallway ahead of *Frau* Hamster for once, opening the door to find Robert Levers in a lather. "Good sir!"

With a flushed face, he waved what appeared to be a broadside. "I bring good tidings."

"Good tidings are always welcome—as are you. Come in."

"Only for a moment." Levers bowed as the women of the house, framed by Joe, Andrew, and Jacob, started piling up behind Peter. "There has been a declaration of independence!"

Peter heard himself gasping, along with the rest of his family, each of them glancing quickly from face-to-face. "When?"

"The document was approved on the second, and John Hancock signed his name on the fourth. The Congress ordered copies to be sent to all Assemblies, Conventions, and Committees for public readings. On the sixth, Pennsylvania's Committee of Safety instructed all the counties to read the pronouncement at noon on the eighth. I got here as quickly as I could."

"Mr. Levers, you must come in and sit down. You are fatigued." Catherine led him into the parlor where their visitor sat before the idle fireplace.

He patted her hand. "Thank you, madam. How are you faring?"

"I feel quite well, thank you."

"I am happy to hear this. Your child will arrive soon, I think?"

She nodded and sat across from him, looking relieved to lower her bulk into the chair. "Perhaps by the end of the month."

Levers shot Peter a look, which he couldn't bring himself to return. *Frau* Hamster scurried off to the back of the house with Joe on her heels, apparently for refreshments.

"We are independent of Great Britain then?" Jacob was sitting on the edge of his chair.

"We are, my young friend."

Andrew murmured, "It's all over but the shouting."

"Yes, well you might say." Levers placed his hands on his knees. "Colonel, remember what we spoke of several days ago?"

Peter nodded. "I do."

"Can you have everything ready by tomorrow at noon?"

"Yes, my friend. This will be a celebration our villagers and all those who come after us will long remember."

He nodded to Andrew Drunkenmiller to begin the tattoo of the drum, signaling the fifers. Word had spread throughout Easton since Levers's return, and villagers crowded the courthouse square waiting to hear Congress's decision. Falling in line behind him, Peter couldn't have been prouder of his men if they'd been arrayed in British scarlet with not a scuffed button or shoe. Despite their farming and hunting gear, the soldiers of the First Battalion were arrayed in honor and courage.

The piercing notes of the fife and a steady drumbeat trailed after him and Captain Sidman as they processed on horseback behind Easton's new standard—from Shannon's, formerly the Bachmann, Tavern up Northampton Street and to the courthouse. Women and children waved as they passed. Men young, old, and in between stood at attention, working pipes in their mouths, here and there the sunlight reflecting off a tear. He wondered whether he might be dreaming, but the perspiration under his heavy uniform was very real. When they reached the Square, Peter and Sidman led their horses to the right of the courthouse entrance, while behind them their field officers fanned out. On the other side of Robert Levers, who stood in the doorway, the musicians and soldiers gathered. The marching ended, Levers started prancing around as he lifted his voice to the crowd.

"My good people of Easton and Northampton County! I have just come from Philadelphia with a declaration of independence from the Continental Congress, which I have been charged to deliver on this day at noon." He lifted the document and began to read. 'When in the course of human events it becomes necessary for one people to dissolve the political bands which have connected them with another and to assume among the powers of the earth, the separate and equal station to which the Laws of Nature and of Nature's God entitle them, a descent respect to the opinions of mankind requires that they should declare the causes which impel them to the separation.'"

Levers had allowed Peter to read the broadside the night before, but hearing the words delivered in this solemn assembly made his left calf tingle. He sat even straighter in his saddle, feeling as if he could reach the top of the courthouse.

"'We hold these truths to be self-evident, that all men are created equal, that they are endowed by their Creator with certain inalienable Rights, that among these are life, liberty, and the pursuit of happiness. That to secure these Rights, Governments are instituted among men, deriving their just powers from the consent of the governed.'"

He scarcely breathed while his colleague delivered a list of grievances against the King—demanding compliance of his subjects; forbidding them representation; introducing standing armies and quartering the troops wherever and whenever he pleased; imposing taxes; not allowing the colonies to trade with other nations or expand to the west; stirring up the native inhabitants against the colonists.

"'He has plundered our seas, ravaged our coasts, burnt our towns, and destroyed the lives of our people.'"

The charges came rapidly, salvos fired against a tyrant and his minions. Abelard shook off a fly from his mane, breaking Peter's near-trance. He gazed at the crowd, whose rapt faces absorbed every word Levers said as he spoke with an actor's flair, until his eyes fell upon Susannah, standing where the throng wasn't quite as thick. What was this? She was supporting Catherine, holding her by the elbow, both of them as stalwart as any of his men. His wife caught his eye, and she flashed a sober smile containing not a hint of apology for coming today when he had expressly told her she shouldn't. The weather was too hot, the crowd too heavy, and who knew whether they might become unruly. Suddenly his anger dissolved.

He bowed his head in her direction, a tribute to her spiritedness, her own ardor for liberty.

Levers was beginning to wind down.

"'We, therefore, the Representatives of the United States of America, in General Congress, Assembled, appealing to the Supreme Judge of the world for the rectitude of our intentions, do, in the Name, and by Authority of the good People of these Colonies, solemnly publish and declare, That these united Colonies are, and of Right ought to be Free and Independent States, that they are Absolved from all Allegiance to the British Crown, and that all political connection between them and the State of Great Britain, is and ought to be totally dissolved; and that as Free and Independent States, they have full Power to levy War, conclude Peace, contract Alliances, establish Commerce, and to do all other Acts and Things which Independent States may of right do.'"

He caught Robert Traill's glance. Knowing if he continued to look at his dearest friend, he would blubber like a child, Peter turned his head once again in Levers's direction.

"'And for the support of this Declaration, with a firm reliance on the protection of Divine Providence, we mutually pledge to each other our Lives, our Fortunes, and our sacred Honor.'"

His eyes scanned the crowd. Would there be any dissent, any ...

"Huzzah! Huzzah! Huzzah!" As if they had their own script, the villagers cried, "May God long preserve and unite the free, independent states of America!"

He not only heard, but felt the courthouse bell tolling as he signaled his men to fire their cannon. Easton had never heard such a din. Even the cows and sheep wallowing in the July heat bleated and mooed as if cheering for liberty. Peter almost shed his dignity and started shouting himself. Instead, he led his men in a parade toward the church, enjoying himself vicariously.

Chapter Fifteen

She was caught in a whirlwind of epic proportions. Trying to get herself and her son out of the house on time to arrive at her in-laws' to make their flight out of Philadelphia International was right up there with landing a lunar module. Jim had always been so much better at organizing and making sure their bags were packed just-so into the trunk, that all TSA regulations had been meticulously observed, while at the same time adjusting house lights, thermostats, and the hot water heater to vacation settings.

"Ethan, are you sure you packed your toothbrush and other toiletries?"

He came down the staircase bumping his suitcase behind him. "Yes, Mom."

"Not the big toothpaste, the travel size."

"Yes, Mom."

"Do you remember if we put two swim trunks in with your clothes?"

"They're there, Mom, with my swim shirts." He rolled his eyes. "You're going to have a stroke if you don't chill."

She didn't know whether to reprimand him or laugh. Her heart was racing. Her head did feel just short of exploding. She cast an apologetic glance at Mia, whose parents had readily consented to the coed's staying at Erin's house over Thanksgiving. "I'm not usually like this."

Mia grinned. "My mom and dad get like you are when we go on trips." She petted Toby, who already seemed to have sworn his canine devotion to the sweet-spirited young woman. "There's so much to remember, but they always tell me—'If we forget something, there are stores where we're going.'"

Erin's mouth fell open. *Jim used to say the same thing!* A giant eraser glided across her emotions, removing all the exclamation points and upper case, bold, letters. In their place, a smooth sort of calm spread over her. "Okay, then, you have all the instructions about the house and Toby." Her voice sounded less shrill in her ears.

"I do."

"Oh, did I give you my new cell number?"

Mia nodded. "I added it to my contacts."

"Great. I haven't memorized the number yet myself."

In the great debate about whether or not to let Ethan have a phone, Al and Pat Miles had stepped in. Their meat packing business was upgrading employee phones and plans, and because of the system's requirements, everyone's numbers had to be changed. Erin appreciated how her in-laws were allowing her to participate in the package as a family courtesy, since Jim had always had his cell coverage through the business. As a result, she'd replaced her four-year-old fossil of a phone with a dazzling model she had yet to understand beyond text messaging—she kept hanging up on people when they tried to call her—and Ethan now had a simple, non-smart phone. He had balked at the absence of bells and whistles, but there was no way Erin was going to let her son turn into an adolescent cellphone automaton.

She surveyed their rolling suitcases and carryons, then opened her backpack to make sure she had her laptop. She planned to spend some of her time in Orlando trying to find out where her Grandfather Peter had lived in Easton.

"Well, then, I guess we're ready." She bent down and gave Toby a hug. "You be a good boy. Feel free to text or call if you need anything, Mia, or just want to talk."

"I will. You guys have a great time."

Ethan wrapped his arms around the dog. "Bye, old boy, I'm going to miss you." For a moment he seemed to waver. Then he rose. "Let's go, Mom!"

Her legs felt as if she'd been on the Summit Plummet ride one too many times. On the other hand, Ethan had energy to spare, even after the drive to Lansdale, then to the airport, the flight, arrival at the hotel, and thrusting himself whole-hog into the Magic Kingdom before closing time. Al gamely volunteered to stay with the boy.

"You girls go back to the hotel. We need some guy-time, don't we, champ?" He ruffled the top of Ethan's head.

"You don't have to twist my arm, Dad."

"Mine either," Pat said. "Al, do you have Ethan's room key?"

He checked his wallet. "I sure do."

"Why can't I keep the key, Grandpa?"

His blue eyes twinkled. "Because I might forget it."

"Wh-what?"

"Don't stay out too late now," Pat said, chuckling.

Back at the Contemporary, Erin said good-night to her mother-in-law, whose room was just across the hall. "Sleep well, Mom."

"I fully intend to. Now, go relax." She kissed Erin's cheek.

Inside the comfortable room, Erin unpacked the suitcases and set out Ethan's pajamas near the sunshine yellow Mickey Mouse pillows. His toiletries went in the ultra-modern bathroom next to his own sink. Then she filled and eased herself into the tub with a generous helping of vanilla-scented bubble bath, feeling relaxed for the first time in the last twenty-four hours. She lolled in the water until the temperature grew tepid and the last bubble had disappeared. Ten minutes later, she was in bed, enjoying the crispness of high-thread-count sheets when she had a sudden realization. She was supposed to call or text Paul, who had left the day before, after arriving in Orlando. She reached for the phone on the nightstand and checked her messages—voice and email. Although she was the one who was supposed to have contacted Paul, she felt disappointed he hadn't reached out to her. He had already had time to settle in at his parents' house in the suburbs.

She was too tired for a conversation, so she texted him.

Hi, Paul. We arrived in Orlando in time for supper. I'm about to go to sleep after dragging myself around the park as soon as we got here. Ethan and my f-i-l are still out there going strong. Oh, for the energy of a ten-year-old! We plan to do the park tomorrow. Let me know your plans.

She wondered whether to sign off with an emoji or other sign of affection. The truth was, they'd just skimmed the surface physically with kisses on the cheek, moderate hugging, a bit of hand-holding. There was a line they hadn't crossed, one Erin was profoundly grateful he respected while she took the necessary time to travel through grief and possibly toward a serious relationship. She looked down at her left hand, noting the absence of her wedding band, which she'd put in her jewelry case, unsure where she was on her particular journey. She selected a sleepy face with z's and hit "send."

Ethan surprised no one when he announced he wanted to eat breakfast at Chef Mickey's. No one objected. A concierge had told them when they checked in that they should eat there at least one of the mornings of their stay since "You never know who might drop by." The only problem was, Erin couldn't get her son to focus on his meal—mini-Mickey waffles and an assortment of fruit and meats. The distractions of the spectacular Bay Lake view, the regular junket of the monorail zipping by, and visitations by Pluto and Goofy had left Ethan open-but-empty-mouthed. Nearly an hour later, having eaten way too much herself, she dug in her heels.

"Ethan, we can't go into the park until you've put some food in your stomach."

"Aw, Mom. I'm not hungry."

"She's right, champ."

"Okay, Grandpa."

Not for the first time, Erin realized just how much a boy needed a man in his life.

At the monorail, Erin once again checked her messages. Melissa wished her a Happy Thanksgiving—"Be sure to text photos!" Mia sent a selfie with Toby, saying all was well. Her dad requested, "Say 'hi' to Mickey for me!" Nothing from Paul. *How strange. I hope he's alright.* She decided against sending him another text, not wanting to be pushy. She thought maybe she should put her wedding band back on.

She had known from the start of the trip where she would be eating Thanksgiving dinner since Pat and Al had made reservations at The Wave. Conversely, Paul would be with his parents, sister, and her family. Their discussion about seeing each other included the possibility of getting together Friday or Saturday, possibly just the two of them, or with members of his family. He had twelve- and fifteen-year-old nephews, who would be good company for Ethan, kids who knew the Disney parks like experts. They had told each other they'd be in touch once she'd arrived in Orlando to firm up plans. Besides, wasn't touching base just common courtesy? She knew something was wrong when, by the end of Wednesday night, still she hadn't heard from him.

Hi again. I'm wondering whether you got my text yesterday. You usually respond fairly quickly, so I'm getting concerned. Is everything alright? Let me know.

By Thanksgiving morning, she was downright worried and decided something needed to be said to her in-laws. They'd been in on the plans and would be wondering what was going on.

"I've only met Paul a couple of times," Al said over a light breakfast, "but this not answering texts or calling isn't like him."

Ethan smirked. "Maybe you should get your shotgun, Grandpa."

Erin shook her head and gave a short laugh.

"Did you try calling?" he asked.

"Yes, but I just got a message that his voicemail hadn't been set up."

Al patted her hand on the table. "Try not to worry, Erin. I'm guessing we can give him the benefit of our doubts. Let's just pray all is well."

The benefit of the doubt. She'd learned to do that over the years with Jim after a bumpy start when they were first married. Too often, her brain reverted to a childhood place in which her family ate cold or over-cooked food once her mom had concluded Tony wasn't coming home for dinner. He'd never bothered to call, just headed to a bar with his buddies after work. He'd come home stinking drunk, resulting in a fight, cold shouldering, or all of the above. Erin had hated both means of communication. "I'm not your dad," Jim would tell her. "If I'm ever late and I don't call you first, which doesn't normally happen, I will have a very good reason." He had never let her down. She could either start this relationship with Paul on

Jim's steady foundation, or build on the old one. Hands down, Jim's solid rock beat her parents' sinking sand.

The Thanksgiving Day plan included rides and attractions in the morning and early afternoon, returning to the hotel around three to rest and prepare for their holiday meal at six. The grown-ups preferred dining later, but they knew a hungry boy might not be able to wait until seven or eight. Erin went on a number of rides with Ethan after breakfast, avoiding the more aggressive ones in spite of her son's taunting. "I'd rather be called 'chicken' than toss my cookies," she told him.

Al gamely did the Tower of Terror with his grandson, afterward looking like he'd actually seen a ghost. "I'm getting too old for this, champ."

Ethan looked ready to get back in line to do the ride again, but Erin frowned and held up her right hand. "I think we should all slow down." *If Paul can deliver his nephews tomorrow or Saturday, Ethan would love going on those rides with them, and we grown-ups would have a great 'out.'*

When they'd first arrived at the Magic Kingdom two nights earlier, Erin had noticed the ubiquitous presence of background music playing throughout the park and how the tunes shifted to reflect the themed areas. She wouldn't have chosen to take a breather in this particular place in which the music sounded like something out of "Psycho," but Al had needed to "sit for a spell." Ethan remained standing, his body twitching, eyes darting about. She closed her eyes beneath her sunglasses and sank into the bench, trying to find a tiny space of quiet, nearly achieving relaxation when Ethan shook her shoulder.

"Mom! Mom!"

She sat up. "What?"

"They just announced your name over the loudspeaker."

She screwed up her lips. "Very funny."

"I'm not trolling you! Listen!" He pointed up at the sky.

"Would Dr. Erin Miles please report to guest services?"

She looked at Al and Pat. "What in the world?"

They raised their eyebrows in tandem.

Erin pulled out her map, trying to find the location while the announcement ran again. Realizing the place was a good ten-minute walk away, she offered to go herself. "You just keep relaxing, and I'll text or call to let you know what's going on."

Ethan was hopping up and down. "I'll go with you, Mom."

"You know, this music is really getting to me," Pat said, standing. "We'll follow in the same direction. Ethan, you stay with us and make sure we don't get lost."

"But …"

"Let your mom go ahead." She telegraphed a "Be careful" look to Erin.

She could almost hear her son deflate as she took off, grateful she'd chosen her most comfortable Sketchers for the trek through the park. A few times, she bumped into people in her state of distraction. When she reached guest services and realized what was happening, she did her best Roadrunner imitation, skidding to a halt. "Paul!" For once he didn't look put together.

"Oh, Erin, I'm so glad I found you. This is the—"

"I've been really worried. Are you okay?"

"Now I am." He took a step closer. "Can I hug you, or perhaps you're not speaking to me?"

She gave a laugh and moved closer. "I'm so glad you're okay, at least you seem to be."

"You know when people say 'You wouldn't believe what happened?'" She nodded. "Well, I'm about to say 'You wouldn't believe what happened.'"

"So, what happened?" She debated whether to text Al and Pat right away, then decided to hear Paul's story first.

"After I arrived at the airport the other day, I went to the rental car desk and signed out a vehicle. I put my bags in the trunk, got into the driver's seat, and started the engine. I was backing out of the spot when I heard a crunching sound under the tires."

Erin's eyes widened. "Ooooh. What did you run over?"

"My cellphone."

"Your cellphone!" She clasped her hand against her chest.

"Yup. I had put it on top of the car while loading my things."

"Not good."

"At all. My phone was deader than Jacob Marley."

"No wonder you didn't answer my texts or calls."

"I am so sorry, Erin." He squeezed her right hand. "Please forgive me."

"Well, there's really nothing to forgive."

"I must've caused you some uneasy feelings, though." He stared into her eyes.

"Mostly about your welfare. I was striving to give you the benefit of the doubt."

"A very wise and caring thing to do."

She paused. "So, do you have a phone now?"

He rolled his eyes. "So, I found a store for my carrier not too far from my parents' house, and three hours later, I had a new phone. The problem was their system wasn't working properly, and they couldn't transport my contacts. I have to go back another time."

"Bummer."

"I tried to call you, but a message told me your number had been disconnected."

She let out a long, "Oh."

"What?"

"I just got on a new plan and had to get a different number. I must've forgotten to tell you! But you did get my texts, right? I called, but I got a message about your voicemail not being set up. Now I understand why."

"You texted me?" he asked.

"Yes, a couple of times."

He slapped his palm to his forehead. "I'm still figuring out my phone, and when I saw a number I didn't recognize, I was a complete doofus and hit 'delete.'" He reached for her hand again. "I am so sorry."

"Me too." She smiled at him, joy bubbling inside. "Technology failed, so you came looking for me!"

"I couldn't remember what hotel you said you'd be staying at, but I thought Ethan had mentioned something about the Magic Kingdom. On the off-chance you might be here, I came and had you paged."

She inched back a little for a better look at him. "Let me get this straight. You bought a ticket, which I might add isn't cheap, on the chance you might find me here and not at one of the many other Disney parks?"

He nodded sheepishly.

"On Thanksgiving day."

He closed his eyes, gave another nod.

"Were you going to track me down at one park after another?"

He gazed at her. "If that's what it took to find you."

Chapter Sixteen

The glow he felt from the previous day's proceedings didn't start dimming until he walked to the courthouse the following day. The impending proceedings would be a far cry from the Continental Congress's Declaration of Independence from Great Britain. There would be no cheering crowd, no cannon fire. There could, however, be shouting. Truly, he didn't know what to expect of a man who'd spread such vicious lies and refused to recant. As he walked through a curtain of humidity, he wondered how a person could become as hardhearted as Pharaoh.

Seeing Robert Bell coming in his direction was as welcome as a mosquito bite, but he managed a curt "Good day." Bell sniffed as if he smelled pig flatulence, then grunted. Peter held back a laugh, which turned into a smile when he fell in step with Robert Traill a few paces ahead.

"Good morning, my friend."

"Good morning to you, Robert. How are you faring?"

"Quite well. The question is, 'How are you?'"

"I'm also well, thank you. Hopefully there will finally be some closure to this unpleasantness." He hoped he didn't sound as if he were fishing for information.

"We will know soon; I believe there's only one other matter on the docket. So, how is Catherine after yesterday's merriment?"

"She's taking a rest." He didn't mention how he'd had to talk her into not coming with him this morning.

"She's a plucky woman."

"Yes, and in spite of my concern for her and the baby, I must say I am proud of her."

Traill clapped him on the back. "She's strong, a good helpmeet for you." He mopped his brow. "A son of the Highlands has difficulty with these Pennsylvania summers."

Out of charity, Peter didn't add, "Nor does a man of your heft."

Ziba Wiggins greeted them with his usual smile and bow. "Good day, gentlemen! What a day this is. Independence at last!"

Peter shook his Associator's hand. "Yes, indeed." He knew Wiggins realized the hard work of winning that independence still lay ahead. A small gathering had collected around the building's perimeter, and he tipped his hat to them as he followed Traill into the courthouse. Since this was not to be a public meeting, the room felt almost empty, except for Peter, Traill, and six committee members. Mercifully, Wiggins had cracked open the windows.

Lewis Gordon waved him toward the small enclave, apparently feeling well enough to preside. "Good morning, Colonel, Mr. Traill."

"Good morning, Mr. Gordon." Peter removed his hat and greeted each of the other men, seating himself a few steps away from the committee's table out of deference to their authority. Under normal circumstances, he might have joined them, but since his name and case were on the agenda, he didn't want to make any appearance of currying favor.

"Well, then, gentlemen, this standing committee shall come to order on this auspicious day after the Declaration of Independence was read just outside these walls."

The other men nodded their agreement, then Cornelius Weygandt spoke. "What a day! I am so pleased the Congress took this bold step."

"Hear, hear!"

Gordon was all business. "Yes, well, since Congress did take such a step, we have work to do. The very same Congress has requested counties to form Flying Camps to aid General Washington whenever and wherever he shall need their assistance. Now then, with the concurrence of Northampton County's commissioners and field officers, in order to encourage a sufficient number of volunteers to turn out to serve in the defense of their Country, we are prepared to contribute to this Flying Camp. A bounty of three pounds will be given to every able-bodied man to enlist in this service and remain so until the first of December next, unless Congress discharges them sooner. This bounty will be raised by a tax on the inhabitants of this county."

Abraham Berlin spoke. "May our present Associators join the ranks of this Flying Camp?"

"Indeed, Mr. Berlin," Gordon said. "They have been training for months and are in just such a position."

Peter wanted to jump into the conversation, but since he was no longer part of the Committee, he knew he needed to remain silent unless asked for his opinion.

The other committeemen accepted the recommendations, then selected officers for this Flying Camp. For the most part, these were already leaders of the existing four militia battalions, Peter included.

"Now that we've established the officers, there remains the matter of choosing a colonel," Gordon said. He gazed at each of the men. "I believe we should table this measure until the next meeting since we have some important business to attend to first."

Peter bristled but didn't care to give away any indication of annoyance. While he seemed to be the most logical choice, surely his good name needed to be cleared first in this public forum. He wasn't angry at Gordon, but he did begrudge the man who had created this infernal problem.

Gordon cleared his throat, sipped from a heavy mug, then began reading a document heavy with legalese. "Upon the complaint of Peter Kichline, Lieutenant Colonel of the First Battalion of Associators in this county, representing that a certain John Musch of the town of Easton had falsely and maliciously calumniated and slandered him by circulating a report that he, the said, Peter Kichline, was proffered the quantity of two thousand acres of land as a bribe or reward to use his best influence and interest to keep up and support the Assembly of this province, and the said Peter Kichline farther represented that the courts of law being now shut up, he could find no redress or remedy from thence, he therefore prayed this committee to take the same into consideration."

Peter felt the need to take a breath for Gordon.

"As all of you know, this committee has, indeed, looked into Colonel Kichline's complaint." Gordon looked over at Peter, then back at the men around the table. "We immediately heard evidences from both parties, including testimony from Mr. Weygandt, who solemnly declared Mr. Musch told him Colonel Kichline had been offered a bribe of land in exchange for his influence in upholding the Assembly of Pennsylvania. The committee adjourned for three hours to consider this matter to the fullest extent, and our conclusion was in favor of the colonel. We told Mr. Musch he was to sign a written acknowledgment of his fault for circulating so injurious a report, which greatly hurt Colonel Kichline's character through the whole county. Not only so, but his work as an Associator and officer was also harmed. We drew up the paper, but Mr. Musch still refused to sign."

Peter listened with the focus of a hunting dog, waiting for the final outcome. So far, he'd already known most of what Gordon was saying, but where were all these prior steps leading?

"This was not our only attempt to get Mr. Musch to comply with our decision of Colonel Kichline's innocence in the matter. We repeatedly summoned Mr. Musch to appear before this Committee, and he constantly refused to pay any obedience." Gordon sat up taller. "Therefore, this Committee does hold up Mr. Musch to this entire county as a designing, dangerous, and refractory person, and the public are desired to beware of him accordingly. Mr. Traill, see to it the above transaction be published in the English and German newspapers."

Peter caught the approving glances of the committeemen and nodded his appreciation. His good name was publicly cleared, for the record, yet he couldn't help but feel some disappointment. John Musch also deserved the stocks.

Not much had changed for him when he went to his men the following day. He wasn't sure whether they knew about the Committee's decision, nor did he particularly want to speak about Musch's condemnation. He was content to have the heaviness on his chest and in his step lifted. He had always been an honest man and his good name had been forever cleared by other honest men. As he stood before his Associators, he explained the Committee's decision to form a Flying Camp.

"We are in an excellent position to supply General Washington as he prepares to engage the enemy, likely very soon, in the defense of New York. You are skilled riflemen, your patriotism is unmatched. I appeal to each of you to consider signing up." He nodded toward his aide. "Captain Sidman will assist you as you come forward for this purpose. Let me say before you do, I am proud to serve as your colonel. I hope you will continue in defense of your country in this new capacity. If you cannot, for your own good reasons, I still count it a privilege to have served with you."

To a man, his Associators became members of Northampton County's Flying Camp. Including Jacob.

He appeared before the Committee with his colleague, Colonel Jacob Stroud, on the thirteenth to recommend a first lieutenant for the fourth Battalion. Then came the last of the day's business, which was to choose by ballot a Lieutenant Colonel for the newly-formed Flying Camp. He excused himself quietly, believing since he was such an obvious choice, he shouldn't be present during the election. Instead, he lingered outside where he and Ziba Wiggins talked in the shade of an oak tree. Peter tried to keep his mind on his friend's discussion about the price of ale, but he kept asking Wiggins to repeat himself when the man's words fell unheard to the ground.

When the Committee members began filtering out of the courthouse, Peter wondered why they weren't making eye contact with him. Shouldn't they be stopping to congratulate him? Puzzled, he watched as Robert Traill emerged, striding in his direction. "May I have a word?"

"Yes, of course. Will you please excuse me, Mr. Wiggins?"

"Certainly. Good day, sirs." The keeper of the keys bowed and removed himself.

Traill walked briskly down Julianna Street toward the Lehigh River. When they reached the bank of the slow-moving water, he spoke at last. "My friend, the committee has chosen a colonel, and I wanted to tell you the news apart from everyone else." His eyes combusted. "Isaac Sidman."

Peter's feet felt suddenly rooted to the ground. "Sidman?" His thoughts stirred. Isaac was so young, the same age as Peter Jr. He'd never led men in battle. He was highly regarded by one and all, a capable enough fellow, but an untested man commanding untested troops, a man who couldn't even speak German.

"The Committee decided you'll continue as head of the First Battalion, but some members preferred a more youthful leader." He spat on the ground. "Since he's been learning straight from you all these months, he seemed to them the right choice."

The initial shock was lifting. "I understand how they could think so."

"Honestly, my friend, I don't think this had anything to do with the Musch affair," Traill said, addressing an unspoken question.

The shouts of children playing along the river drifted their way.

"Peter." Traill looked into his friend's eyes. "The decision was not unanimous."

"Thank you." He stared across the forks of the two rivers. "I guess we need to get straight to work then."

Traill was in a huff. "I can't believe you're not livid."

"Why should I be? The Almighty has his very good reasons for everything. I would be wrong to accept the things which appear favorable, then complain when something happens beyond my understanding, or desire. Besides …" He grinned at Traill. "… I think you're angry enough for two men."

His friend shook his head. "You amaze me."

The scene for drilling to the west of Easton hadn't changed. The former commander, however, now stood to the side while his former subordinate took his place before the troops. Sidman's face, barely able to sport a beard, was ruddier than usual. He constantly wiped sweat from his brow and forehead.

"Good day, men." Sidman raised his voice. "I am honored to have been chosen to lead our Northampton County Flying Camp and will do my best to serve you and our country."

Peter noticed his men frowning.

Sidman seemed to remind himself to speak slower, as if to dull-witted men. "Today we will begin with a review of facings, starting with a right-face." He lifted a small pamphlet and read aloud: 'First, turn briskly on both heels to the right, lifting up the toes a little, and do a quarter circle.'" He looked up. "Right-face!"

They gaped. Sidman repeated himself, to no avail. A sudden gust caught his hat, and he reached up to prevent the covering from blowing off. "Now, then, what was the word for right in German?" He seemed to reach inside himself and brightened. "*Richt! Richt!*"

Peter's heart constricted. He wanted very much to rescue Sidman, but decided not to interfere unless the commander asked for his help. He didn't want to undermine what little authority the man clung to.

Sidman was looking at the booklet again, muttering. "'Right-face. Then bring back the right foot to its proper position, without stamping. Then, to the Left-face in two motions, first turning to the left as before to the right. Second, bring up the right foot to its proper position.'" He suddenly dropped, then retrieved the pamphlet, brushing dust from the cover, fumbling to find his place.

By this time, the men had given way to whispered grumbles spoken from the corners of their mouths. Peter caught various men's eyes, communicating to each they were to remain at attention. Sidman walked over to him then. "Perhaps you could assist me, sir? I need to have them understand me."

"Yes, of course, Colonel." Peter followed Sidman to the center of the group, and immediately the men pushed their shoulders back and sucked in their stomachs. He waited for the commander to take the initiative.

Sidman spoke loudly. "Colonel Kichline will be assisting me this morning with our drills."

No one really understood what he was saying, except for the word "Kichline." This was something they could hang their hats on.

Chapter Seventeen

"Tell me everything."

Erin scooched herself up further on the bed and relaxed against the headboard in her quiet hotel room. She'd been preparing to take a shower when her phone rang, and "Melissa" popped onto the screen. This was a call she really wanted to take.

"Hello to you too!"

"Enough with the niceties, young lady. I want details."

Erin laughed, pulling the coverlet over her legs. "So, you got my texts?"

"Yes, but too skimpy. No, Tim, the red bowl goes on the middle shelf in the cabinet next to the oven. Sorry about that, Erin. We're still cleaning up after Thanksgiving."

"Did you have a good one?"

"Yes, all the usual suspects were here. We ate and watched football, ate again and played football, had dessert and watched two more football games. I told my family I don't want to cook, or hear the word 'football' for at least a week. Now then, you spent Thanksgiving with Ethan, Al, and Pat, but you saw Paul at Disney. I didn't quite get everything."

Erin told the story of how Paul had showed up at the Magic Kingdom quite unexpectedly, his gesture covering a multitude of prior lack-of-communication sins. "Then we hung out for a few hours at the park until we both had to get ready for dinner."

"I'm really glad the whole mess got straightened out. He's right about the perfect storm thing—how you got a new number just before you left Pennsylvania, and he ran over his phone with the rental car. Sheesh." She started making crunching sounds, and spoke around whatever she was eating. "So, what happened on Friday?"

"What are you eating, Melissa?"

"I'm trying to be good after all the fat and sugar I've consumed. I have celery sticks with peanut butter."

"Since you're snacking while talking, I'm going to join you."

"Might as well. What are you having?"

"White wine with jalapeño crackers and marshmallow fluff."

There was a momentary silence. Then, "So, tell me about yesterday and today."

"Okay, let me get my days straight, they're all running together. Yesterday was Friday, so Paul's sister, Laurel, and her husband, Dennis, brought their boys to the park to hang out with us. Gavin is twelve, and Joey is fifteen."

"How did they get along?"

"Really well, at least Gavin and Ethan did. Joey spent most of his time with his phone. He wasn't a bad kid, just acting like he was too cool for a couple of middle schoolers."

"And Paul's sister?"

"Very nice. We sort of danced around each other, you know, gathering facts about our lives, connecting over songs and movies we'd seen and liked, talking about our work, normal chit chat. I liked her. Dennis was nice too—fun with the boys but also hanging back and letting them do their own thing."

"So you were comfortable with them?"

She was in the middle of biting and swallowing a cracker. "Um-mm. Excuse me."

"What did you do today?"

"Today was wonderful, like the perfect cup of coffee at just the right temperature."

"Sweet! What happened?"

"The boys ended up having such a good time, Laurel decided to team up with Al and Pat to take her kids and Ethan to Universal, mainly for Harry Potter. I hesitated because honestly, I am theme-parked out! Even with my good shoes and sandals, I have two blisters, and I will shoot straight to the moon if I hear the song from 'Beauty and the Beast' one more time."

"I had that song as an earworm once. I think I could hear the loop in my head for a week. Did you know I can get an earworm out of even a slip of a commercial or a TV show theme? I remember when Ryan was little, he used to watch 'Sponge Bob,' and there was a piece of busy music they always played, which just about drove me to distraction. Erin? Are you there?"

"I'm here."

"I went off on a tangent—again."

"No problem." She picked up the thread of her prior comments. "I was just about to tell you, Paul asked if I'd rather get away from the whole Disney-Orlando thing and have a quiet day. Did I ever jump at the chance! My in-laws thought this was a good idea, and Ethan hardly noticed I wouldn't be tagging along."

"I like this man more and more."

Erin sipped her wine and continued. "Paul wanted to know if I'd be interested in hanging out at his parents' house or would rather go out somewhere. I wasn't nervous any more about meeting them, not after being with his sister and her family, like meeting the Bassetts would just be a natural thing to do, so I said I would."

"Ooh! What were they like? Where do they live?"

"They were quietly friendly, not all over me with hugs and kisses, but still welcoming and comfortable. More bassett hound, pardon the pun, than springer spaniel."

Melissa laughed until she snorted. "You're a hoot."

"Yes, well, they live in a retirement community with a golf course, pool, and recreation center. Their ranch house is all soft green tones and white accents. Quiet, like them."

"How old would you say they are?"

"Mid-to-late seventies."

"Did you have lunch there?"

"We did. Mrs. Bassett—Louise is her name—made turkey sandwiches, and we had pumpkin pie for dessert. Then they left to play golf with some friends, and Paul and I had a great visit together."

"The parents left you alone?"

Erin laughed. "Honestly, Melissa! Oh, guess what? He found out some great information about my Grandfather Peter!"

"Of course he did."

"Are you making fun of us?"

"Just a little. I enjoy hearing about your ancestry. What did he discover?"

"I've been wondering where Grandfather Peter lived in Easton. There are maps from his time period showing lots and who lived on them, but his name doesn't show up."

"That's pretty strange, I mean for a man who was doing all the things he was doing."

"I know. He did own a good deal of property, though, including the mills and a house near one of them where some of his indentured servants lived. He also had a tavern when he first came to Easton, and there's actually a record Paul showed me this afternoon—he took a picture with his phone—from a book about Benjamin Franklin. He'd been a member of the Pennsylvania Assembly during the Indian uprisings in 1755, and the book says he stayed in one of the taverns. According to Paul, there were only a few in Easton then, and one of them wasn't very reputable. The most highly regarded ones were the Kichlines' and the Bachmanns'. Courts used to meet in both, but my relatives' place was bigger, and Franklin said he stayed in a large room."

"Do you know where the place was, or is?"

"Yes, the book gives a good description of the building and location, between Centre Square and Fifth Street, on the left." Erin's right leg started jiggling.

"How cool is that!"

"I know."

"Dare I ask, is the tavern still there?"

"Paul has to dig a little deeper, but he suspects the structure could be there but under layers of additions."

"Oh, wouldn't that be exciting!"

"Yes. I feel like an infomercial saying this, but wait, there's more. When Grandfather Peter became sheriff, he had to give up selling spirits, meaning alcohol, and Paul thinks he and my grandmother Margaretta may have moved a little further to the west of town, turning the tavern over to another couple to run. My grandfather Peter Jr., his son, ended up building a house in the area to the west after the Revolution, and he had a tavern there at the crossroads."

"And is that one still there?"

Erin sighed. "Unfortunately, no. Sometime in the late seventies, the tavern was torn down, and an appliance store was built."

"Oh, ugh, and double ugh!"

"I know. I felt so sad when Paul told me, as if the event had just happened, and I was in mourning. He said the place was a restaurant and bar pretty much until the end. Maybe my parents remember. I'll ask them when I get home."

"Well, my friend, you are having a banner day and a great vacation."

"Yes, I am—made all the better since you called. I was dying to tell you everything. I miss you."

"I miss you back. How about if I come to Easton in a couple weeks, or are you swamped for Christmas?"

"I'm never too swamped for you."

"So, you're coming home tomorrow?"

"Yes, and Paul will go to the airport with us. His flight leaves an hour after ours, but we're coordinating our travels so we can ride together to Orlando, then from Philadelphia to Lansdale to Easton."

Melissa didn't say anything for a long moment. Then, "You like him, don't you?"

"Yes."

"A lot?"

Erin held a cracker in mid-air, not liking feeling pressured. "I think so."

"Erin?"

"Yes?

"I think Jim would want you to be happy."

Tears stung her eyes. "I know."

"Love you."

"Love you back."

Erin stood in her kitchen feeling like something the cat, if she had one, would have dragged in. There'd been a flight delay, two bouts of heavy turbulence, a forty-minute Philadelphia-style traffic jam, and a pummeling rain from Lansdale to Easton. Mia was standing there saying something. *Focus!*

"I'm so thankful you asked me to house and dog sit, Dr. Miles. This really did me good. Oh, I'm sorry if I wasn't supposed to, but I ate your last Dove bar. Was that okay?"

Erin was happy to see a spark in her student's eyes again. "More than okay. I told you to have anything you wanted."

"I know, but a Dove bar is a Dove bar. All of your mail is in a box on the desk in the hallway, and I gave Toby his flea and tick medicine on Saturday. He's a great dog." She bent over and patted his head.

"Yes, he is. Any time you'd like to come over to see him, just let me know."

"Oh, thank you." She looked down. "Um, I would like to tell you something. I can see you're tired and all, so I won't take long."

Erin sank onto a stool at the island. Ethan snatched his backpack and ran upstairs, Toby on his heels. "You look peaceful."

"I took some long walks with Toby, and I spoke to my parents a few times, and well, I prayed too. I realize Lafayette is a great school, and I was really fortunate to get accepted because it's so competitive."

Erin sensed a "but."

"But, this isn't the right place for me. I just don't fit into the culture, you know? I'm a Midwestern girl with pretty traditional values, maybe even old-fashioned ones. There's a small Christian college not quite an hour from my family, and I'm going to apply to transfer there. My dad knows one of the trustees, and they spoke. Dad doesn't think, after being accepted at Lafayette, I'll have difficulty getting in." She sighed, smiling. "I think I'm finding my place."

"I'm so happy for you, Mia.

"Honestly, Dr. Miles, if it hadn't been for you, I probably would have bolted last month. But you were right—completing a semester is better."

While this was about her student, Erin was taking the lesson very much to heart.

She had promised to let Audrey know of her and Ethan's safe arrival, so after driving Mia back to her dorm in the rain, Erin called her mom. "Hey, it's me."

"Erin! Where are you?" This as if she expected to hear her daughter had been on an expedition to Bora Bora.

"We're home now."

"You're home? When did you get in?"

"Oh, about forty-five minutes ago. I just got back from taking my student home, the one who housesat for us."

"Are you alright? Did you have a good time? How's Ethan?"

Erin laughed. "We're both doing well, tired but happy. We had a really nice time." Out of all the fun things she'd done on the trip, her mind drifted back to the quiet afternoon she'd spent with Paul. "There's so much to tell you, and I brought something for you from the Magic Kingdom."

"Did you see Mickey and Minnie?"

"Yes, and Pluto and Goofy and all the Princesses. Did you enjoy yourself at Allen's?"

"Oh, yes, Tanya made so many different side dishes I couldn't eat them all. Of course, I couldn't see them too well either, but everything tasted wonderful. Except the Brussels sprouts. I could never stand them, they taste like iron."

"How late did you stay?"

"How late did I stay? I was there until about nine o'clock. All the kids and grandkids were there, too."

"Well, I'm glad you had such a nice time."

"Yes, but I missed you and Ethan."

"Uh, I missed you too." *Sort of.* "Will you be around on Tuesday? I can stop by to take you shopping, and just to see you."

"I'll be here."

She only had forty minutes to get to her first class after Ethan got on the bus, but she couldn't wait until later in the day to go down the hill to see the place where Paul had confirmed Peter and Margaretta had once lived. Dodging the usual morning traffic, she was at least able to find a parking spot along Northampton Street across from the building Paul had mentioned. She got out of the car and waited for a LANTA van to pass before crossing the street. Near a parking lot for the Pomfret Club stood a three-story, free-standing building with a stucco façade and nineteenth century trim work running across the top at the roof line. Simple. Elegant. Unlike the fancy-schmancy edifices on Millionaires Row near First Church. *Like Grandfather Peter.* Her breath formed a miniature cloud. *This was where they lived. My ancestors. My family. This place has so many stories to tell.*

A few men and women passed by her on the sidewalk, then someone came over and stood beside her. Paul. They smiled at each other, and he took her hand. She only had fifteen minutes to get to class, but Erin wasn't concerned. Like Mia, she was beginning to see other possibilities.

Chapter Eighteen

He had dragged himself out of bed and picked his way through breakfast, avoiding his sons' knowing looks before heading off to the parade ground. Afterward he sat in the parlor, morose and tired. Isaac Sidman's drilling had been as uncomfortable as constipation. Maybe he was prejudiced, but Peter Jr. was more adept than Sidman, who constantly referred to his pamphlet and whose lack of German wedged an ever-widening breach between him and the Flying Camp.

These are good men, though. In spite of what's happening, they are trying their best to comply.

He'd heard their grumbles afterward, however, and fought his own temptation to join the complaints. The Committee had chosen Sidman, and Peter needed to support the man. He began praying silently for the new commander to rise to this very important occasion.

"Peter. Peter!"

"Yes? What?" He looked up from his chair as if awakened from sleep.

"You're grinding your teeth."

Newly aware of the tension filling his jaw, he flexed his facial muscles. "Yes, I suppose I was, my dear." He smiled at his extra large wife. "How are you this afternoon? And how is our *kleines Mädchen?* "

"Elizabeth and I are fine, husband. It's you I'm worried about." She lowered herself slowly onto an adjoining chair. When he didn't say anything, she spoke again. "You don't need to tell me about the situation." She placed her hands across her stomach. "I already know. I just can't understand the Committee's decision."

"Isaac is a good man. He's just …" He couldn't bring himself to say any of the adjectives parading across his mind. In time the young man could become a good leader, but now …

He saw *Frau* Hamster cruise down the hall with Joe at her heels when someone knocked on the door. "*Ja. Ja.* Come!"

Moments later, Peter's eyes widened at the sight of Isaac Sidman. "Good day, Colonel Kichline, Mrs. Kichline." He reminded Peter of a toy soldier whose paint had peeled off.

"Good day, Colonel Sidman. I was just going out to the kitchen." Catherine rose slowly, pushing herself up with her hands against the chair, wobbling to establish her balance as Peter guided her. "If you will excuse me."

Sidman bowed as she left the room, then shook Peter's hand. He waved to the chair his wife had vacated. "Please have a seat."

"Thank you, sir." Sidman worked his hands over a button on his waistcoat. "I need to speak with you."

Peter's heart rate escalated. "Of course. What's on your mind?" He resisted tacking on "son" to the end of the sentence.

Sidman bent his head. "I'm a failure, sir, a big fat failure."

He didn't wish to pour salt on an obviously opened wound. He decided just to let the man talk.

The young officer's face was the color of a bleached dish towel. "I don't know what the Committee was thinking, sir, but at first I was so honored by my appointment I couldn't see past my inexperience. Then I became terrified. I can't lead these men, not like …" He paused, then dropped his voice. "… not like you can." He slapped his right hand against his leg. "I can't even speak their language."

When Peter guessed Sidman had said all he'd intended to say, he spoke. "Coming here, telling me … this is hard for you."

"Yes, sir, but no harder than trying to lead men who deserve better."

Peter served a small portion of a smile to the distressed Sidman. "I believe in time you will be ready to lead. There's something in you, something the Committee also saw of this nature."

"I have a favor to ask, sir." His clear green eyes met Peter's gaze. "I wonder if you would stand for me tomorrow morning while I seek Mr. Gordon to discuss this matter."

"Yes, of course."

"What will you tell them?"

Peter would need to think about this. "I'll come up with something."

"Thank you." As he rose, some color began returning to his face. Peter also stood, and felt the millstone roll off his back.

The men gaped openly when Peter stood before them, appearing to be very much in charge. Beside him stood his subordinate, Sergeant Peter Horn, whom he'd apprised of the situation a few minutes earlier. The grin on Horn's face wasn't lost on his commander.

"Colonel Sidman has asked me to take his place this morning." Although he maintained his signature composure, Peter couldn't help but notice the men's expressions. They reminded him of his daughter Susannah's face when she'd received her first horse, disbelief mixed with utter joy.

As he approached the edge of the village, Peter saw his oldest son approach along with Joe, who called out "My hair! My hair!" Peter had grown used to the mangled German expression.

Peter the younger was laughing as he playfully cuffed the back of the boy's head. "Just say 'sir.'"

Joe nodded, somber. "Sir. My hair, sir."

"No, Joe, just 'sir.' Forget the German."

Peter saw the sweat of the drilling field still shimmering on his son's face. "Well, hello! What is happening?"

Joe stretched out his hand, giving Peter a crumpled note—"Please come to my home at once. L.G." He looked into his son's face for an explanation.

"Mr. Gordon sent for Joe to deliver this message, and he intercepted me while I was heading home." He tilted his head. "What is it, Father?"

"I need to see him immediately."

"I see." A smile began dawning on his face.

"If you will excuse me." Peter picked up his pace as he crested the hill along the top of Northampton Street. Turning around, he called out, "Thank you!"

Peter stood in Lewis Gordon's stifling office, feeling a kind of static in the room. The Committeemen were either jiggling legs or coins in their pockets, or tapping their fingers on waistcoats and chairs. The only person seated was Gordon, who addressed them in a hoarse voice, his face the shade of lard. His eyes sank like a sunset into his forehead.

"Thank you, gentlemen, for appearing on such short notice. I needed to see you apart from a formal Committee meeting about an urgent matter."

Robert Traill glanced at Peter, who nodded at his friend.

"Colonel Sidman visited me early this morning. He was quite downcast about his abilities to lead the Flying Camp and asked to be dismissed from his duties."

Gasps echoed in the room. Peter let out a puff of air. He hadn't expected Gordon to come so directly to the point. Then again, perhaps Sidman hadn't minced words either.

Robert Levers spoke up. "What happened, my good man?"

"Perhaps Colonel Kichline would like to address your question." Gordon looked at Peter, followed by everyone else's glances.

"Yes, of course, good sir." Peter determined to keep his tone on high ground. What would complaining or any amount of "I told you so" accomplish? "Colonel Sidman is a fine young man with unwavering devotion to the Cause. By his own admission, however, he is untried in leading men toward battle."

Levers interrupted. "Did he tell you this, or did you witness his lack of proficiency?"

Peter stepped around temptation. "I would say both, Mr. Levers. Colonel Sidman has strong though undeveloped qualities. With time, I'm confident he will be a fine leader."

Abraham Berlin crossed his arms. "I heard he didn't communicate well with the men."

"He doesn't speak German, Mr. Berlin. This impeded him."

"I can only imagine!"

Children's laughter filtered into the room from outside. "Colonel Kichline," Gordon said, "these few men from the Committee have discussed our current crisis and come up with a solution, one which Colonel Sidman also suggested." He ran the tips of his fingers across his desk as if playing a pianoforte. "We made a mistake in choosing Sidman to lead the Flying Camp. We thought he was further along and hadn't considered his inability to speak German as an issue."

His left calf tingled. *Not when most of you speak English.*

"We believed the Flying Camp could be best served by a young man, but …" Gordon halted briefly. "… we were clearly in the wrong, and all of us beg your humble pardon, Colonel Kichline."

Peter nodded, guessing at what was coming.

"We would like to make this desperate situation right by choosing you as colonel of the Northampton County Flying Camp at tomorrow's regular Committee meeting." Everyone turned toward Peter. "Would you be amenable?"

He wasn't one to hold a grudge. "Yes, of course, Mr. Gordon. I'm available to promote our Glorious Cause in any way I can."

Gordon half-smiled, his sigh of relief repeated by the others, who had just eaten humble pie.

On the way out, Levers intercepted Peter and slapped him on the back. "Old reliable."

Reliable, yes. As for old, Peter begged to differ.

He held his new son in his arms, marveling once again at the miracle of birth, grateful beyond words Catherine was doing well, and the boy seemed strong. She lay against the pillow, depleted, her damp, dark brown hair framing a radiant face.

"He is handsome," Peter said, looking into eyes just opening to a new world, a world his father was in a position to make right.

She murmured, "Like his father." She drifted back into sleep while *Frau* Hamster stroked her forehead, her gentle touch belying her crusty exterior.

Susannah moved closer to her father and the tiny boy. "I agree, Papa. I think he's going to have your light hair and eyes."

He didn't trust himself to speak but caressed his darling daughter with a smile. She responded with tears in her eyes. He wouldn't have long with them before he had to go. Troops were already making their way through New Jersey to New York, poised to strike against the British. In a matter of days, he would be marching the Flying Camp across the Delaware into New Jersey, leaving behind all their domestic scenes and the people so dear to them. He gazed into his son's face and knew the only way to make this child's life flourish as he lived out his purpose was to secure the independence the United States had declared. If Peter had anything to do with the matter, this boy, like Elizabeth, Susannah, Jacob, Andrew, and Peter Jr. would not live under tyranny as he and his family had back in Germany. They would bow to no prince, except for the Prince of Peace, to no god, except the God of Abraham, Isaac, and Jacob.

"Abraham."

Susannah looked at him, her head to the side. "What did you say, Papa?"

"Abraham is a good, strong name for this little fellow." The baby curled his right hand loosely around Peter's index finger. "You will help Mother Catherine while I'm away."

"Yes, of course, Papa. You can count on me."

He nodded. "I know, *liebling*. My dearest Susannah."

Tears shimmered in her eyes. "I promise I'll be strong, Papa."

"Remember the words of our Father in Heaven, 'Never will I leave you. Never will I forsake you.'"

"I know. I will depend on him."

"I love you so very much, darling Peter. I will pray for you always."

"And I for you." He held her hand, and her gaze, saying nothing about the possibility of never seeing her again this side of heaven. The prospect, however, occupied the space between their unspoken thoughts.

He kissed her tenderly, held her hand for a long moment, then rose and went to the door. Before descending the stairs, he turned one last time, to fix in his mind the image of Catherine and baby Abraham. He smiled, and she did as well. He didn't see her cascade of tears as he headed downstairs. His housekeeper handed him his hat, looking down. "*Danke schoen, Frau Hamster.*"

Joe helped him attach his belt and sword around his waistcoat. His other children were at the courthouse with the throng seeing the Flying Camp off.

"You are a big help to *Frau* Hamster and Mrs. Kichline, Joe. Keep up the good work."

"Yes, hair!"

Peter smiled, chucked the boy's chin. "Keep working on your English, my fine fellow." His eyes searched the housekeeper's, but she wasn't returning the look, seeming as if she were holding back a dam of tears with sheer willpower, of which she had an abundant supply.

"*Frau Hamster, Sie sind eine wundersame Frau.*"

She curtsied, wordless.

Although he longed to run back upstairs for once last look at Catherine and wee Abraham, Peter knew he must go. When he would see this place and these people again, only God knew.

Chapter Nineteen

Her dad had been a little slower to recover from his heart attack than Erin expected. He no longer went fishing every day. His bike collected dust. When he called to ask if she would take him grocery shopping, she was surprised, and she agreed, having two hours between her Wednesday classes. He wore his Korean War Vet baseball cap to the store, and people stopped them in the aisles, reaching out to shake his hand and say "Thank you for your service, sir."

After the third time, Erin laughed. "I feel like I'm with a celebrity." Tony responded with a closed-mouthed smile, and she sensed nothing more needed to be said. He'd never talked about his war experiences, and he'd just begun wearing the hat in recent months. On one of his apartment walls, he now displayed his medals in a case Allen had given him last Father's Day.

Their shopping trip went quickly, Tony not being one to dawdle, and he asked if she'd like to have lunch. Erin checked her watch. "Sure, Dad. I could do a quick one, but then I need to take you home and get to my class."

Now he smiled fully. "That'll be nice, daughter."

"Where do you want to go?"

"How about Carolina Chicken?"

Erin blinked twice. Her mother called the fast food chain by the same wrong name! *How could two people with so little in common make the same strange mistake?* She didn't have an answer, but she did have an alibi. "Gosh, Dad, I don't really have time to go there."

"It's on your way."

He was right. She tried a different approach. "You know, there's a chicken place across the street. Then we can shoot right down Main Street to your apartment."

"Okay, you're the boss."

One thing she liked about this particular restaurant was how a server brought your food to the table. She was sitting at a booth with her dad when a worker came over carrying a tray, paused and stared at Erin. The woman turned her head slightly and squinted. "Erin?"

She looked up and grinned. "Meg?"

"Yes! Wow, I haven't seen you in, well, since we graduated from high school."

"I know!" An image popped into Erin's mind of herself sitting in history class dressed in a toga Meg had helped her put together. "I remember how creative you were."

"And you were so smart."

"Uh, Meg, this is my dad, Tony Pelleriti. Dad, I went to school with Meg." She went fishing mentally for a last name and came up empty.

"Nice to meet you, Mr. Pelleriti." She turned to Erin. "You don't live around here, do you?"

"I lived in Lansdale pretty much since grad school, that's where my husband was from, but I recently bought a house in Easton."

Tony straightened his back. "She's a professor at Lafayette."

"How cool is that! What does your husband do?"

"He passed away a year ago last spring."

"Oh, I am so sorry. That's really sad."

The familiar awkwardness floated between them.

"I'm on my second husband, but I was divorced," Meg said. "And here I am, an assistant manager at a fast food place."

Erin couldn't quite tell if Meg was proud of this or regretful.

She looked over her shoulder. "I better get back to work. It was great seeing you, Erin, and meeting you, sir." She stopped herself short. "Oh! Our high school reunion will be next spring. Since you're back in the area, maybe you'll come?"

Erin had never been to one before, and she wasn't about to commit herself on the spot. "Thanks for letting me know."

"No problem. Enjoy your lunch!"

"She was nice," Tony said while Erin sorted out their items.

"Yes, she was always a nice person."

"She's your age?"

Erin tried figuring out which was the sweet and which was the unsweetened iced tea. "Uh-huh."

"She sure looks a lot older than you."

Erin winced, hoping in this bustling restaurant, Meg hadn't heard. Her dad was right though. Meg's brown hair carried significant gray now, and she wore the kind of stretchy pants Audrey favored, along with the preferred footwear of Clymer Village's matrons. Clearing her mind of such thoughts, she introduced a conversation she'd been hoping to have with her dad for several days. "Dad, do you remember a place call the Fountain House in Easton?"

He popped a waffle fry into his mouth. "Say, this is good. I like these potatoes." He ate another one then asked, "The Fountain House, you said?"

"Yes, a tavern along the Bushkill Creek."

"At Twenty-fifth Street?"

"Yes."

"I sure do. Haven't thought of that place in years, though."

"Did you ever go there?"

"Of course, I went there," he said as if a history professor should know better. "I used to go there all the time. A spring ran underneath the place. Man, they had good trout." He sat quietly for a moment. "I used to take your mom there."

She felt as if she'd struck a nerve.

"They tore the place down a long time ago, put up some ridiculous store instead." He shook his head. "Why do you want to know about the Fountain House?"

"My five-times great-grandfather built the tavern in the late 1700s."

"Well, I'll be."

"I wish the building were still there."

"Yeah, what a shame. A lot of local history has been paved under parking lots."

She began thinking about Peter Kichline Senior's original Easton home and the possibility of its being somewhere under the façade of the current building. Her father interrupted her thoughts.

"There's still a lot left, though, and we should save everything we can. This is a really special place, you know."

She gazed at him, knowing he didn't mean the fast food restaurant. "Did you ever want to leave this area?"

He swallowed a bite of his sandwich and leaned back. "Well, I spent two years in the Army, and I saw a lot of the world. I always used to tell my buddies I couldn't wait to get home."

"Why did you love this area so much?"

Another look of disbelief crossed his olive features. "Why? Because this is God's country. Why would I ever need to go anywhere else?"

She had no answer for this. Growing up, she couldn't wait to leave, to find peace among peaceful people, "to be somebody," someone she felt she never could be in her hometown and among her own people. Easton and P'burg had seemed so small, so insignificant, and her family so ensconced in dysfunction. She'd wondered how anything good could ever come out of there. For a moment, she felt almost panicky to think she'd come back to such a place. Then images of her Grandfather Peter and her many other noble ancestors settled her spirit. Their contributions toward life, liberty, and the pursuit of happiness, their fortitude and faith were the legacy she was seeking to reclaim for herself and her son.

She almost missed her father's next words, quiet and uncharacteristic coming from her shoot-from-the hip parent.

"I've been thinking about something." He looked at her, then down at the napkin next to him on the table.

"What, Dad?"

"What happened between your mother and me was a long time ago." He raised his eyes. "Do you think she'd be willing to see me sometime? I'd like to, you know, be at peace with her."

For some strange reason, pieces of an old song played in her mind while she crossed the Quad toward her office, a song about being in a peaceful place. She couldn't remember the recording artist's name or the last time she'd heard the tune, but its meaning rang true. Life had become more sedate since Marty Lee's expulsion. Nevertheless, her spirit wasn't entirely at rest since she didn't know how, or even if, she'd be staying at her alma mater beyond the current academic year. She wasn't even sure she wanted to stay.

At the main office, the History Department secretary looked up from her computer. "Good morning, Dr. Miles. How are you today?"

"Just fine, Ginnie. How are you?"

"Doing well."

"Great." She moved to her mailbox and after removing the slim contents, went upstairs to her office. She had unlocked the door and distributed her things on the desk when her cell phone rang. Nudging the light switch on with her elbow so she didn't spill her take-out tea, she answered. "Hello, this is Erin Miles."

"Hello, Erin Miles! This is Connie."

She went over to her chair and sat down, smiling. "Hi, Connie. How are you today?"

"Just dandy. And you?"

"I'm well, thanks. I just arrived at my office."

"Oh, did I catch you at a bad time?"

"Not at all."

"Super. Listen, I'm calling to let you know how much I enjoyed your article about Colonel Kichline. We're just about ready to go to press."

"Oh, I'm so glad." She fist-pumped her left hand at the enthusiasm in Connie's voice.

"You filled in a lot of gaps in my knowledge—I didn't know he didn't immigrate to America with his father, like some of the records say."

"I think they got mixed up because he, Peter, came with his mother and stepfather."

"You really made him come alive with your writing style, as if you actually knew him. What a decent and winsome person he was! Oh, I just wish we had a portrait of him. You know I'm always searching for one. In the meantime I think we'll use the Kichline coat of arms or something along those lines."

Erin smiled at the Easton flag she kept on her desk. "Sounds good, and I so appreciate your efforts looking for a portrait."

"I showed the article to a few others here, and they raved. You're a really good writer, young lady."

Erin laughed. "Why, thank you for saying so."

"I almost hated to come to the end of the story."

"Me too. There's so much more I want to know, especially about the Battle of Brooklyn. There are a lot of books about the engagement, and

I just haven't had time to read them." She took a sip of tea. "By the way, Connie, I've actually made a really cool discovery about where he lived in Easton."

"You have?" She sounded as eager as Toby when he scented a squirrel.

"Paul told me he's been uncovering documents related to a building about a block up Northampton Street from the Sigal Museum. Grandfather Peter seems to have owned the property when he and my Grandmother Margaretta settled in Easton. There's a store on the spot now, and the owner is about to sell. The manager of the property told Paul he's pretty sure the original foundations can still be seen, and some of the upstairs rooms may be under layers of drywall and plaster."

"Oh, how exciting, Erin!"

"I can't wait to get inside. Paul is trying to arrange a visit for me."

"So many of our colonial buildings were lost to so-called progress …"

"Like the Fountain House."

"Erin, do you think you'd like to write a sidebar about the building? The thing is, we're about ready to go to press, so I'd need the filler ASAP. Maybe you could take some pictures too."

"I sure will. I'll get a tour as quickly as I can and take photos." She promised herself she'd make time to dig into a book she'd found in Skillman Library about the Battle of Brooklyn. They spoke a few minutes longer, and she hung up just as Herman Weinreich appeared in the doorway.

"Good morning, Professor Miles."

She mirrored his playful mood. "Good morning, Professor Weinreich. Come in."

"I waited until you finished your call. You sound excited."

She cleared a spot on the chair, but he leaned against a wall with his "I Love Grandpa" mug. Erin wasn't sure how he would receive the news, but she plunged ahead, feeling reckless. "Connie from the historical society let me know how pleased they are with the article I just handed in about Colonel Peter Kichline."

He sipped his coffee, nodding. "You always were a good writer."

She briefly filled him in on the discovery of the downtown building's connection to her six-times great-grandfather.

"How wonderful you're here to enjoy all this local history."

For some reason, she cringed when he said "local history," as if this couldn't be significant. The thing was, she understood—this had been exactly her attitude when she went to Lafayette as an undergraduate—one she'd just been thinking of in the context of her present life. Herman was speaking again, and she willed herself to listen.

"I'd love for you to write something for the *Academic Journal of American Historiography*. I know the editor, and she's looking for submissions for next fall's edition, mainly about the economic interpretation of the mid-Federalist Period and its bearing on early 20th century historical research." He was glowing, offering what he surely must consider a golden opportunity to one of his all-time favorite students. "May I tell her you're interested?"

Erin bit the inside of her cheek. That would be worse than grading four classes' worth of Intro to English Comp essays. She knew history departments valued such research highly, but the unvarnished truth was, she did not. *Is this what teaching is all about—writing historiography and coddling dangerous students and keeping my mouth shut during faculty meetings because only one viewpoint is acceptable?* She didn't want to share these misgivings with her boss, who held the strings to her future at Lafayette. She heard herself say through a smile she managed to conjure up, "How nice of you to invite me to contribute to the journal. When is the deadline?"

His eyes sparkled. "I'm afraid next Monday. Sorry for the short notice. I know one of the other professors has something he's been working on, but I wanted to give you a shot to beef up the old CV."

Her words leaped ahead of her thoughts. When she spoke, Erin felt as if she were hearing someone else. "I really appreciate the offer, Herman, but I'm not quite finished with the piece for the historical society. They've added another component, and I need to complete the article this weekend to meet their deadline. I'm not sure I could do both things justice in such a short amount of time. If you'd like me to try ..."

He waved her objections away. "No, no. You go ahead and finish your story." He fixed his eyes on her for a moment, and she had the distinct impression she was being examined and found wanting. Why, then, wasn't she more upset?

Chapter Twenty

He read General's Orders, a cluster of gnats buzzing around his right ear. He managed to get two-for-one when an unfortunate mosquito caught the brunt of his hand. Washington's words would go far, he believed, in stirring his men's spirits.

Ziba Wiggins stuck his head inside the tent. "Excuse me, Colonel Kichline, your son is here to see you."

Peter rose from the campaign chair. "Thank you, Private Wiggins. Send him in."

Wiggins stepped to the side, allowing Peter Jr. to enter. His father grinned when his son whacked at a fly near his face. "We seem to have a welcoming committee." He cuffed his son's shoulder and shook his right hand.

"Or perhaps an 'unwelcoming committee' is more accurate. How are you, Father?"

"Keeping quite well, and yourself?"

"I'm also well."

Peter gestured toward a second folding chair. "Won't you have a seat?"

"Thank you." He lowered his tall frame onto the chair.

"How are Captain Arndt's men faring?"

"We're managing life in the field quite nicely," his namesake said. "I think they're far more disciplined than other units I've seen." He shook his head. "Some of those men are acting like this is a holiday, drinking into the late hours and, well …" He dropped his glance.

Peter had also witnessed the revelry of some New England troops encamping nearby, including more than a few scenes with local women. He knew General Washington would not be pleased, confident the news was getting back to him. "While I'm unhappy about this state of affairs, I am more than pleased with the order and decorum of our Northampton County men."

"I agree, Father. We have good men, principled men."

Peter clapped his hand onto his left forearm where a mosquito bit through his linen shirt. A tiny spot of blood appeared where the insect had expired. "Thank you for coming to see me this morning since I realize your hands are full. I wanted to have a private word with you before we head across the river."

"I'm glad you sent for me, Father. I, too, was hoping to have some time alone before …"

The prospects lying before them dangled wordlessly between them.

Peter cleared his parched throat, reached for a pewter jug of water and offered his son a drink, which he declined. After Peter drank, he put his mug on a small table and rose to retrieve a folded and sealed paper from his desk. He sat back down and handed the item to his oldest son. "I'd like you to keep this for me."

He accepted the paper, looking at his father. "Is this what I think?"

Peter leaned back into the chair as far as he could without tipping over. "I couldn't bring myself to write my will in Easton or to speak of my possible demise with Catherine. Not until we'd been here a few days did I collect my thoughts into a coherent enough piece to write my last wishes down. If we were home, I would've given this to Robert Traill. Since we're not, I'm entrusting the document to you."

Peter ran a finger over the red seal. "I understand. Father," he looked up, "What if I shouldn't return?"

He had considered the awful possibility. "Let Captain Arndt know. My hope is one of your men would find the will and follow the instructions." He propped his arms against his thighs and smiled. "Son, I don't have any of *Frau* Hamster's premonitions. While I don't believe you or I are doomed, I have been in battle and know the risks. I also believe when we have fulfilled our God-given purpose in this world, we are then called to our heavenly home. No one knows when this will be, of course. As we face battle, we must be prudent in considering our families."

Peter Jr. nodded. He placed the will inside his officer's coat and produced a similar piece of paper. "I have been thinking along the same lines, Father." He handed the document across the space between them, grinning. For a long moment, neither of them spoke. Then the young officer stood, followed by his father. They gazed at each other, clasped each other's shoulders, and Peter Jr. stepped outside of the tent into the blazing New Jersey sun.

Peter stood before his men at the beginning of a new day, perspiring under his military garb, hearing a droning sound just above his head. Sergeant Horn was calling nearly three hundred members of the Northampton County Flying Camp to attention on a dusty parade ground, rugged fellows looking more like a company of medieval peasants with pitchforks than official troops of the United States military. Nevertheless, Peter felt his chest expand as he gazed upon their stalwart faces. *I'd rather lead them in battle against the British than be Lord Howe himself with all his soldiers in full regalia.* Beside Horn, Pastor Rodenheimer stood tall, ready to give his blessing to the troops, men he'd told Peter he would have gladly joined except for his pastoral duties back in Easton. He'd traveled with the company across New Jersey and planned to depart after they embarked on their campaign.

Peter stepped into position to address them, feeling a sudden yellow jacket sting on his right cheek. He thrust the bee from his face and pried at the stinger with his forefinger. Without missing a beat, he said, "Good day, men. Before we begin our exercises, I have information, as well as General Washington's Orders, to share with you. The British have at last begun to come ashore on Long Island, and we must be ready to engage them at any time." He left out the part about their vast fleet and menacing firepower. Peter's men remained at attention, only a rise of their eyebrows gave away their thoughts and emotions as the news sank in—the time of battle was drawing very near.

His cheek swelled as he held up the paper bearing Washington's now-familiar script, tight and purposeful, and began to read.

> General Orders for August 23, 1776. The hour is fast approaching, on which the honor and success of this army, and the safety of our bleeding country depend. Remember officers and soldiers that you are free men, fighting for the blessings of liberty—that Slavery will be your portion, and that of your posterity, if you do not acquit yourselves like men. Remember how your courage and spirit have been despised and traduced by your cruel invaders, though they have found by dear experience at Boston, Charlestown, and other

> places, what a few brave men contending in their own land, and in the best of causes can do, against base hirelings and mercenaries. Be cool, but determined; do not fire at a distance, but wait for orders from your officers—It is the General's orders that if any man attempt to skulk, lay down, or retreat without Orders, he will be instantly shot down as an example, he hopes no such Scoundrel will be found in this army, but on the contrary, every one for himself resolving to conquer or die, and trusting to the smiles of heaven upon so just a cause, will behave with Bravery and Resolution.

Peter looked up from the paper, saw his men's earnest faces including his sons', Sergeant Horn and Captain Arndt, Zibba Wiggins, Peter Horeback, Michael Gress and his son, and Andrew Drunkenmiller. These were no shirkers or cowards. They might not be men of learning, but they were men of valor. He continued reading, his left calf tingling, ignoring the pain in his cheek.

> Those who are distinguished for their Gallantry, and good Conduct, may depend upon being honorably noticed, and suitably rewarded. And if this army will but emulate, and imitate their brave countrymen, in other parts of America, he has no doubt they will by a glorious Victory, save their Country, and acquire to themselves immortal Honor.

After finishing Washington's last housekeeping details, he lowered the paper and turned to his clergyman. "Pastor Rodenheimer, I believe this would be a good time for you to offer a prayer."

The lanky man nodded and raised his voice with its lisp so recognizable to many from his congregation. "My dear friends, let us commit this righteous enterprise to the Almighty. Let us pray." Every head bowed. Even the bees and mosquitoes seemed to observe a moratorium on their feasting.

Samuel Miles clasped Peter's hand and shook vigorously. "My good friend! How very pleased I am to see you!"

He broke into a grin the size of Long Island at the sight of his friend's face. "Not half as pleased as I am to see you. How are you?"

"Never better. And you?"

"The same. How is your family?"

"Everyone is keeping well. I understand you had a recent addition."

Peter's smile expanded along with his chest. "Yes, my dear wife presented me with a healthy young son just two weeks ago."

His friend's expression bore the joy of new birth mixed with the sorrow of parting. "Then we must see to matters here so you may return to them as quickly as possible."

Today's meeting with many of the top officers would go a long way toward determining what kind of outcome the battle might have for their men and their country.

Miles turned to a pleasant-faced, rather doughy man of late middle age. "General Putnam, I'd like to present my dear friend, Lt. Colonel Peter Kichline, commander of the Northampton County Pennsylvania Flying Camp."

Putnam reached out his hand. "Glad to meet you, Colonel. Yours would be the mostly German troops, then?"

"Yes, sir."

"I hear good things about them. Perhaps they will be able to act as translators for the Hessians we'll be taking as prisoners." His stomach jiggled as he laughed at his own joke. "Do I detect a trace of the Fatherland in your own voice, Kichline?"

"Yes, General. I am of Swiss and German descent."

Putnam sized him up, in a not unfriendly way. "Grow them big over there, do they?"

Peter smiled. "Yes, sir."

"How long have you inhabited these shores, my good fellow?"

"I came with my family nearly thirty-five years ago, General."

Putnam pressed his ample lips together, then he grinned and elbowed Peter. "I'm glad I'm not the only old man in this army."

"No, sir, you are not."

"Have you ever seen action before, my good man?"

"Yes, sir, in the French and Indian War."

"He also served two terms as Sheriff of Northampton County," Miles said.

Putnam glanced sideways at Miles. "Impressive credentials. We need all the experienced officers we can get." He failed to add, "As I am not one myself." He paused, looked around the muggy room filled with men sweating through their uniforms. "Very well, then. Gentlemen, if you will excuse me, I need to greet some others before I get this meeting started."

Peter frowned after his retreating figure. When Miles met his gaze, he whispered, "I thought General Sullivan had taken over after General Greene's unfortunate illness." He'd seen John Sullivan earlier, the same General who'd just returned from the northern campaign in which Peter's brother Andrew had participated.

Miles inclined his head to the left, indicating Peter should follow him to an unoccupied part of the room. When they were slightly more private, he said, "You're right about Sullivan. Then General Washington abruptly changed his mind and switched out Sullivan for Old Put."

Although Miles hadn't offered any commentary, Peter read the doubt in his friend's expression. His own inclinations were in a similar direction. He knew Israel Putnam had a strong reputation for bravery and camaraderie, but he wasn't battle-tested like John Sullivan, nor did he inspire the deepest respect. In a strange twist, General Washington had done what the Northampton County Committee had done in choosing Isaac Sidman, except in reverse. The thought felt like yet another bee sting for Peter—the wrong officer had ended up in charge.

No sooner had Sunday services ended than the strains of martial music, including the drumming of purposeful, wide-eyed Andrew Drunkenmiller, accompanied the troops across the bay to Brooklyn. Once the men reached the other side, Peter witnessed all hell break loose—loud laughter, jokes the Old Pig Drover would have blushed to hear, men groping the few women among them. Some soldiers drove horses and vehicles helter-skelter, kicking up sand, causing men to leap to the sides so they didn't get run over. Other soldiers discharged their firearms and field pieces at random, wasting valuable ammunition as they lent to the general mayhem. The Northampton County unit conducted themselves in a far more worthy manner, many of them bug-eyed at what was happening around them.

Miles ventured over to Peter. "Good heavens! What is happening here?"

Peter shook his head, ducking to avoid a flying shoe. He didn't need to say, but thought his friend might also be thinking, "This would never have happened with General Sullivan in charge."

A few hours later, Colonel Miles sent word to Peter through a dispatch.

My dear Colonel Kichline,

General Washington and his party arrived some two hours after we did and witnessed the outrageous behavior for himself. I assure you, our Commander was in a major huff. He has ordered General Putnam to see to the immediate ceasing of all irregularities and to reinforce the need for a well-regulated army, as opposed to the undisciplined and disorderly mob we observed. Let us hope and pray this can be accomplished.

Your obedient servant,

Samuel Miles

Not Peter, nor the officers, nor the miscreants, nor the men who did maintain their honor and discipline knew five thousand Hessians were converging upon the island in a state of perfect martial order. Lord Howe's experienced and well-furnished forces now numbered twenty thousand.

Chapter Twenty-One

Just after lunch on Friday, Sol Levy met Erin and Paul at the corner of Fourth and Northampton Streets. The two men clasped hands like the old friends they were, and Paul introduced Levy to Erin.

"I'm very glad to meet you," she said, feeling surprised by the Hulk Hogan grip of a man built more like a starving artist.

"The pleasure is mine." Levy looked from her to Paul and smiled. Then they began walking toward the old building. He pointed at the gray stone façade and a display window filled with Christmas-themed nostalgic wares. The store was aptly called Yesterday's Gone.

"Have you ever been inside, Erin?"

A gaggle of brown leaves skittered around her feet. "I'm not sure, but I think so. When I was a girl, I believe there was a clothing store in here, something like Little Sister?"

Levy nodded his head as he led the way toward the front door. "Yes, there was. The place was called Little Mister, Little Sister, and my grandmother owned it."

"I remember!" She had a sudden image of a coin-operated horse she'd begged her mother to ride just outside the store along the sidewalk. "If my memory serves me correctly, there used to be a mechanical horse just outside."

He smiled. "Come inside. I have something to show you." He opened the door for Erin and Paul, then he pointed toward the corner of the left display window. In the background, satellite radio was playing "Sounds of the Sixties," featuring Jay and the Americans. "There's your old friend."

"The horse!" Erin broke into a grin as she strode over, seeing part of the mane was missing, and the "saddle" was worn to a nub by generations of local children. "My mom always made sure she had quarters when we came in here or I'd pitch a fit."

"Somehow I can't imagine you pitching a fit," Paul said.

"Oh, just ask my mom. Then again …" She laughed. "I loved this place because of that dear horse."

"And maybe the lollypops?" Sol asked.

"Yes, green lollypops!" She could almost taste the deep lime flavor of the candy she remembered savoring on trips to this place in the late seventies.

"My grandmother once refused to open the store because her shipment of green lollipops hadn't arrived, and no customer ever left without one." He laughed, pushing dark-rimmed glasses up on his nose. "My grandfather pitched a fit then, to borrow your expression. He said, 'Why don't you just give the customers double the lollypops the next time they come in?' She wouldn't budge, though. Bubbe put a sign in the door, 'Closed. No Lollypops. Open Tomorrow.'"

Erin and Paul laughed almost in harmony as a man with a gray ponytail walked over to them.

"Hey, Sol, good to see you!" He shook hands with the owner, then Paul, who also greeted the proprietor by name.

"Mickey, this is Dr. Erin Miles from Lafayette." Erin extended her hand and found this shake far less strenuous than Sol's. "She's doing research on the original owner of this building."

Mickey nodded his head. "This place sure goes way back. I've done some exploring myself, and I can tell you, it's old. Real old."

Erin nodded toward the merchandise, everything from linen handkerchiefs to Radio wagons, Flexible Flyers featuring red and green bows, coin-operated banks, lunch boxes with The Monkees and Dukes of Hazzard, and a maple dresser very much like one her Grammy Ott used to have with the same kind of curved mirror attached.

"I can see you enjoy being around old things," Erin said.

"I sure do." He winked at her and gave a short laugh. "I've started fitting right in. One lady even asked me recently if I was for sale."

Erin blushed, realizing she had set him up inadvertently for such a remark. She was glad he hadn't taken offense.

"Well, if you will excuse us," Sol said, "I'm going to give Paul and Erin the grand tour."

"Of course. It was nice to meet you, Dr. Miles."

"Same here."

Sol led them through a long front room smelling of lavender and dust. She noticed on the right side part of what appeared to be stone peeking through. "Is the wall original?" she asked, pointing.

"I think so. As I show you around, you'll notice a lot more stone walls, especially upstairs. Let's start up there." He led them toward a door, which concealed a wooden staircase, then climbed the unswept steps. Erin brushed away a dangling cobweb at eye level. The open room they entered ran the entire length of the building, and as they got their bearings, Erin sneezed once, then twice, reaching for a tissue in her bag.

"Are these floorboards original?" Paul asked.

"They appear to be in this section of the room, but if you look closely, some of the wood seems to have replaced the earlier parts, probably after they rotted. You'll need to watch your step because here and there nails are sticking up."

The room offered a plethora of crazily-stacked wooden and cardboard boxes dating back to the administration of Calvin Coolidge, as well as barrels, cans, mannequins, vacuum cleaners, display cases, piles of newspapers, and coat racks—all dust-enshrouded. Erin wondered whether the proprietor of Yesterday's Gone had been through this jumble in search of treasure, or even the American Pickers. *This may have been where men lodged or the courts had their sessions.*

Sol Levy appeared to be oblivious to the backlog of inventory.

"So, then, is this is where Benjamin Franklin would have stayed in the 1750s when he came to Easton?" Erin's question contained a drop of awe.

"I haven't heard that particular story," Sol said.

Erin dove into the tale. "According to a volume about Franklin, during the Indian massacres in 1755, he came as a commissioner to Easton to see how the Pennsylvania Assembly might be able to help the settlers. There's a reference to him staying at a certain tavern, which fit the description of my ancestor's place. This place."

Sol folded his arms across his chest, nodding. "Very impressive." He seemed to be looking at the room with new eyes. "If these walls could talk, I'm sure they would have many great stories to tell." He paused. "There's actually a smaller room on the third floor under the eaves, probably where some of the household stayed."

Erin was suddenly struck by the idea of her many times great-grandparents standing in this very place, their own voices echoing through their lives and experiences. She caught a flash of sunlight filtering through a set of streaked windows. "These aren't original," she said.

"What?" Sol asked.

"The windows. But they do appear to be old."

"Right on both counts. I think my great-grandfather installed those, maybe a hundred years ago."

Paul spoke. "How long has your family owned this building?"

Sol let out a puff of air. "Oh, ages. Let me see … my grandparents had the children's store, then my parents started leasing the space sometime in the eighties." He looked up at the ceiling with cobwebs and pieces of insulation protruding through rain-streaked plaster bulging at the center. "My father says his great-grandfather, Saul Levy, bought the place in the 1870s, and for a while he kept the tavern-hotel thing going, but then he began a store, and there have been stores here ever since.

"I've been digging around a bit and discovered Saul Levy bought the building from a man named Wiggins," Paul said.

Erin laughed. "Like Mrs. Uh-Wiggins from the *Carol Burnett Show*?"

He smiled. "Precisely. Before them, a family named Eckert ran a tavern and before them, your ancestors."

"And you're sure this is the right place?" Erin asked.

"According to a deed I found, yes," Paul said.

For the next hour, they toured cubbies and corners, top to bottom, Erin making notes on a pad she kept in her bag, her imagination running away with her as she pictured the men and women of colonial Easton conducting their lives in this very place. In the moldy basement, another collection of boxes and containers large and small held either someone's junk or buried treasure. *I wonder what might be found here if there was ever to be an archaeological dig? What sorts of artifacts might there be?*

"I hate to sell what has been in our family for five generations. Nevertheless, I'm losing interest in keeping the building up from my new home in South Carolina, and no one else in the family wants to take my place. We need to move on," Levy said, shrugging his shoulders.

"Did you ever apply for historic registry?" Paul asked.

"Gosh, I don't know. I could ask my dad."

"This place definitely should be listed."

"Yes, you're right. There are a lot of things that should be done, including fixing up the leaks and broken flooring and the walls ..." He sighed. "I've done my best to put bandaids on the problems, but I don't have the energy anymore, especially since I moved down south." He looked around for a long moment. "I just hope whoever buys the place will appreciate its historic value."

"Have you had any offers?"

"No offers, but a developer contacted me. He's interested in tearing down the building and starting with something entirely new, actually in this section of Northampton Street."

Erin clenched her teeth. *Over my dead body.*

With Ethan spending the night at his cousin's house, Erin purchased a drive-through meal and headed home. She sat at the kitchen table plucking fries from their paper cone while typing the sidebar about the Kichline tavern, combining historic facts she'd gleaned from documents with Sol Levy's stories about his family's ownership of the building across parts of three centuries. She quickly reached her five-hundred-word count, then put the piece aside until the next day when she could put fresh eyes on the story and do the necessary cutting. She didn't know what she could omit, though—every part fascinated her.

At ten o'clock, she took Toby out one last time, then headed upstairs to wash up for bed. She wasn't sleepy, though—her mind racing at the thought of saving her ancestor's historic building from demolition. She wondered whether the place could be restored to its colonial-era appearance, the way so many buildings in Williamsburg had been. Were there any descriptions of the place in documents? What lay under the current walls? Who would be able to find out? Were any secrets among the scads of boxes and barrels? How much would such an undertaking cost? Although the questions circled her thoughts, one came in for a landing—there was no way she would stand by and watch the place get torn down. She pictured herself chained to a supporting beam while a wrecking ball came within inches of her head, like Steve Martin in *Father of the Bride*.

She climbed into bed and saw the book on her night table related to the Battle of Brooklyn, along with a copy of *The Kichlines in America.* Placing a mental bookmark in her thoughts about the tavern, she reached for the volume and settled in, Toby curling up at her feet. Soon, she was completely immersed in the first battle after independence had been declared, in which the odds were completely, overwhelmingly against the American forces.

She was eager to share what she'd read the night before with Paul and to get more information about exactly what had happened at Brooklyn. She wasn't especially adept at military terms or the direction of the battle in general, but she knew based on earlier conversations Paul was. They met for brunch at the Easton Public Market and sat across from each other, Paul with a bagel and lox. As she shrugged out of her coat, she followed his eyes to her creation of sushi and a chocolate éclair, grateful for his understanding smile. He didn't even wince when she sprinkled a tiny, paper-cup sample of peach-flavored balsamic vinegar over the pastry. She only took a few bites to settle her grumbling stomach, then promptly forgot her meal as she dove into a discussion about the Battle of Brooklyn.

"The numbers differ in various accounts, but do you agree the British had about four hundred ships plus warships and nearly thirty-thousand troops?"

He nodded while chewing and swallowing a bite of his bagel. "I believe so. Theirs was the largest invasion force in the world's history until then."

"And General Washington's army wasn't in very good shape."

"I know Washington's best general, Nathaniel Greene, was deathly ill, and some sort of sickness had broken out in the American ranks." Paul wiped a trace of cream cheese from the corner of his mouth. "He had only a small portion of able-bodied soldiers left to face the British, and remember, most of them had never seen battle before. I remember one author said something like, "A bleaker situation is difficult to imagine. It was David vs. Goliath, the high school varsity vs. the Chicago Bulls."

Erin picked up her copy of *The Kichlines in America.* "I wonder if you can help me understand what happened in the battle, based on what's in this account, that is, if you think this is accurate."

"There are more thorough descriptions, but I think this one gives an excellent overview."

"Alright then, for starters there's a lot of talk about a wooded ridge and various passes. I keep picturing the top of College Hill, right around the Lafayette campus. Do you think that's accurate?"

"I'm not sure the ridge at Brooklyn was as steep as College Hill, but if we lowered that a bit, you'd have the right idea."

"So, the passes were roads through the ridge?"

Paul reached for a napkin and a pen he kept in his coat pocket and began drawing a simple illustration. "Okay, here's the ridge, and the passes were roads and paths. Sullivan and Sterling set up their units along the ridge in order to cover the main roads and passes."

"My Grandfather Peter served under Sterling, right?"

"Right. Sterling, followed by Attlee and Miles."

"Didn't Grandfather Peter's Northampton County men number around three hundred?"

"That's about right, with something like one hundred from the Easton Company."

She glanced at the simple drawing. "Was Peter at the foot of the ridge?"

"For the main part of the battle, yes. His men were specialists—sharpshooters—and they were used as such."

Erin leaned back in her chair, frowning. "I don't quite understand this military part—sharpshooters—and his company is often called a Rifle Company."

"Right. They didn't have muskets, which could fire more rounds, more rapidly. They had rifles, which were more accurate weapons than muskets, but they could only get off one shot at a time. Therefore, a general wouldn't use them for one-on-one warfare, like ranks facing each other and firing."

Erin moved her head back. "This is making more sense to me."

"Early in the battle, then, Peter Kichline and his riflemen, along with some of Attlee's unit, were guarding a coast road from the bay to the Brooklyn Ferry."

"And during the night," she cut in, "my Grandfather Peter discovered an advance of General Grant's men and sent word to General Putnam."

"Right."

"Would he have been on horseback? Didn't colonels lead from that position?"

"You're right about colonels having horses, but there are accounts saying he commanded on foot, probably because of the nature of the terrain and the battle itself." He paused, then continued. "So, then, Old Put ordered Sterling to reinforce Kichline with regiments from Maryland, Delaware, and Connecticut, and early in the morning, they engaged in battle."

Erin read from the document. "'Atlee's skirmishers were driven out of the orchard and retreated along the Gowanus Road.'"

"Yes, on the far right flank. Kichline's riflemen were by that time at the base of the ridge. Their sharpshooting allowed Attlee to retake their position from the rear."

Paul started drawing arrows on the napkin to illustrate what was happening. For Erin, the Christmasy sounds and scents of the Public Market receded, and she imagined herself along the lines with her ancestor and his men.

"When Attlee's men left, Grandfather Peter would have been unaided, right?"

"Exactly," Paul said. "As one document says, he and his men were 'in the jaws of death.'"

She spoke quietly. "I know he was wounded, but I don't know exactly how."

"Nor do I. Actually, I'm amazed he survived at all."

They both observed a long moment of silence.

Chapter Twenty-Two

August 26, 1776

At four o'clock, he and his company ate under a scorching sun. Peter hardly tasted the stew, swallowing large bites without much chewing, intent upon seeking out Colonels Attlee and Miles one more time. He caught up with the men after the meal, standing next to each other at close range, arms crossed. Attlee was speaking, and Miles was nodding his head as he gazed at something in the distance. A small gathering of seagulls swooped and squawked within a few yards of their hats, but the men appeared not to have seen or heard. Peter approached his colleagues slowly, respecting whatever confidences they might be sharing until Miles noticed him and summoned Peter with a quick jerk of his head.

Attlee greeted him. "Good evening, Colonel Kichline, please join us."

Peter nodded and shook their hands. "Have you further news?"

Miles looked at Atlee, who turned to Peter. "Let's just say Clinton and Cornwallis's invasion forces are far more numerous than we had been led to believe."

Peter knew, having observed the spectacle of the King's Royal Navy in full sail across the bay, carrying highly regimented troops, and greeted by throngs of Loyalists. One thing was for sure, General Washington's army would receive no help from the locals.

"Besides those British, there are several thousand Hessians," Atlee said. "They were observed crossing the Narrows two days ago."

Peter pressed his lips together knowing there was no use wishing the situation wasn't as bad as it appeared. This was a sobering circumstance, and the Americans would have to do the best they could with what little they had, God help them.

"At this point, I'm guessing there are between five and ten thousand troops on the island," Miles said.

Attlee grimaced and spat on the ground. "I wouldn't be surprised if there were more."

"I'm inclined to agree with you, Colonel Atlee," Peter said. In his heart, he believed ten thousand was far more likely. Statistical information had been maddeningly slow to come, as well as inaccurate. Nor was Peter certain how many forces General Washington actually had at his disposal. He doubted Atlee and Miles knew either. Maybe even Old Put himself didn't know. The man hadn't been in charge but for a few days. According to some unofficial reports, the Continentals and militia numbered upwards of forty thousand, but from what Peter had seen, there were but a fraction here and now. General Greene hadn't been the only soldier laid low by sickness in the extreme heat of a New York summer.

Washington had concluded a few days earlier the British were only using Long Island as a sort of feint, and the bulk of the battle either would be at New York or further up the Hudson River. Peter wondered if by now, the commander in chief might have changed his mind.

He spoke again, scratching his cheek where the bee had stung him. "According to my observations, the British are now about six miles inland, around the wooded ridges."

Miles nodded. "Allow me to bring you up to date, Colonel Kichline. I was just telling Mr. Attlee I rode earlier today with General Washington."

Peter ignored the persistent seagulls and concentrated on this bit of news.

"We rode to the Heights of Gowan and observed the British setting up their tents at the Flatlands."

This was the kind of intelligence Peter had been craving to hear, information direct from the General of the Continental Army.

Miles continued. "The general has placed Putnam at our Brooklyn Heights fortifications, which will serve as his command post. Generals Sullivan and Sterling, who is of course, our immediate senior officer, are to cover the roads and passes through the wooded ridge." He pointed in the direction to which he referred. "These are fairly narrow and can be defended rather easily and not far from the coast road."

"About how many men are at the fort?" Peter asked.

Miles shrugged his shoulders. "About six thousand, I believe."

"Are they available to us?"

His friend removed a well-used handkerchief from a pocket and wiped sweat dripping from his forehead. "General Washington suspects the British will come through the center, which is the Flatbush Road. As for us …" he paused, dodging Peter's question, "… General Stirling will use all of us near the Gowanus Road, with General Sullivan at the Flatbush, or center road, as well as on the left flank, the Bedford Road. General Washington wants above all else for us to prevent the British from passing the wood and approaching the forts."

Peter disliked the sound of this, but he didn't think voicing his concerns would contribute anything of value. Miles and Attlee were likely thinking along the same lines anyway. Neither Old Put or Sullivan knew Long Island very well. Of the available American troops, most had never seen battle, and many of those had exhibited the most blatant disregard for military protocol or discipline. Those very men were supposed to hold a four-mile-long ridge against some of the world's most elite troops while the majority of Washington's men stayed within Brooklyn's fortifications. There was precious little communication. There was no cavalry. In some places the woods along the ridge were so thick a man couldn't see beyond a hundred feet. He took a deep breath, then emptied his lungs slowly to steady himself. He suspected Miles knew something he wasn't saying, but Peter wasn't about to force the issue.

Miles added one last detail. "Since most of our men do not have uniforms, the general has instructed us to have all of them wear a sprig of green in their hats for identification."

Peter almost let out a nervous laugh as he looked toward the water and an armada of tall ships. This did not inspire confidence.

About seven o'clock, with a pitiless sun blazing down untempered by clouds, he returned to his Flying Camp. Sergeant Horn greeted him with a salute, his face pink with sweat, his dark brown eyes expectant.

"Sir, would you like me to gather the troops now?"

"Yes, Sergeant, would you please?" He might have wished for some private time in his tent before addressing them, but concluded there was no use delaying what was unavoidable.

"Yes, sir."

Peter waited along the periphery while Horn, aided by Andrew Drunkenmiller's drum, called the men to order, watching as they assembled into their ranks. Their appearance may not have been crisp, but their comportment was flawless. He was proud of them. He pushed back a dark foreboding in the vicinity of his heart, willing the phantom menace to be gone. He'd enough reality to deal with, without adding fear to the mix.

Horn slid next to him. "Colonel Kichline, the men are ready for you."

"Thank you, Sergeant." He strode to the front and center of his unit. With his legs astride and hands behind his back, he spoke as if to each one individually. "Gentlemen, we will soon be facing the enemy, and I want to give you an overview of our position, as well as your orders."

After completing the technical part of his speech, including the instruction to wear a bit of greenery in their hats, he became more personal. "I want you to know I have every confidence in you." His eyes fell upon Peter Jr., looking so very much like his late mother in his face, but in his carriage, the image of his proud father. Then there were the Gresses, Conrad Fartenius, and Ziba Wiggins among the many other fine farmers, shopkeepers, and craftsmen from Easton. He permitted himself a thin smile in their direction, feeling a streak of perspiration slip from the top part of his lip into his mouth.

"I am certain each of you has the courage, fortitude, and faith to meet these British and Hessians, no matter how formidable they may seem. You may not have the benefit of their impressive uniforms and weapons, but your stout hearts and sure marksmanship are every bit a match for them. I would rather lead you into battle in the coming hours than any one of his Majesty's soldiers." He cleared his throat, surprised when he heard a similar sort of sound echo sporadically throughout the ranks. "Always remember those battles of old in which the Lord's armies defeated those of far greater numbers. Ours is a righteous cause, and I believe he will go before us, and deliver us." He noticed Peter Horeback standing with his chin jutted out.

"Since we will be heading toward our positions during the night, I want you to get some rest now. I commend you to the care of the Almighty, who neither slumbers nor sleeps." He turned to his subordinate. "Sergeant Horn, you may dismiss the troops."

He lay on his cot trying to relax for an hour or two, the heat an invisible blanket. He hadn't closed his eyes for more than ten minutes when he opened them again and reached for the letters he kept inside his uniform waistcoat. He'd only received them just yesterday, but already they were threadbare.

My darling Papa,

We are all well here and hope you are the same. I have only a few minutes to write you before the post goes out, but I want to assure you of my everlasting love and devotion. No daughter could be prouder of her brave Papa. Please do not worry about us. We are Patriots, too, bound together in this Glorious Cause. I will pray for you until you safely return, you and my brother and all our dear friends. Oh, I must go now, but know how much love goes into this letter from your affectionate and obedient Daughter, Susannah

He folded the note in half, then again, savoring its sweet innocence and robust conviction. Then he reached for the one from Catherine, one he'd almost committed to memory.

My dearest Husband,

I greet you from our beloved Easton where the hearts of so many are turned in thought and prayer to the Island of New York. Indeed, it seems as if the better part of myself is away, with you. Please do not worry about me or baby Abraham as we are both well and receiving the best of care from dear Susannah, Frau Hamster, Phoebe Hansen, Sarah Kichline, and Elizabeth Traill. Indeed, the entire village would be in our home if they had their way, so much do they care for us and you! I want for nothing, except to pray most earnestly that our Glorious Cause will be upheld by the Almighty and that He will see fit to grant you and our brave men success in every endeavor against the enemy.

You may count on my love to be with you, even as our great God will never leave nor forsake you. Go in His strength.

Your devoted Wife, Catherine

He folded the letter, then took the one from Susannah, along with his son Peter's will, and placed them inside his waistcoat, close to his heart.

Just after midnight, Peter could no longer ignore a hunch nagging at him. Captain Arndt quickly rounded up a small contingent of Peter's troops, including his son, men who came quickly, not a trace of sleep on any of their faces. Peter led them through dense woods thick with the sound of owls and crickets, ignoring relentless mosquito bites, single-minded in his pursuit of any information about a British advance. When they came to Martense Lane, passing through Gowanus Heights toward Flatbush, he saw what he expected, a significant gathering of British troops. To be more specific, an advance of General Grant's force encroached, their movement like stealthy bobcats.

Arndt leaned over his commander's shoulder. "What are you seeing, sir?"

"Take a look." He handed over his field glass and after a moment, heard the captain whistle almost inaudibly. "I want you to take two men with you, and get word of this to General Putnam as quickly as you can."

"Yes, sir."

As Arndt prepared to depart, Peter watched his son Peter join the officer. "Be vigilant, and may God be with you."

Peter sighed with relief when at five a.m., Captain Arndt and his men returned, accompanied by a large contingent of unfamiliar soldiers. He briefly wondered where his son was positioned. At this point, Peter and his unit were posted in the woods at the foot of the Greenwood Hills, toward the rear of Colonel Attlee's skirmishers. He was relieved to see his scouts come back, their clothes and faces smudged, men wide awake in spite of the hour and lack of sleep. There would be no time for breakfast this day.

"I'm glad to see you, captain."

Arndt and his men saluted. "Sir, may I present Captains Chalmers of Maryland, Perrin of Delaware, and Brown of Connecticut."

Peter received and returned their salutes. "Gentlemen, I am pleased to make your acquaintance.

"Thank you, sir," Perrin said. He was a stocky, dark-haired man who looked as if he'd quit smiling in boyhood. "General Stirling has sent us and our troops to reinforce your line. May I say, I'm relieved you speak English. I'd heard yours was a mostly German outfit."

"What are your numbers?" Peter asked, ignoring the remark.

Chalmers stepped forward. "Sir, we total one-hundred-fifty."

He was heartened by the presence of extra men, which had come just as the British began their offensive. Quickly, Peter ordered his men to support Colonel Attlee's rear flank, pleased he'd listened to his instincts so the Americans weren't surprised. Nevertheless, Attlee's skirmishers were swiftly driven out of their position in an orchard as if they were of as little account as ants under a boot heel. Those who hadn't fallen under the assault began retreating along the Gowanus Road. His heart rate accelerated—the Flying Camp and its reinforcements were now in the crosshairs.

He lost track of the hour and thirst, how his inner garments were so wet they'd become one with his skin. Peter and his men fought with the bravery of lions while storming the hill in order to keep the British from occupying such an important position. Amidst screams and the sharp reports of muskets, he watched his tailor fall, followed by a fellow who worked at the Shannon's Tavern. A cannonball removed a Williams Township farmer's head. Peter called out orders, Andrew Drunkenmiller's drum beating them out in the din, mixing with the smell of gunpowder.

He'd lost track of Attlee, didn't know Stirling's position, was cut off from all communication with his superiors. There was only himself and his troops, who didn't give up the fight even when they discovered the British had already taken the critical hill. There was nothing to do but charge, or disperse like some of the regiments had done. Peter wouldn't stand for such cowardice. Nor would his men.

Twice, they withstood British counteroffensives, unwavering in their quest to cut off the King's finest from their position. Twice, the Red Coats drew back, only to reappear, their numbers seemingly endless. The German marksmen with their frontier rifles inflicted severe damage, their fire rapid and unbroken, not a man among them wavering. Constantly, they looked to Peter, who held them steady as he commanded on foot. At one point, Peter was delighted to see Colonel Attlee's men emerge and reoccupy their original position, due to the steadfastness of Peter's company. But this was only temporary.

By midday, General Cornwallis was leading his troops through the unguarded Bedford and Jamaica Passes. Peter sensed and heard their advance before he actually saw the men approaching his sharpshooters. The British General Grant sent volleys into Peter's unit, while to the rear, the Hessian general DeHeister encircled the Flatbush Pass. The impact of the fierce battle was upon Peter's regiment. He stared for a long moment when he saw Ziba Wiggins go down, a dark red stain filling his chest and mouth.

Sergeant Horn ran up to him, breathless. "What now, sir?"

Peter blinked a few times, his heart pounding in his ears. For some reason he tasted his own blood. "Stand your ground, Mr. Horn! The longer we hold out, the more damage we inflict, the better chance our men have of escape."

"Yes, sir!"

Peter watched as Colonel Atlee's remaining men fell, human dominos, one against the other, some intact, others brutally slaughtered. Horn and Chalmers reappeared.

"Colonel Kichline, we've lost most of our men. We're totally exposed." Chalmers spoke as if he were placing an order for flour at the mill.

Peter admired the calm assessment. "How many men are left?"

"Roughly two hundred, sir."

"Mr. Chalmers, Mr. Horn, gather them to me as quickly as possible."

"Yes, sir!" they echoed.

Time took on an odd dimension as Peter watched the red-coated British and fierce Hessians encircle them. He was soaked to the skin, but he felt nothing, suspended from any personal awareness. He was more focused than he'd ever been in his life. When the men reappeared with his unit, his son and closest friends among them to his great relief, Peter addressed them.

"Men, you have fought bravely and well. As you can see, we're quickly being surrounded. Our only chance of escape is to break through the British lines ahead and advance toward New York." He pointed in the right direction. "I will go first up the hill, then you follow. Remember, the objective now is to break through the British to freedom. We'll regroup in New York." A muscle twitched under his right eye. "Godspeed, gentlemen."

His heart thumping and ears ringing, Peter stormed up the hill, feeling, rather than seeing his men following close behind. He wasn't more than halfway to his goal when a Hessian emerged at his left, rushing at Peter with a bayonet. He felt the stab through his uniform waistcoat, pain searing through his upper left arm as he stumbled. The German's fierce expression accompanied the yanking of his blade from Peter's body, and he drew back as if to strike at his chest. Peter found enough strength to raise his other hand and cry out, "*Schlage nicht! Ich bin Deutsche!*"

The young Hessian stood frozen, bewildered, while Peter slipped into unconsciousness.

Chapter Twenty-Three

Erin had decided to invite her mom to the George Taylor Chapter's Christmas party the first Saturday in December. While she wasn't sure of the outcome, she sensed this was the right thing to do. How could she live in the same area as her mom, who was as clearly qualified for DAR membership as herself, and not bring her on board—if she wanted to be brought on board?

At first, Audrey hesitated."I'm not sure I have the right clothes."

Erin had assured her. "This group is pretty informal." Inwardly, she hoped her mom wouldn't wear, say, or do anything to embarrass her.

The event was scheduled to begin at eleven-thirty, so Erin got Ethan and Toby in the car, picked up hotdogs at Jimmy's over the bridge, and dropped them all off at her dad's apartment. She smiled to herself, standing in his place. *What a concept! My father babysitting.*

"Where are you going again?" Tony asked as she headed for the door.

"There's a DAR Christmas party in Easton."

"DAR, eh?" He frowned.

"Yes."

"I don't think I'd like that crowd."

Erin ignored the remark. "See you, Dad. Bye, Ethan. Have fun! I'll be back around three."

Ten minutes later, she found her mother waiting in the Clymer Village lobby, dressed in a tan pants suit with ivory-colored heels and carrying a small clutch purse. She'd painted her nails and applied her makeup almost flawlessly.

Erin kissed her cheek. "Mother, you look wonderful!" Why had she doubted? Audrey had grown up with a mother and grandmother who wore dresses or suits, hats and gloves when they ran errands.

"Do I look alright then?"

"More than alright."

"I'll fit in?"

"I guarantee it."

Audrey smiled. "I like your dress, what I can see under your coat." She bid good-bye to the women sitting on the sofas and chairs, including Aunt Fran. "I'll see you later. We're going to a DAR luncheon."

"Have fun."

"Well, la-de-da."

"Have a good time."

Once they were settled in the minivan, Audrey asked the inevitable. "So, where's Ethan while you're out today?"

Erin cleared her throat, as ready as she could be for the question. "He's with his grandfather."

Audrey twisted her lips to the side. "I wonder how that will go. Does Ethan see much of him?"

"I'm not sure what you mean by 'much.' They do see each other from time-to-time." She attempted to change the subject. "So, Mom, on our way to the Pomfret Club, I want to show you something special."

"Yeah, what's that?"

She brought her up-to-date about the Kichline tavern, what she'd seen, how the building was for sale, and her brief article about the place.

"And where is this?"

"Remember the old Little Mister, Little Sister store?"

"Of course, I do. They always had some kind of mechanical horse you rode when we went there, and they gave out lollipops. Oh, I used to love coming over Easton." Her expression was long ago and far away.

"Yes, Mom, that's the place.

"You're kidding. You're saying that was the Kichline tavern?"

"Yes. We'll be there in just a few minutes."

After the light at Fourth and Northampton Streets, Erin took a left turn into the Pomfret Club's parking lot. She pulled into one of a few spots left and because they had ten minutes to spare, walked her mom to the front of the Kichline building. As they stood there, she explained what she'd seen on her tour with Paul.

"So," Audrey said when Erin finished the story, "what's going to happen to this? I certainly hope they're not going to tear this down the way they did the Spring Brook Tavern."

Erin set her jaw. "There's no way that's going to happen."

She might have known her mother would be "the belle of the ball." Audrey's face shone when Connie introduced guests during the luncheon. "We'd also like to welcome our new member Erin Miles's mother, Audrey Pelleriti. Both of them are descendants of Colonel Peter Kichline. Audrey, would you please stand?"

Erin helped her mom pull her chair away from the table and smiled as Audrey accepted the applause of some sixty women. She leaned into Erin after sitting back down. "Well, wasn't that nice?"

She squeezed her mother's hand and smiled, feeling very much like she was beginning to belong to this chapter. They enjoyed polite conversation at the table over chicken piccata and salads, and after cheesecake was served, Connie introduced a few of the Bachmann Players. Three men and two women, who did colonial dinner theater at the old tavern, looked straight out of Williamsburg as they performed old Christmas songs. Then came tombola.

"What in heck is tombola?" Audrey addressed the entire table.

A portly woman with at least ten supplemental pins on her wide ribbons gave a man-sized laugh. "I'd never heard of tombola either before I became a DAR." She went on. "Did you buy any raffle tickets when you came today?"

"Yes." Audrey picked up a strip of red paper.

"When your number is called, you get to go to the tables along the wall over there, and choose any item you want."

"Anything?" Audrey's eyes widened.

"Anything. Of course, people who get called first get the best pick."

"Where do the items come from?"

The woman continued explaining as Connie prepared to read off numbers. "Everyone brings something, either new or used, but always interesting."

"Did you bring anything, Erin?"

"Yes, a children's book about George Washington I picked up at the Sigal Museum Store."

Connie called out five numbers, then on the sixth, the sequence matched one of Audrey's tickets.

"Hey, Mom, that's you!" Erin lifted her voice and pointed to her mother. "My mom has this one."

"Super! We love when our guests win," Connie said.

"Mom, I'll go up with you and help you pick something."

Audrey slipped out of her chair and walked over to the tables filled with mirrors, prints, books, linens, toys, soaps, candles, wines, holiday items, even a fairly-new-looking camera.

"I hardly know what to get. You know I can't see so well." Audrey moved closer.

Erin was about to describe some of the possibilities when a strawberry blonde about her age squinted at her, then broke into a smile.

"It is you! When I heard your mother's last name, I realized you were Erin Pelleriti."

Erin cocked her head. The face was familiar, maybe a little sun-damaged, but she was able to identify her old classmate from past years. "Uh, I recognize you, too, but I'm sorry, I can't recall your name."

"Christa Arndt. My last name is Harcus now."

"How nice to see you!" They embraced, and Erin introduced her mother, who also remembered Christa. A bell rang in Erin's thoughts. "Arndt. Who is your patriot?"

"John Arndt."

"He was Captain of the Easton Company during the Battle of Brooklyn!"

Christa smiled. "Yes, he was. I'm amazed you could just pull that out of your head."

"She's a history professor at Lafayette," Audrey offered by way of explanation.

"Well, I'm impressed."

"Do you belong to this chapter, Christa? I haven't seen you at meetings before."

"I do, but I usually work on Saturdays. I'm going to try to get my schedule changed so I can start coming again."

"Are there other women from school who are DARs?"

Christa pursed her lips then said, "I don't think so."

Then again, how many of them have no clue about their ancestry, like I once didn't?

At the end of the Christmas luncheon, Connie rushed over to Erin and Audrey, hugging the latter. "Oh, Mrs. Pelleriti, we just loved having you here today. Did you enjoy yourself?"

"Very much."

"We're so happy Erin is in our chapter. You've never joined the DAR, have you?"

Erin knew where this was going, and suddenly, she didn't mind.

"Well, do please consider it. I would be more than happy to help with your application. Oh, Erin, wouldn't it be lovely to have your mom be part of our chapter?"

She wasn't lying when she answered, "Yes, very nice."

"Erin, one quick thing before you go. Actually two. Your article will be coming out next week."

"Super."

"You're going to love it. The other thing is, I keep thinking about the Kichline tavern. I don't know what's going to happen to the property, but let's keep something in mind—the DAR offers historic preservation grants. I'm not sure if we could make anything happen because a lot depends on who buys the property, but let's just tuck the information away for future reference. I really don't want anything bad to happen to the old place."

Erin's wheels had begun to spin, but she had no idea what direction they were taking her.

She walked her mother to her apartment, helping her carry a medium-sized Father Christmas statue, her tombola treasure.

Audrey shrugged out of her coat and hung it in the hall closet. "Thanks again for taking me, Erin. I had a great time. You have very nice friends."

"They can be your friends, too, if you want."

She nodded her head. "Maybe I will. Does joining cost a lot?"

"Not so much. There is an application fee, then annual dues, which don't amount to much."

"Would you take me to meetings since I wouldn't have any way of getting there?"

"Of course, Mom." She looked at the clock above the kitchen sink. "I'd better get going." She started toward the tiny hallway.

"Erin, I wanted to ask you, when you take me to the store again, next week I think, could we do a little Christmas shopping? When I drove, I used to be finished by early December, and I haven't even started this year."

"Sure, Mom." She kept walking.

"Where will we have Christmas this year?"

Erin didn't know yet. She hadn't spoken to her nieces or her brother, let alone her dad. Not wanting the joyful day to be ruined, she said quickly, "I'll talk to Allen. Don't worry, we'll figure out the details."

"Erin? Thanks again. I'm so proud of my daughter."

"Allen? Is this a good time?"

"This is so weird, Erin. I was just getting ready to call you."

She plunked herself down on the family room sofa, having just cleaned up after Sunday lunch. Ethan was taking Toby for a short walk around the block. "Well, you know what they say about great minds thinking alike."

Her brother chuckled. "How are things?"

"Good. I took Mom to a DAR Christmas party yesterday, and she had a great time."

"Where was it?"

"The Pomfret Club."

"Nice place. I've been there a few times."

"So, how are you and Tanya?"

"Busy. Good. So, I wanted to talk to you about Christmas this year and when we can get together."

"The same reason I called you."

"We usually have the family come here, but this is Tanya's year to host her brothers and sisters on Christmas Day. She doesn't think she can manage back-to-back parties."

"I don't think anyone could, and I know Tanya goes all-out." She paused. "I would love to have the family come to my house this year. I was going to offer to give you guys a break, anyway, and to celebrate at my new home."

"What a great idea," Allen said. "Let's see, Christmas is on Monday this year. I don't know what the girls' schedules are like, but they tend to spend Christmas Day with their husbands' families. Saturday might be good for them or Sunday. Which is best for you?"

"I would slightly prefer Saturday since we have two services on Christmas Eve, and I'd like to go to both."

"How do you like the church?"

"Very much. At first, I wasn't used to the smaller size, but now I feel part of a family there, and Ethan has made a couple of friends in the Sunday school. I love the pastor. He's very warm and gives great sermons."

"Good for you. Okay, so Saturday would actually work a little better for us. Do you want me to contact the girls, or do you want to?"

"I'll give them a call. Let's make the date Saturday then, how about two-ish? I can be flexible, though, if we need to make the time earlier, or later."

"Sounds great." A moment later he spoke again. "Uh, Erin, I've been thinking about Mom and Dad."

"What about?" She twisted a tassle from her throw blanket around her right index finger.

"Which one should we invite?"

Erin sighed. "I really wish they would both come."

Silence. Then, "Do you think they would, I mean if we asked?"

"The thought never crossed my mind. What makes you think they would?"

"Well, I was talking to Dad the other day, and he was saying he doesn't hold any grudges against Mom. I don't know how she feels since I try never to bring up the subject of Dad. I just wonder since Dad's on his own now, Mom might be more open to seeing him at family functions."

Erin needed to collect her thoughts. Then she said, "I'd love having them both here. How could we, though?"

"How about if I ask Dad, and then you ask Mom?"

Part of her would rather take a high dive off the Northampton Street Bridge into the freezing Delaware. Something inside, however, told her this was the right thing to do. "Okay, I'll try."

"Oh, by the way, will your friend be joining us?"

"My friend?"

"Peter or Paul, sorry I forget."

"Paul. I was leaning toward including him." She laughed. "If Mom and Dad both come, though, I might not want to subject him to our particular version of the Addams Family."

Chapter Twenty-Four

"Well, now, me lads, it looks as though we've captured some Deutsch." The commanding officer put his hands on his skirted hips and snorted. "So, then, who's in charge of these ruffians?"

Peter heard the words but couldn't quite understand their meaning, filtering as they were through a kind of brain fog. He struggled to get to his feet, but someone was pushing him down, or was the heat, or perhaps his trembling body keeping him prostrate? Maybe the heat was coming from his left arm. Heat and pain. He didn't have strength to resist.

Irritation replaced the Scotsman's banter. "Don't any of you Dutchmen speak English?"

"Yes," Peter answered, but he wasn't sure if his lips had uttered the word, or merely his thoughts.

"You there." The senior officer pointed at Andrew Drunkenmiller, then at Peter and spoke slowly. "Is-that-your-commander?"

"*Ja*. Uh, yes."

"Finally." He turned to his men. "Do any of you speak German?" A crow cawed in the near distance. "Sergeant Black, go find one of the Hessians and be quick!"

Peter sat against a tree in the shade. Someone was lifting a canteen to his lips, which felt stuck together. He tried moving them apart, but he couldn't seem to lift his right hand. Why did such a simple task require such a staggering effort? Then he felt wetness, a drop at first, running down his chin, resulting in a small mudslide down the front of his shirt. He swallowed. Oh, the coolness of the water. He sipped, then gulped, the liquid spreading across his face. He could conquer the entire British Army if he just had enough water. Too soon, there was no more.

♛

The voice was robust. If *Frau* Hamster's beef stew could speak, it would sound just like this. A certain joy rose in his spirit to hear his native tongue. Was he in Easton? He opened his eyes and gazed through a crusty coating at the unfamiliar landscape. Andrew and Sergeant Horn were talking in German to the Big Voice. Peter strained to hear. Something about him. Yes, Peter was their colonel. From Pennsylvania. He attempted to rise, but when his left hand pressed against the dusty soil, he heard a loud cry coming from somewhere, then blacked out.

The scene had changed—when he didn't know, but the German with a big voice was gone. There was a feeling of being closed in, and he wondered if he might forget to breathe. In and out. In and out, he willed himself. Humidity united with the sour scent of unwashed men. So much dirt. So many flies. Another big voice, but not like the German's. He strained to see. Red coat. Powdered wig. Large eyes, a pinched mouth. Then, a familiar voice.

"His name is Lt. Col. Peter Kichline, and we served under Lord Sterling."

Harsh laughter. "Lord indeed. Where are you from?"

"Pennsylvania."

"Your unit?"

Peter thought he heard "Flying Camp," but then he might just be thinking about the fly buzzing in his right ear. He tried to lift his hand to strike the insect but failed.

"Miles. Colonel Samuel Miles."

His friend! Peter managed a smile through his parched lips. His friend was here, wherever "here" was.

"What's the matter with him?"

"He's obviously been wounded, General Howe," Miles said. He sounded as if he were speaking to a daft person.

The British commander scowled. "The man is delirious."

"A bayonet wound will do that."

"Impudent rebel," he muttered.

Peter heard so many words now he couldn't possibly piece them all together to make sense of them, hard as he tried. His mind wandered … Catherine sat before him with their baby and Elizabeth, smiling. Like the

Madonnas in German Catholic churches. His sons at the mills, except their faces appeared larger than the mills themselves. Robert Traill was shaking his hand, but Peter's arm ached, and he couldn't quite find words to beg him to stop. The roar of battle …

When he awakened, he thought he might be in church because he was flat against a wooden bench, maybe a pew. But where was Pastor Rodenheimer? Something was wrong. The pews faced in the wrong direction. When had they been switched? Shouldn't he have been told?

"There you are, my friend."

A soothing voice. Concerned eyes.

"There's no need to speak."

"Where?" He pushed the single word through his lips.

"New York. We're safe now."

"M-miles?"

"Yes, my friend. I'm going to need to remove your jacket. You've been stabbed in the arm. We're going to dress the wound."

Peter felt as though frantic squirrels were darting through his head and chest. He couldn't let anyone take his jacket. He must hold on to the letters.

"He's got a tight grip on his waistcoat," Miles was saying to someone. "Don't worry, Peter, we're not going to take away your coat."

Brown eyes, truthful eyes gazed down at him. He began loosening his hold.

"Thank you, my friend. I promise, we'll keep your coat nearby."

Blazing pain as he half-sat in the wooden pew and felt the coat being removed. *"For he was pierced for our transgressions."*

He'd been in church such a long time. He liked going to church, but he also wanted to go home afterwards. This service never seemed to end, like the pain in his arm. Funny, though, he couldn't remember any preaching. There'd been a pastor, though, a large man bringing a little food and water, but no message from the Word. He looked to the side where his friend sat, looking disheveled. He wondered why Samuel Miles would let himself go when he'd always been so orderly. Peter didn't mind, not as long as Miles didn't go away.

He heard someone talking nearby, another Big Voice clothed in bright scarlet, the piercing sound making Peter's arm throb even more.

"Who's the commanding officer here?"

"I am Colonel Samuel Miles of Lord Stirling's Division."

The red-coated man knit his brow. "Miles? From Philadelphia?"

"Yes, sir."

"I was stationed there and knew of you. I'd like to ask you some questions."

"Of course, but as you can see, my friend and fellow officer is badly hurt and not making a good recovery. He needs a doctor, but also water and food."

The Voice gazed at Peter. "Good God! This man looks just like someone I knew a decade ago." He turned to Miles. "Who is this?"

"Lieutenant Colonel Peter Kichline of the Northampton County, Pennsylvania, Flying Camp."

The officer gasped. "It is Sheriff Kichline."

Peter responded to his name. "Yes?"

The man drew closer. "I am Stephen Hough—Captain Hough, who married Greta Schmidt."

Peter tried sitting up so he could greet his old acquaintance.

"No, no, you just lie back there," Hough said.

"How-is-Greta?"

"She is well, sir."

Peter missed the startled look between Samuel Miles and Peter Horn when this British major called him "sir."

"Which is more than I can say for you, my friend. Do not worry. I'll send for help." He rose and turned toward Miles. "What happened?"

"A bayonet wound to his left arm. We don't have anything to clean and dress the site properly. He's been feverish for at least a week. How do you know him?"

"I was stationed in Northampton County years ago, when he was Sheriff. He, uh …" Hough cleared his throat and looked away. "… He introduced me to my wife and then gave us a nice wedding."

Peter wondered what had made Samuel Miles smile so broadly.

He would never tell his wife, but this beef tea tasted better than any she had ever made, and she was especially adept at broths. The salt revived him, and the fresh water he drank afterward was almost as sweet as the Bushkill's springs. The doctor had been so pleasant, and although he caused pain when caring for Peter's arm, the discomfort felt somehow purifying. Soon, he would be able to feed himself. For now, though, Andrew Drunkenmiller was perfectly timing the spoonfuls, his hand and Peter's mouth moving in harmony.

"Thank you, son," he said. "That will be all for now." He looked around the church, which smelled something like the courthouse pond on a muggy day, marveling at how many men filled the pews, aisles, even the chancel. He'd heard they were in New York City, prisoners of war. He could recall some of the battle now, leading his men through the woods and passes, the noises and smells of war. They seemed to have happened yesterday, but then again, a long time ago, when the intense heat had become one with a man. This place was musty, but no longer like steam rising from a pot. "Where is Captain Horn?"

His subordinate moved closer to the pew on which Peter now sat. "Yes, sir?"

"What day is this?"

"September 30th, sir."

He calculated this news in his sponge-like mind, which was growing slowly more supple. *Many weeks have passed since the battle. Perhaps four? No five, at least.* He spoke again. "How many men are here?"

Horn scratched his head with a dirt-tipped fingernail. "I'd say a few hundred, sir."

"Our men?"

"Yes, sir, ours and those from other colonies, uh, states."

Peter looked past Horn and noticed some of his men gazing back at him, their faces grimy but smiling. "Is this a hospital of sorts?"

"Well, no, sir, not exactly, although some have been wounded, like yourself."

"A prison then?"

"Yes, sir. We are prisoners of the British."

Peter absorbed this information. "How many of our men are here?"

"There are twenty-nine, sir."

"Twenty-nine." Something was wrong with the number. He'd started with some three hundred. Maybe the others were elsewhere. "Where are the rest? Where is my son?" His heart began pumping fear into his spirit.

Samuel Miles came into view, and he whispered to Horn. Then he came over to Peter and sat at his feet on the pew. "Well, my friend, you are looking much improved this morning."

"I feel much improved." Peter smiled crookedly. "I was just asking about my men and my son."

Miles didn't address the remark. "How is the pain?"

He touched his right hand to his arm. "Better as well. But, Samuel, what exactly happened? I need to know about Peter—and my men."

"You don't remember?"

Peter pressed his lips together for a moment. "I remember being in battle, then a hill, I think, and a kind of spike driven into my arm. A bayonet?"

"Yes, a bayonet, in battle." Miles touched Peter's foot in a parental gesture. "All in due time we can discuss what happened and what is happening now. You were very sick for weeks, so let's take this slowly, yes?"

Peter disliked being put off, but he didn't yet have strength to argue.

"There continues to be good news, and we will hope for more." Miles smiled at Peter, then at Horn and Drunkenmiller. "Your trunk has been recovered."

"My trunk?" Actually, he hadn't known the piece was even missing, but then again, if they had been in battle, and he'd been captured, of course his personal belongings would have been blown to the four winds.

"Yes."

"And my possessions?"

Miles tilted his head. "Your Bible is still here."

Peter became aware of the clothes hanging from his reduced frame, the dirt-encased wrinkles and dried sweat smelling like vinegar. He stroked his face and felt the serious makings of a beard, a look he'd never much cared for. He suddenly could barely stand himself. Maybe in the next day or two he'd be able to bathe in some fashion. "Do I have other clothes?"

"Your friend, Major Hough, had a new set of basics sent to you, breeches, socks, shirt, underclothes."

He frown-smiled at the realization of his scant belongings and the kindness of an old friend, now on the other side of this war. Peter looked up at Miles and the others. "What of yourselves? Do you have adequate clothes and food?"

Miles didn't answer right away. "We are managing, so you are not to worry."

Peter sat further up so quickly he winced. Ignoring the pain he asked, "What of the letters in my waistcoat?"

"Still there, and I'm told there are one or two new ones. Would you like me to read them to you?"

He allowed himself to slump back. "I would, very much." He closed his eyes as his friend chose one from the small pile.

Miles began, "'My darling husband …'" Coloring furiously, he put the letter down as if he suddenly found himself on the receiving end of a live cannonball. Once he worked up some courage, he'd tackle the first one. He selected a different note, in another's handwriting. "Here you go."

> *My dear Father. I hope you are in good health and good spirits. We are all well at home, awaiting news from New York about the battle. There have been prayer services each day at noon at the church, and we have all attended, except for Mother Catherine and Baby Abraham, who are both doing just fine.. We eagerly await news. I hope to join you one day in fighting for our country, a cause we both believe in so much. You should see Susannah—if she were a man, well, I wouldn't like to be facing her in battle! She is as zealous for independence as you or I, or my brothers. If you happen to see …*

Miles stopped for a long moment, then read on.

> *I send you my very best wishes, along with those of our family. We entrust you to God's good care. Your devoted son, Jacob.*

Miles appeared slightly rattled. "Perhaps that will be enough reading for now. Peter, my friend, try to get some sleep. You are still fighting a battle, this time for your health."

Peter nodded, then slipped into sleep more contented, but still wondering what had happened to his son and his men.

Chapter Twenty-Five

She didn't feel like the forty-something, independent woman she was. No, sir. Asking her mother whether she'd agree to celebrate Christmas in the same room with her ex-husband had reduced Erin to a five-year-old about to ask her mom if she could play in traffic. Actually, asking to play in traffic felt safer. Allen had definitely got the better part of this deal.

"Dad was pretty enthusiastic about the entire family being together, Mom included," her brother had reported. "Dad said, 'I buried the hatchet a long time ago.'"

Erin decided to approach her mother while taking her Christmas shopping.

Audrey picked up a glass jar from a cosmetic department counter. "Do you think Alana and Zoe would like these bath salts?"

Erin bent forward to take a look. "Uh, Mom, those are candles."

"What?" She lifted the object to her eyes, straining to see.

"They're candles, but very nice ones," she hastened to say. "The bath salts are on the next shelf."

"I'm telling you, Erin, it's miserable not being able to see."

She'd heard the refrain many times, in many places. What more could she say except "I know," even if she didn't, even if what she said made no difference? "I think the girls would be pleased with candles or bath salts. Your choice."

By the time they hit the food court two hours into the Lewis-and-Clarke-style shopping expedition, Erin's blood sugar had taken a dive, especially after not eating breakfast. She chose chicken nuggets and fries for her mom, then a double burger with a side of jalapeños and ice cream, which she slathered between the buns. At least, her mother couldn't see what she was eating. She ate faster than normal, eager to get some food into, and the six-million-dollar question out of, her system. With

"Grandma Got Run Over by a Reindeer" playing in the background, she whispered a prayer and leaped off the high dive.

"So, Mom, Allen and I have been talking about our family Christmas celebration, and we agreed to let me host this year. Since I have a new house, and he and Tanya will be throwing her family's party on the same weekend, this makes sense." She swallowed. "What do you think?"

Audrey nodded. "What day is Christmas?"

"The twenty-fifth," she said slowly.

"I know that, Erin. I mean, what day of the week?"

"Oh, Monday. We would have the party on Saturday." She felt like she was tip-toeing on eggshells.

"What about Christmas Eve or Christmas Day?"

"Those are times when the rest of the family are with in-laws and cousins."

"Well, I like being with you on those days. Could we still do that?"

"Uh, sure, Mom. Maybe you could go to church with Ethan and me on Christmas Eve and spend the night so you could see him open his presents." Where had those words come from?

Audrey clapped her hands together. "I would love to! I like the whole idea. Your house is so beautiful, and besides, we used to have Christmases there when your Aunt Jane and Uncle Howard lived there. Do you remember?"

"Oh, I remember. Those were some happy times."

"So, who would be coming?" She bent closer, spreading her elbows on the table.

"Well, you, me, Ethan, Allen and Tanya, the girls and their families …"

"And Paul? Will you invite him?"

Erin narrowly averted quicksand. "I'm not sure what his plans are."

"Oh. Well, I hope he'll come. I like him." Her hazel eyes reflected the Christmas lights overhead.

Go ahead, Erin. Get this over with! "Mom, there's someone else Allen and I talked about inviting. We, uh, would kind of like the whole family to be together this year, you know, since getting everyone together with our busy schedules is challenging, and since this is my first year in the new house. Allen asked Dad whether he'd be willing to come if you were at the party, and he said he would like to, so we were wondering whether you would be okay if Dad were there too." She waved her hands in front of her as if to clear the air. "Of course, if you're not good with him coming, I'll just have you there."

"Whose idea was this?"

"Uh, I'm not really sure. The subject just sort of came up as we were thinking about the holidays." She wasn't about to throw her brother under the bus.

Audrey pinched her lips, sat back against the bench, crossed her arms. "Well, I suppose I could go along." Her eyes and nostrils flared. "As long as he behaves himself, I will too."

And if he doesn't?

♛

"Oh, Melissa, I'm so happy to see you!" Erin threw her arms around her best friend, who'd come to Lafayette to see Erin's digs, then go to lunch.

"I'm happy to see you, too! You look great."

"You too." Erin couldn't help but admire her fashionable friend's peach-hued scarf, expertly tied, her stylish coat and leather ankle boots.

"I love your office." Melissa scanned the room. "The campus is so beautiful. I've only been here once before, when Ryan had a swim meet."

"You've come at a wonderful time. I just finished the last of my grading, and I'm ready to close the door on the semester." She looked toward the entry when she heard a knock and saw Mia standing there. "Well, hello, Mia. Come in."

Melissa stepped to the side, and Erin introduced them. Then Mia said, "I just wanted to stop in to say good-bye. My flight leaves at three this afternoon."

Erin walked over to the young woman and hugged her. "You take good care of yourself. You have a bright future ahead of you. You will keep in touch, right?"

"I promise."

Herman Weinreich was right behind Mia and also wished her the best. "And I came to wish you happy holidays," he told Erin after the young woman left.

"Thanks, Herman. This is my dear friend, Melissa Grey, from Lansdale. Melissa, my favorite Lafayette professor and current department chair, Herman Weinreich."

They shook hands. "I'm very glad to meet you, Melissa." He faced Erin. "I also wanted to congratulate you." He produced a small booklet with a tan and black cover—the historical society bulletin. "I just read your piece about Peter Kichline. You always were a good writer."

"Why, thank you. I haven't received my copy yet." She took the one he held and thumbed to the spot he'd bookmarked. "Colonel Peter Kichline—Unsung Easton Hero, by Dr. Erin Miles."

"I was especially fascinated about the building downtown being the site of his tavern. You say the tavern's bones, as it were, are still there?"

"More or less, under all those layers."

"Where is the tavern?"

"Just above the Sigal Museum in the next block of Northampton Street on the left. There's a consignment and antiques store there, at least for now. As I mentioned in the sidebar, the owner is selling the building." She followed his gaze out the window, wondering what he was thinking.

After a short time he looked back at her and smiled. "You must be very proud of your ancestor. He was quite a man, and I'm glad he's finally getting the attention he deserves. Well, then, you two have a good visit and a wonderful holiday. It was nice to meet you, Melissa."

"I wonder what he was thinking?" Melissa mused as he retreated down the hallway.

Erin plucked yet another olive from the dish at Sette Luna as they waited for their paninis to arrive. "I would like to invite Paul to celebrate Christmas with my family, but at the same time, the thought terrifies me." She opened a packet of Stevia and poured the contents over a dark green olive. "I mean, what if my parents act up? I would die of embarrassment."

"This is a hard decision. Has Paul met them yet?" She corrected herself. "Actually, I know he's met your mom, I was there, but what about your dad?"

Erin shook her head, suddenly aware of what seemed a glaring oversight. Not only had Paul not met her father, her father hadn't been to her house yet.

"Well, this is a tough thing then, Erin." She suddenly grinned. "You know, having Paul there might just make your parents be on their best behavior."

She hadn't thought of such a possibility.

"Oh, Erin, the article is so well-written, and we're getting great feedback," Connie said over the phone the next day."Normally, we hear about the magazine in dribs and drabs, but this one is getting an immediate response."

"I'm so glad."

"Some of the directors and I were talking about having you do a presentation on your ancestor. Would you be interested?"

The energy pulsing through her was the equivalent of a double espresso, minus the jitters. "I'd love to!"

"Great. We just happen to have an opening in February, which is short notice, but could you do Saturday the seventeenth at one o'clock?"

"Let me check." Erin went to her desk and opened her pocket calendar. "Yes, I could do the seventeenth."

As far as Erin was concerned, Christmas had already come.

Ethan had just gone to bed, and Erin went to her home office to get the tapestry-covered box in which she kept her papers about Peter Kichline. She kept thinking about the Battle of Brooklyn and something she'd read about Washington's amazing retreat, which some writers said her many times great-grandfather had, in part, made possible. By holding back the British and Hessians as long as his small unit could, the bulk of Washington's army was able to slip behind the lines.

Then she remembered the story wasn't in her box, but in a book she'd read during college, the cover featuring a variety of scenes from America's past. She found the volume on her U.S. History shelf. Grabbing the book and her reading glasses, she sat in her recliner with a throw and a cup of tea.

> The survivors either ran back to the fort or surrendered to the British. Now it was up to Washington to keep the 4,000 soldiers inside the fort from panicking as massive British forces advanced toward them. One can only imagine what went through the Americans' minds. With the Brooklyn Heights fort at his mercy, General Howe delayed. Although his men outnumbered the patriots, the

> Americans had dug formidable earthworks. If the British stormed them, they would suffer heavy losses. No, it would be better, Howe reasoned, to employ heavy artillery against those earthworks to maximize the damage to the Americans while minimizing his own casualties …

> A praying man and a wise man, General Washington informed his officers that he was going to remove the American army from Brooklyn to Manhattan. They may have gaped as Washington explained that the evacuation would involve a flotilla of small boats ferrying group after group of soldiers for the two-mile round trip. The small craft, manned by capable Massachusetts fighters who had grown up near the water … nevertheless would be up against the world's greatest navy.

Erin felt transported back to the critical night when the Revolution itself hung by a loose thread.

> All that storm-tossed night of the 28th, the men from Massachusetts evacuated the American troops in choppy, windy conditions. When the wind dissipated around midnight, however, the moon illuminated the scene. Although more men could now flee per boat because of the calm conditions, the British would now be able to hear and see the troop movements. Also working against the Americans was their troops' fractious mood, with soldiers arguing noisily amongst themselves as they waited along the shore for their rescue. However, even under those circumstances, the British remained ignorant of Washington's evacuation.

She sipped her chamomile tea and gazed out the window toward the back yard where branches of oak trees her uncle had planted decades ago swayed in the wind. The skeletal tendrils of a forsythia bush tapped at the window. She tried to put herself in those soldiers' shoes, in her ancestor Peter Junior's shoes since, according to a document she'd read, he would have been there too, having escaped death and capture. She was reading the account from the perspective of someone who literally had skin in the game.

As dawn broke, Washington knew he needed at least three more hours of darkness to complete the removal. Only a miracle could save his men—and the newborn United States.

American Major Ben Tallmadge, an eyewitness at the scene, described what happened next:

> As the dawn of the next day approached, those of us who remained in the trenches became very anxious for our own safety, and when the dawn appeared there were several regiments still on duty. At this time a very dense fog began to rise (out of the ground and off the river), and it seemed to settle in a peculiar manner over both encampments. I recollect this peculiar providential occurrence perfectly well, and so very dense was the atmosphere that I could scarcely discern a man at six yards, distance … We tarried until the sun had risen, but the fog remained as dense as ever.

When General Washington finally took the last boat to freedom, the fog began to lift. The stunned British realized what had happened: 8,000 Americans had fled under their very noses, and it was too late to do anything about it. Someday Howe and Washington would face each other again. But not that day. The hand of Providence had guided the infant nation to safety.

Erin left the book open on her lap as she looked toward a shelf containing generations of her family's photos. *If events had happened otherwise during the battle and the evacuation, I might not be here.* She gave a small laugh. *Heck, the United States itself might not be here!* Although she hesitated to think so out of arrogance or vanity, Peter Kichline and his Flying Camp had played a significant role in keeping the Revolution alive.

She stood in the kitchen, which was imbued with aromas of cinnamon, pine, chocolate and vanilla, roasting beef, garlic, and an intangible feeling, joy. The last time she'd celebrated Christmas in this house was a few years after her parents' divorce. Her aunt and uncle had gone their separate ways before Audrey and Tony, and Erin's cousins were too hip to get anywhere near the Christmas spirit. A verse popped into her mind—*I will restore the years the locusts have eaten*. Accompanying this testament to renewal, her eyes zoomed in on a scene from the family room, Audrey and Tony sitting on the sofa nearly shoulder-to-shoulder, *and they were laughing*. Not devouring one another with sharpened tongues. Not staring hatefully. Laughing. Sitting at their feet were Ethan and Toby, while Paul assembled her son's new stop action camera, a gift from Alana and her family.

Erin heard a voice behind her. "I never thought I'd live to see the day when your parents would be in the same place at the same time," Tanya whispered.

Alan walked over to them, far more blunt in his assessment. "It's a freakin' miracle."

Audrey's eyes misted after they finished singing "Hark, the Herald Angels Sing."

"Oh, I just love being here. I remember when I was a little girl, and I came here for Christmas Eve services."

Erin's eyes reflected the glow in her mother's, the two of them side-by-side in the church of their ancestors, in Grandfather Peter's church. The time had come for communion, and she followed her mother into the aisle, Ethan and Paul coming behind them. They waited their turn while the first group received the elements, then they spread across the front, and Pastor Grube spoke over them.

"We celebrate the Lord's Supper in this holy place where generations of families have worshiped down through the ages, as we wait for his glorious reappearing."

Erin thought about her Revolutionary War-era family, how they had spent the Christmas of 1776 in this very church, apart from Peter. Catherine would have been with her little Elizabeth and new baby. Where had Peter spent the holiday? Who was he with? Had the Nativity even been observed?

The minister reached Erin and held out the loaf for her to break a piece. "The body of Christ, broken for you, Erin."

After eating the bread, she took a tiny glass goblet from the tray the minister offered.

"The blood of Christ, shed for the remission of sins."

She let the sharpness of the wine fill her throat as she walked back down the aisle and into their pew. Erin began thinking of the year ahead, wondering what was going to transpire with her work situation, and with the kind and caring man sitting beside her. The last of the communicants slipped into their pews when all at once she knew whatever happened, this church, this town, this quirky family, were truly home.

Chapter Twenty-Six

The remnants of the Northampton County Flying Camp hadn't had much to cheer them during three months of cramped, smelly, vermin-infested captivity. The smiles brought about by a two-dollar allotment from the Continental Congress, however, did much to cheer the early-December gloom.

"Thank you, Colonel Kichline, thank you so much." Conrad Fartentius grasped Peter's hand as if he were General Washington himself.

Andrew Drunkenmiller grinned, his teeth as yellow as his eyes. "We can buy food."

Peter managed a smile, but he knew the money wouldn't go far, not nearly enough to fill their malnourished bellies and under-clothed bodies. He wouldn't openly second guess the Congress, believing their intentions had been for the prisoners' good, but did they really understand how rugged these conditions were? Were they taking the British at their word when they told American officials even their own soldiers received a modest allocation of rations, when available, and prisoners were to get two-thirds? Peter had never seen a quarter of the rations, let alone two-thirds, and food so poor Easton's pigs would have grunted in disgust. His men's gaunt frames and pallor bore testimony to a diet of moldy bread and chunks of under-cooked pork crawling with maggots.

When the last of his troops had accepted the notes, Peter addressed them. "You are all free to use your allowances as you please. I'm planning to find out where we can buy food and clothing. As soon as I know, I'll be happy to provide information, as well as assistance."

Most of their heads nodded. They knew their leader had some "pull," given his friendly interactions with the church's minister and a certain British major who visited sporadically.

"Excuse me, Colonel." Trinity Church's dark-haired pastor came over to Peter.

"Good day, Pastor Burton."

He lowered his voice. "Don't you want to be keeping some of those funds for yourself?"

He'd hoped no one would notice.

Burton put his hand on Peter's shoulder and steered him away from the Northampton County contingent, tripping at least twice over the gaunt forms of men lying in the aisle. "You are in need too, my friend," he said quietly. "You really need to take better care of yourself."

Peter looked into the minister's earth-colored eyes. "I appreciate your concern, Pastor, but I am doing fine now." Didn't this man of God realize to whom much was given, much was required?

"May I remind you, you've only recently recovered your strength, sir?"

Peter needed no reminding on nights when pain shot through his arm as he lay awake listening to the nasal cadences of two hundred men catching whatever sleep they could. Or when another kind of ache, just as real, raised images of his missing and dead troops and the awful ignorance of his son's whereabouts. Or when he changed out one of his two shirts and breeches for a "fresh" pair and struggled to keep the bottoms from slipping completely down his scarecrow legs. At least Peter had received a letter from home, which had also included a generous amount of money. His men didn't know their officer had used most of the funds to purchase shirts and socks for them, as well as modest portions of properly-cooked beef. They didn't know the food had come from the major's wife, whom Peter had not yet seen, or at least from her cook.

The minister seemed to sense Peter didn't wish to belabor the subject of his health. "Would you like to assist me this Sunday in leading worship? I've truly been blessed to have you and Colonel Miles, both of you elders in your churches, helping me."

Peter gave a small bow of his head. "I would be delighted. Thank you." On the occasions when he'd been able to lend a hand, the church became for him its intended place of worship, rather than a place of suffering, especially during this season of Advent. He often considered, however, what better place to be detained. This sanctuary bore constant witness to God's presence and what the Almighty had sacrificed by sending his only son to redeem human affliction. Although the church's members literally had been put out by the multitude of unwashed soldiers, there had been a surprising fellowship between the two groups on Sunday mornings. Some even brought fresh biscuits and breads for the men, although the food was more on the order of the two loaves and five fishes among so many, minus the miraculous multiplication.

In those moments when Peter read the Scriptures or prayed during services, he was no longer a prisoner of war, but an elder at the new church in Easton. He could almost see his family seated in the pews smiling back at him and smell the beeswax candles.

"My text will be Matthew One, verses eighteen and following, on Joseph's dream and instructions." He looked at Peter with widened eyes. "For now, Colonel Kichline, I truly believe you need to lie down."

Flickers of light before his eyes signaled to Peter the necessity of rest, the ocular headaches having become a familiar companion since early November. "Yes, I believe I will." He excused himself and returned to what had become his pew, wondering how long this one would last, and how long before he and his men would cease being a captive audience in this church.

Christmas cheer came for Peter in the form of letters and money from home, along with a rather large wooden box filled with molasses cookies, cakes, breads, and dried fruit. After choosing two cookies and a palmful of fruit, Peter distributed the food among his men, eager to devour his letters. Maybe there would be news of his son! Might his family know anything about the war's progress?

My darling husband,

I greet you in this season of Advent, praying not only for our good Savior's coming again, but for your own return to Easton and home. I am zealous for your health and pray for you and your men many times each day as I go about my tasks.

The happiest news I have to share is that Sarah has received word from your dear son, Peter! It seems he was able to escape from the battle and rejoined another unit. He is currently with General Washington's army somewhere in New Jersey, I do believe. How we all rejoiced! I know this will strengthen your spirit as well.

Peter wanted to jump up and down, to shout for joy, but there was no room. Instead he bowed his head in gratitude for several moments. Then he continued reading.

Baby Abraham looks more like you all the time, and he and Elizabeth are growing so quickly Frau Hamster, Susannah, and I keep our needles busy to clothe them. Speaking of Susannah, our dear daughter has just become a communicant at church. I know you will share my pride in the woman she is becoming.

As he read the last part of the letter, heat filled his cheeks.

My dearest, before you share the food we send from home, be sure to take some for yourself. If I know you, you are giving away everything to your men. This letter comes with all the love in my heart, and my dearest desire to welcome you home soon. All of us at here send our affection. May the Lord watch between Thee and Me while we are apart.

Your loving wife,

Catherine

He carefully placed the letter inside his battered waistcoat's pocket , along with the others. Then he began reading the next one, recognizing Robert Traill's distinct handwriting.

My dear friend,

This letter comes to you with all my best wishes for your health and welfare. Elizabeth and I were pleased to hear by way of Sergeant Horn about the recovery you have made from your wound. We ask the Almighty daily for your soon release and for grace-upon-grace while you are detained.

The villagers are eager for all news of you and your courageous men, as we have mourned the loss of those who gave their lives for this Sacred Cause, including our dear friend Ziba Wiggins. His wife soldiers on with her indomitable spirit, and their young children continue to assist her at the tavern.

We all soldier on as well, giving our best to God and Country, knowing in our hearts He is with us.

I am enclosing some funds for your use, hoping these will help meet some of your and your men's needs.

Your wife and family are well. They ask me to remind you of their steadfast affections and join me in wishing we may soon be reunited.

I remain, Dear Sir,

Robert Traill

A lingering morning fog penetrated the sanctuary, lending a spectral aspect to their quarters. Candles flickered bravely against the gloom. They'd just finished a breakfast of cold, watery porridge, and not much of that, when a guard came for Samuel Miles. Peter watched him put down his battered tin bowl and make his way through the listless ranks huddled in the pews and on the cold floor, rubbing their arms across their chests.

Those who noticed Miles leave whispered among themselves, their breath mingling with the chilly fog. Peter had never been one for sinking moods, thank God, not even in this place of imprisonment, pain, and deprivation. This morning, however, as he watched his friend disappear, Peter felt as bereft as a child left behind by his parents. He willed himself not to consider the destitution he might experience if his friend were removed elsewhere, or even released, so much had he come to depend on Miles's companionship and steady encouragement. Surely, though, he would rejoice for his friend if the latter proved true.

The best thing to do is talk with my men, perhaps have them share their letters from home with one another, as well as a Psalm or two. Yes, there was nothing better to do with glumness and worry than take care of the needs of others.

An hour or so later, the same young guard who'd come for Miles reappeared, glancing around the back pews where Peter and his men had stationed themselves. Pointing, he barked, "You, Kichline! Come with me."

Peter stood and hitched up his breeches as inconspicuously as possible. He smiled at his men, whose upturned faces reminded him of his own mood after Miles left.

"This way."

Peter followed the soldier out of the sanctuary to the back of the church and a room with a desk and a few chairs. His eyes needed to adjust to the brightness of the British officer's uniforms in such pointed contrast to his own clothings' dullness. A sharp odor of perfume clung to the space, and Peter hoped he wouldn't get another piercing headache. An unexpected stab of pain exploded through his left arm when the soldier shoved him toward the front of the desk where Samuel Miles stood. The two friends nodded at one another as Peter took a few deep breaths to steady himself.

The man sitting behind the desk, looking as if he owned the islands of New York, addressed the guard without looking at him. "That will be all."

As the young soldier slipped next to his colleague near the exit, Peter studied the superior officer. The fleshy appearance angered him, a testimony to no lack of provisions while Peter's men daily battled starvation. The powdered wig had not a hair out of place—clearly his routine had not been terribly interrupted by war. Although Peter guessed the man was younger than himself, his jowls belied his age. Peter's nostrils twitched from the officer's heavy cologne, and before he could help himself, a loud sneeze ensued, which made his arm hurt even more. The younger officer put his forefinger above his mouth as if to cover a snigger. The commander's lower lip jutted. Since Peter didn't have a handkerchief, he sniffed, hoping to forestall a dripping nose and further embarrassment.

The head officer gave Peter a thorough once-over, tilted his head toward his subordinate and muttered, "Big fellow, isn't he?" His New England accent gave away his American roots.

Loyalist!

"Now then, I have brought the two of you here to offer a parole." He kept his eyes fixed on Peter, but addressed Miles. "Perhaps you can translate for me. I don't imagine a German *officer* speaks English."

Peter noticed the strange way in which this loathsome man suddenly took on the appearance of Easton's renowned hater of Germans, Robert Bell.

Miles straightened himself. "I'll have you know, sir, this Lieutenant Colonel is a Heidelberg University man, and he speaks English quite fluently."

The officer raised his chin in tandem with his watery blue eyes. "Well, Lieutenant Colonel," he consulted a paper on his desk, "Kick-line, as the King's representative, I am prepared to offer you parole. If you and your friend here will agree not to take up arms against His Majesty and swear you will not try to escape, you will be free to find lodging in New York with people authorized by His Majesty's government at a cost of two dollars per week. You will stay there until a proper exchange can be made for you."

Peter bowed his head out of respect for the man's office and for the mercy being extended. "Thank you." He asked, "And what will become of my men?"

Miles spoke up. "I have the same question, sir."

A man who appeared to be a junior officer leaned closer and whispered something to the commander. The older man nodded, light flickering in his eyes. "Ah, yes, of course." He addressed Peter. "I am reminded Major Hough has for some reason taken an interest in your welfare. He has informed us there is a place not far from the docks where you two can board. I can arrange for your men to be taken to one of the nearby sugar houses." He leaned closer, his body spilling across the desk, and poked a few papers. "If you will agree to these terms." He shoved a document towards the two men. Peter picked up his page and read silently.

I, Peter Kichline of the County of Northampton in the Province of Pennsylvania, hereby pledge my faith and word of honor to General Howe, that I will not bear arms, nor do or say anything contrary to their interest of his Majesty or his Government, and that whenever required so to do, I shall repair to whatever place His Excellency or any other of his Majesty's Commander in Chiefs in North America shall judge expedient to order me, unless I should be regularly exchanged for some Person of equal rank—

Given under my hand at New York

This 29th day of December 1776

Witnesses
Joshua Loring
John Loring

When whichever Loring was in charge offered a quill, Peter signed his name.

Chapter Twenty-Seven

Juggling her cell phone, three hefty books, and a tote bag, she reached for the contents of her faculty mail box. The phone slipped from her hand, starting an avalanche of clanking keys, books, and papers, then swept her bag along, out of which rolled hand sanitizer, a Snickers bar, lipstick, and two used tissues.

"Oh, good grief!" She bent down to corral the runaways.

"Are you alright, Doctor Miles?"

She looked up at the history department secretary, whose eyebrows revealed her concern.

"Yes, I'm f-fine, G-ginnie. Just having a … having a rough start." Erin ladled her mess into the tote bag, grateful no one else had witnessed the spectacle.

"We all have those. So, how is your son?"

She stood, sighing. "He's coming along, but a lot slower than I expected."

"So many people are having a hard time getting over this strain of flu. My daughter-in-law was down for three weeks, and my husband hasn't been completely well since Thanksgiving. When did Ethan get sick?"

She did not need to hear this. "Just after Christmas. He missed the entire first week of school after the break, and he's been going to see the nurse every day since then wanting to come home. With our spring semester just starting, well …" She felt as if she were spilling her own contents. "Anyway, I'm a bit distracted as you can see. The nurse calls me a lot, and, well, I'm trying to teach."

Ginnie held up her right index finger. "Here's an idea … what if you leave your cell phone with me while you're in class? Few things can't wait an hour before being addressed, especially if your son is already under the nurse's watchful eye."

"I love you, Ginnie! Many thanks." *If only the secretary could take care of the other problem.*

"Hey, I raised three kids, so I've had plenty of experience with school nurses."

Erin handed her the phone and noticed the side of the case was starting to peel. *One more thing to think about.* "Just slide the symbol to the right if the school calls—the name will come up on the screen."

She headed downstairs to her classroom, trying to focus on the Barbary Pirates, having woefully neglected her preparation the previous night. While Ethan coughed at irregular intervals in his room, Erin had sat up until two-thirty pouring over military documents about the Battle of Brooklyn, compliments of new information from Sydney Stordahl. Then she'd reread papers she had in her Kichline box related to the Colonel's imprisonment and release. At three-forty-five, she'd suddenly sat bolt upright, inspired by a story about his return to Easton with his remaining, ragged men. She would call Pastor Grube as soon as she had the chance.

Now, heading toward her classroom through a swarm of students, she chastised herself. *I should've spent more time on this lecture last night. Is this the way life is always going to be, with me wanting to be doing something other than what I'm paid to do?*

Back when she was completing her dissertation, what she'd wanted most was to find out more about Peter Kichline. And when she was supposed to be applying for teaching positions, she'd longed to excavate family stories and discover long-lost relatives. These afforded her access to pieces of herself, helping her connect the dots to her own narrative. Earning her doctorate had been worthy of the effort, and teaching college had always given her joy, at least at Hatfield, but being a history professor at Lafayette was in a different league, and she wasn't sure she belonged.

When Jim was living, she'd never had to worry about just teaching part-time since he provided more than enough financially. She could do her own thing at Hatfield, and her small paychecks went for extras, not basics. Now Erin was the breadwinner. She couldn't just do as she pleased anymore. Her throat tightened.

This isn't the time for such thoughts. Focus!

She stood at the door to her classroom when a sudden realization came over her. If Herman Weinreich didn't offer her a long-term teaching position, she'd be okay with his decision. She imagined herself being in a stalled elevator when the door slides open. She just didn't know what floor she'd landed on.

An hour later, she emerged from the classroom after sending four students straight to the Sandman and losing her place three times. She wouldn't let such a thing happen again, no matter how sidetracked she was by Ethan's illness or her Peter Kichline research. She had a job to do, and her students deserved better than crumbs from the table. As Erin headed upstairs to the secretary's office, she imagined her tall ancestor standing all splendid in his uniform, smiling at her. The Colonel hadn't been a person to do anything half-hearted, and neither would she.

When she reached the department office, a female colleague was talking to Ginnie, who interrupted the conversation. "Dr. Miles! Here's your phone. The nurse did call."

Her heart skidded. "What did she say?"

"Your son is in her office, not feeling well, and you should call her as soon as you can."

She struggled not to sigh. "Okay, thanks. I guess I'll have to figure out how to teach this afternoon if he needs to come home." She immediately regretted sharing her thoughts out loud.

The other professor, a woman who hadn't plucked her eyebrows since the Berlin Wall fell, nodded energetically. "I'm so glad my son is in daycare. They have an infirmary there, which has saved my butt more than once, but then your son is older, right?"

Erin nodded, then excused herself and went upstairs to her office to call the school.

"Hello, Mrs. Miles, Ethan is with me again. He doesn't have a fever, but he's complaining of a headache and stomachache."

"Do you think he's really sick?"

"Hard to tell," she whispered. "Some kids take longer to recover. Do you want to talk to him?"

"Okay." She waited a moment until her son came on the line. "Hey, Ethan, what's up?"

"I just don't feel well, Mom. Can I go home?"

"Well, I don't know. I have two more classes to teach this afternoon."

"I can stay by myself. I'm no baby."

She wasn't sure at what age kids were legally allowed to be home alone. Her mind worked quickly. If she picked him up now, maybe her mom could come over and stay with him. Then again, if Ethan really was sick, her mom might pick up what he had. Same for her dad. Both of her nieces worked and, who knew, their kids might be sick too. She would definitely have to find a babysitter, but what about right now? Could he stay in her office here until she finished? But there was no place to stretch out.

"Mom? Are you coming for me?"

"Yes, I'll be there in about fifteen minutes. We'll figure something out."

She taught the two afternoon classes, careful to leave her personal concerns outside the room. Between them, she called home to see how Ethan was doing. He was no better by two-thirty, so she called his new pediatrician's office.

"Can you get him in here at four-thirty? Dr. DeLavara has an opening then."

For the first time since moving to Easton, Erin felt homesick for Lansdale, for her in-laws and neighbors, her support system. Most of all she missed Jim, the way they partnered with each other as parents, providing reality checks and wisdom when one of them veered off toward a ditch. Being a parent was hard enough. Being a single parent sometimes felt like getting a thirty-pound turkey out of the oven without protective mitts.

The doctor asked to see Erin out in the hall after a nurse did the initial intake. "I understand you have some concerns you wanted to discuss privately."

Erin explained what was going on concluding, "I'm just not sure if he's really sick. He's never avoided school before, but the thought has crossed my mind."

"How old is he again?"

"Ten."

The thirty-something doctor smiled, and for the first time she noticed he had a small scar on his chin. "You've never been a ten year-old, middle-school boy. He's at an age when academics get serious, and kids get meaner. He's new too, feeling his way around."

Her temples started throbbing. "So, what do I do?" *Besides head for the piney woods with a year's supply of ready-to-eat meals?*

"For starters, let's see how sick he really is. Even if he's not, he may just need a little extra TLC. He may be ten, but don't kid yourself, every adolescent boy still needs his mother."

Dr. DeLavara finished listening to Ethan's lungs, front and back, then relaxed the stethoscope against his neck and leaned against the sink. "Well, my boy, your lungs are clear. I think you're past the flu."

"But I'm so tired."

"Yes, and you've lost some weight because you haven't been eating much."

"My stomach doesn't feel good a lot of the time."

"All these things are normal after having the flu. My advice is to stay home a few more days, eat good food, get your strength back."

Erin prayed silently, *What am I going to do?*

At least dinner was easy. Ethan wanted drive-through chicken nuggets, and Erin was happy to oblige. While he watched *Milo Murphy* reruns, she spread out her books and paper notes on the kitchen table to prepare her next classes. After she prepped, she could work on the Sigal Museum presentation on Peter Kichline. The phone rang at seven-thirty—Paul.

"Well, hello, Paul."

"Hello, Erin. How's Ethan?"

She filled him in, trying to keep weariness and fear from clouding the conversation.

"Too bad he isn't feeling better. The flu can really do a number. So, what are you going to do about teaching while he's home?"

"I think I'll just have to call him a lot from the office and run over to the house between classes and office hours. I thought about having my parents come, but I don't want them getting sick."

"My schedule the next few days is fairly open. If you like, I'll stay with him."

"You will?"

"Of course. I know how to open a can of chicken soup."

"How do you feel about 'Sponge Bob?'"

"My new best friend."

She could have kissed him. "How can I thank you?"

"You just did. Actually, I have something else for you."

Erin heard his enthusiasm. "Really? What?"

"Who's your favorite historian?"

She laughed. "Well, besides you, I'd have to say Derek McCutcheon."

"Bingo! Did you know he's going to be speaking at Lehigh next Thursday?"

"No! How in the world did I miss such news?" Then again, the author of "popular history" books wasn't exactly revered among her Lafayette colleagues.

"There's more. When your article came out in the historical society journal, I gave my friend Dave Ramsey a copy. He works in special events at Lehigh. He was really impressed. He's invited us to meet McCutcheon at a small reception before the lecture."

"No way!"

"Yes, way."

Happy days were here again.

"Hello, is this Dr. Miles?"

"Yes." She put down her coffee mug and hit "send" on an email so she could concentrate on the call, which had come on her school landline.

"I'm Kristen Rinker with the *Express-Times*. Someone gave me your article in the historical society bulletin. I'm fascinated with your ancestor and how his historic tavern is still around. Would you have time for me to interview you sometime this week, tomorrow maybe?"

"Uh, sure." She checked her tight schedule. "If you could meet me between classes tomorrow, I could manage an hour or so."

"How about if we meet at the Public Market? I could take some shots near the building."

"That would be fine." She hung up moments later, not knowing where any of these developments were leading, if anywhere, but all at once spring didn't seem so very far away.

She'd seen Derek McCutcheon many times on TV, making him an oddly familiar figure in spite of their never having met. Up close, he appeared shorter, and his thatch of silver hair, along with pink cheeks, gave him a robust maturity. About three dozen guests holding glasses of wine and small plates of stuffed mushrooms jockeyed themselves to get closer to the acclaimed historian. Some were more discreet than others. For the moment, Erin had his full attention following Paul's friend's introduction as the author of the Kichline article.

"I'm very glad to meet you, Dr. Miles." McCutcheon's pudgy hand delivered an unexpectedly tight squeeze.

"The pleasure is mine," she said, fighting schoolgirl giddiness.

His blues eyes narrowed. "Are you, by any chance, related to Samuel Miles?"

"Just by marriage. He's my husband's ancestor, and I, uh, wrote my doctoral dissertation about him."

"Intriguing." He turned to Paul. "So, you're a descendant of General Miles?"

She spoke up quickly. "If I may, Mr. McCutcheon, my husband has passed away. This is my, uh, friend, Paul Bassett."

The men shook hands, and the author turned his attention back to Erin. "I've become intrigued by men like Miles and your ancestor. I've spent my life writing about American history's icons, and all along the way I've met exceptional supporting actors." He inhaled, then stared into Erin's eyes. "You are a talented writer, Dr. Miles, and you have a strong command of these men's narratives."

A slender fellow in a tight suit and big hair came over to them. "Mr. McCutcheon, I wonder if I might have a word?"

"Yes, certainly," he said, never turning away from Erin. "Just give me a moment here. You see, Dr. Miles, for my next project, I'm planning to write about the unsung heroes. After reading your article, I think there's a good possibility of our collaborating on the project. There are so many of these men and women, and I'm getting up in years. Do you think you'd be interested?"

Erin's jaw fell, then something inside commanded her to abandon the Gomer Pyle imitation. Gathering her dignity she said, "Yes, Mr.

McCutcheon, I would love to talk to you more." She needed to find a place where she could let loose with a scream.

Chapter Twenty-Eight

January 1777

Peter lay on his back staring at the rafters, which he could touch if he raised his arm. He tried not to whenever possible, so as not to disturb an industrious spider. His legs overhung the bed just below his knees, with the bunk bowing in the center despite his significantly-reduced weight. A brood of mice had taken up residence on the other side of the attic space, often in his shoes, crawling in and out of the holes, one in each foot. He could not find, however, a single thing to complain about.

Samuel Miles sat on the side of his bed looking across the trunk-length space between his and Peter's cots. "I can hear you thinking, my friend." His breath created wisps of vapor. "What's on your mind?"

"I don't know how long the men can last in those conditions."

"I think we're doing all we can to meet their needs, but there never seem to be enough blankets, or clothes, or shoes, or …"

"Food." Peter felt relieved his friend was no longer chiding him for what Miles had earlier coined "over-sharing." Peter was as healthy now as he had any right to be under their squalid circumstances, his belly moderately full, if lacking a variety of food. He had two shirts, two breeches, a pair of socks, his uniform waistcoat, and thanks be to God, shoes. He and Miles enjoyed an approximation of bedding and a roof quite literally over their heads. Which was more than he could say for his troops, except perhaps for the roof.

After their breakfast, he and Miles had gone to see their men for the first time since they'd been separated a week earlier. Peter thanked God the men hadn't been required to travel far in the cold while wearing what was left of their summer clothes. Their new prison lay at the northeast corner of Trinity Church's yard, a sugar house the British had confiscated to lodge the captives. These cavernous, freezing New York warehouses had filled quickly as a deluge of grubby soldiers walked, limped, and were carried into every nook and cranny, clamoring for spots closest to the center where a modicum of warmth could be found.

Peter and Miles had smelled the building from two blocks away. When they arrived, they asked a guard where the men from Northampton County and Philadelphia were located. “How should I know?” he’d responded. “All rebels look the same to me.” Under Peter’s firm stare, the youthful soldier’s bravado withered. “You can ask inside.”

The stench of urine, feces, and vomit rose up to greet them, along with the tide of men who had washed over the first floor. The facility was strangely quiet, except for the sounds of coughing and retching. Miniature clouds hung just above the men, one of the few indications they were still breathing. Peter noticed some of the soldiers scratching their bodies with blue-tinged hands made raw by the cold, and fingertips the color of soot.

He and Miles approached another British officer near a stairway with his back completely against the wall. He looked as if he wanted to remove himself as far away as possible from this place. “Where might we find the men from Philadelphia and Northampton County, Pennsylvania?” Peter asked.

The soldier stared at him, then Miles, and jerked his hand in the direction of the steps. “Second floor. Go at your own risk.”

They’d mounted the wide-open stairway and seen much the same conditions as below, though slightly warmer. He and Miles encountered another guard, who pointed toward a far corner of the room. “They tend to hang together.” He added, “They’re the only ones who seem to have any fight left.”

As Peter started walking in the appointed direction, he stepped in a puddle of wet feces. There was no place to remove the filth, so he kept walking, ruing the breakfast he’d eaten. The first person Peter recognized was Andrew Drunkenmiller, whose sunken cheeks and dull eyes testified to his suffering. He appeared strangely young and elderly at the same time. He and his mates seemed shrunken, yet in spite of their misery, they’d brightened at the sight of their commanders and rose to the best sitting positions they could manage. To a man, they each saluted, except for Conrad Fartenius, who was in the throes of fever.

“Colonel Kichline!” Sergeant Horn’s eyes had receded far back into his skull. “How good to see you! How are you, sir?”

He forced himself to see beyond their matted hair and clothes, looking as though moths had enjoyed a bacchanalia at their expense. "I'm well, thank you, so very glad to see you men again." He looked down at what remained of Horn's shoes, hanging in strips like deer jerky. "Colonel Miles and I are staying at a house close to here, and we're able to visit at will." He paused. "Are they allowing you to go outside?"

Horn nodded. "We can go into the yard, but since the weather is so cold, and many of us have taken ill, we stay put."

Fartenius stared vacantly in Peter's direction. Under the soldier's eyes, crusts had formed, his breath was shallow, wheezy. Peter saw in his mind an image of Fartenius's wife and little girl back in Easton, and his gut clenched.

"Has Private Fartenius been ill very long?"

Horn glanced in the man's direction. "Two or three days like this, sir."

"Colonel Miles and I are going to do everything we can to get supplies for you. Are they feeding you?"

Several of the men shrugged their shoulders. Horn spoke up. "We get a little food and water most, but not all, days."

"How about today?" His blood had begun to boil.

"No, sir." He looked down and whispered. "We still had a little flour left from the church, and we, well, we … uh … created some … uh … water with our collected spit and rolled the dough into balls, so at least we had something."

Peter had found himself growling. "I don't see many blankets."

"We have a dozen between our two units, and we take turns using them."

Before they left, he and Miles took turns reading Psalm 139 from Andrew Drunkenmiller's Bible.

> Whither shall I go from thy spirit?
> Or whither shall I flee from thy presence?
> If I ascend up into heaven, thou art there
> if I make my bed in hell, behold, thou art there.
> If I take the wings of the morning,
> and dwell in the uttermost parts of the sea;
> Even there shall thy hand lead me,
> and thy right hand shall hold me.
> If I say, Surely the darkness shall cover me;
> even the night shall be light about me.
> Yea, the darkness hideth not from thee;

but the night shineth as the day:
the darkness and the light are both alike to thee.

The following morning as Peter and Miles finished their breakfast, Mrs. Vink, their landlady, appeared in the doorway. "Colonel Kichline, you've a visitor." Her voice reminded him of a squeaky door hinge.

He wiped the sides of his mouth with his napkin and rose, wondering who might be calling. When he entered the foyer and saw her standing there, he recognized the startled expression at once, although this time, apparently, she truly was disquieted. She dropped her basket, and he stepped forward to help.

"Gre-uh-Mrs. Hough, how very nice to see you." He smiled at his former indentured servant, now garbed as a British officer's wife with a fine woolen cape, fashionable hat, gloves, and boots. He handed the basket to her, which she accepted without taking her eyes off of him. "I can only imagine your shock. Although I lack the benefit of a looking glass, I guess I must appear something like Robinson Crusoe."

"Sher-uh-Colonel Kichline," she said, as if trying to locate her voice from a distant location. "My husband told me I would find you here."

"And I had the pleasure of seeing him while being held at Trinity Church. He was kind to my men and me."

She looked about to sink to the floor, and he moved closer, taking her by the arm and leading her into the empty parlor. They sat across from each other. Mr. Vink had already gone to work, the children of the house to their school.

"How are you?" she asked.

"I am quite well, glad to have been paroled and sharing this home with my dear friend, Colonel Miles." He yearned to tell her about his men's distress, forming ideas about what she might be able to do to help, but he knew he must wait for the right timing. He also decided to act as if he hadn't seen her in Philadelphia two years earlier, a time when she'd all but snubbed him while in the company of British ladies. "And yourself?"

She nodded, looking at her hands wrapped around the basket handle. "I am keeping well. My husband and I came to New York a year ago."

"Are there any children?" He was amazed he didn't know this about a woman who had lived under his very roof for seven years, but then her father didn't either.

"We have two sons, ages eight and six." As if remembering to look at him she asked, "How is Mrs. Kichline, and your children?"

Peter brought her up-to-date, then there was a long silence.

"And my father?"

"He enjoys good health, as well as his wife and children." He waited for her astonishment to register. Since she leaned forward, her mouth slightly open, he provided details.

"When you see him again, please remember me to him."

"I will."

Greta handed him the basket. "I brought you provisions, bread and jam, pickles, some meats. My husband and I would like to help you while you're here."

He could hardly speak. When he at last thanked her, he brought up the subject weighing most heavily on his spirit. "Colonel Miles's men and mine are prisoners in a sugar house with little food and barely a blanket to their names. Their summer clothes are in tatters, their shoes worn to the soles, if there even are soles left." He saw tears spring to her eyes. "You knew some of these men when you lived in Easton. If you and your church friends can do anything to help, I will gladly reimburse you for your time and expense."

She moved her head up and down slowly. "Of course, Colonel Kichline. I will begin this very day."

February 12, 1777

My darling Catherine,

I greet you with the very best of news. Mr. Loring has just informed me of a new condition regarding my parole. My men and I will be able to leave New York by week's end, and I can await my exchange in Easton. Unfortunately, Colonel Miles must wait here for his exchange, and I pray this will come very soon. In my last letter, I mentioned Mrs.

Hough's generosity. Once again, she and her husband have contributed to our welfare by supplying provisions for our journey in addition to a small wagon and horse. I think I wrote earlier about Abelard being lost to me during the battle. Many of my men are weak from sickness and hunger, so the wagon is a great blessing.

Once we leave, I am hopeful we can cover the seventy-five miles in three or four days, depending on weather conditions and how well the men are faring.

Please let their families know we will soon be home, perhaps just after you receive this letter. I keep the image of your face ever before me, drawing strength from your love, longing to hold you and our babies again, and to greet my dearest family.

Your devoted and loving husband,

Peter

He was too numb to feel his beard, frozen like a bird's nest, or his cracked and bloodied lips. His hands, the mottled shade of a cloud-speckled sky, didn't register either. He and his men were going home—home! To Easton. To families and friends. To hot meals and warm beds, to fires crackling in their own grates, and the melody of children at play. To the lowing of cattle lumbering along Ferry Street and sound of the pigs snuffling in the courthouse pond.

Sergeant Horn shot out a hand to stabilize his commander when Peter slipped on an icy patch. "There now, Colonel, maybe you could take a turn riding in the wagon?"

Peter waved him off. "The men are in no condition to walk any more than necessary, especially Private Fartenius." He was doing everything he could to encourage the young man to stay alive. In fact, Conrad was the only one who never had to walk. The rest took turns in two-hour shifts.

Horn opened his mouth to say something, but Peter raised his eyebrows and stared. His sergeant got the message.

They encamped along wagon paths across New Jersey, reaching the central part by that evening. Peter would have liked to continue, but he and his men had begun staggering under a snowstorm which unleashed the Furies with the retreat of the afternoon sun. Seeing a light not too far from the dirt road, Peter directed his men to stop and take cover as best they could around the wagon while he and Horn investigated. Discovering a two-story log dwelling and a barn, they knocked on the cabin door. A dark-bearded man, whose hair seemed to have slipped from the top of his head down to his chin, raised the latch and partially opened the door. "Yes? Who are you?"

"I am Colonel Kichline of the Northampton County Pennsylvania Flying Camp. This is my aide, Sergeant Horn. My men and I have just been released by the British and are on our way home to Easton, at the forks of the Delaware and Lehigh Rivers. They are weak, and some are sick. We wonder if you might shelter us in your barn tonight."

A sturdy woman appeared, glancing over her husband's shoulder. Peter couldn't tell their number, but several young children crowded around their parents.

"Are you sure you're Americans? You sound mighty German to me. What if you're one of those Hess-i-ans?"

Peter almost laughed. "I assure you, although we are of German ancestry, we are all Patriots. Besides, none of the Hessians are outfitted as we are, you see."

Apparently convinced, he asked, "How many of there are you?"

"Besides the two of us, twenty-seven."

The man moved his head from side to side as he made a sharp tsking sound. "The barn is mighty small, but if you don't mind bunking with the animals, you can be our guests."

Peter bowed from the waist. "Thank you very much. We will do our best not to disturb anything."

Horn rushed back to the road to fetch the men, the wagon, and the horse while Peter took a tour of the barn with his host, a Mr. Richard Scattergood. Although his men slept as tightly as a litter of puppies, sleep they did, so deeply Peter wondered in the morning whether Private Fartenius was, in fact, sleeping. He breathed his own sigh of relief when he saw the young man's chest slowly rise and fall. *We need to get as far as possible today, or Fartenius won't live to see his family again.*

Although the Scattergoods had loaned their barn and allowed the men to drink from their mostly frozen well, they did not offer food. The rations Greta had sent with them had dwindled to barely enough for one man's breakfast. The sooner they got to Easton, the better.

When the men had come to within ten miles of home, Peter ordered them to stop near a tiny village where he broke up his trunk for kindling. He told the half-frozen Horn and Drunkenmiller to start a fire as best they could with the wood, which wasn't completely dry. A curious farmer came out to see what was going on and offered them fresh wood, which soon ignited. He also brought each of them an apple from his larder, apologizing for not having more to offer.

"If you stay, my wife can make something."

Peter declined. "I thank you, but my men and I are determined to reach Easton by nightfall."

The man scratched his cheek, frowning.

The last miles were the hardest, the men moving stiffly—frozen likenesses of their prior selves. Peter refused to acknowledge his own pain and discomfort, focused like a hawk on his men's affliction, and their destination. To occupy their minds, he instructed them to share out loud the names of family members they'd soon be seeing, and to recite Psalms they'd committed to memory. Every now and then he checked on Fartenius, who was shivering under several blankets.

When his feet were so numb with cold he couldn't feel them, and his eyes frozen nearly shut, when even the horse seemed barely able to put one hoof in front of the other, sunlight nearly blinded Peter. They were standing on the eastern bank of the Delaware gazing into the promised land, the sun's rays reflecting off the water. A man was waving at them from the Easton side and running toward the ferry. He was shouting something like, "Glory be! I'll have you across as soon as possible!"

Peter heard him calling for his wife, and when she appeared, the man moved his hands up and down rapidly. A moment later, she was running up Northampton Street.

He forgot his hunger and thirst, his freezing face and hands, the frostbitten feet. Joyous cries filled the Great Square as women, men, children, and dogs thrust themselves upon the remnants of the Northampton County Flying Camp. At the sight of Catherine limp-running toward him, holding their baby, little Elizabeth skipping to keep up, everything else receded into the background. His wife was laughing, crying, obviously joyous at seeing her unholy mess of a husband.

"Catherine." He embraced her, breathing into the side of her head, smelling the freshness of her hair, the softness of her face. He had so much to say, yet no words to say them with. He looked into Elizabeth's pink-cheeked countenance and felt tears slipping down his own.

"My darling, darling Peter." Catherine kissed his cheek, not seeming to mind the frosty beard or his fetid odor. They were interrupted by a loud cry.

"Papa!"

He was speechless as this woman—his little Susannah no more—ran, then skidded straight into his arms.

Even he couldn't stop tears from flowing, and freezing, down his face.

After some chaotic minutes, a familiar voice rose about the din. Pastor Rodenheimer was calling out, "*Willkommen! Willkommen zuhause!*" Then he told the men and their families. "Come to the church! There is food and warmth and help for the sick."

"Excuse me," Peter told his family. "I will be back very soon." A look from his wife showed she understood, as always. He backed away from her, slowly at first, then turned and quickly saw Conrad Fartenius' wife and daughter bent over the wagon, their husband and father reaching out to them with what little strength he possessed. Peter called out, "Will someone please give me a hand with Private Fartenius?"

Robert Traill suddenly appeared, hair askew, his waistcoat buttoned in the wrong places. Peter received his friend's light clap on the back. "Oh, how good to see you again!" Traill glanced into the wagon, then at the soldier's wife and daughter. "There is a hospital set up at the church. Let's take him there right away."

Peter and his friend, along with Sergeant Horn, guided the wagon through the throng to the church, the rest of the troops receiving assistance from their loved ones as they followed. When they reached the warm sanctuary, Peter saw what he guessed to be about three dozen men sprawled across the pews, looking as comfortable and well-fed as anyone could under such conditions.

Traill seemed to read his mind. "Come, my friend. There will be time to mingle with the troops later. You must warm yourself and get some nourishment."

The lawyer led Peter to a back room, which had been built in his absence, and where he saw Easton's older *Hausfrauen* bustling around a large table with what appeared to be many loaves of bread dough. *Frau* Hamster raised her wizened face to him with such joy she appeared at least twenty years younger. Then she suddenly frowned, and Peter realized what was disquieting her. With the initial embraces and greetings behind them, his starving men had rushed toward the table and begun stuffing raw dough into their mouths, looking as satisfied as if they were eating warm bread topped with freshly-churned butter. As he stood there watching for some minutes, Peter felt a tug on what was left of his right uniform sleeve. Looking down, he saw the upturned face of Frau Hamster who, smiling, handed him his own loaf.

Chapter Twenty-Nine

She hadn't expected half this many people to show up for her presentation. The Sigal Museum's first floor auditorium boasted nearly-full capacity fifteen minutes before the program. Paul fiddled with the projector while Ethan handed out flyers to people as they entered. She knew she should probably be checking her notes one last time, but then she saw Melissa and Tim come in, followed by her in-laws.

"Is everything okay here, Paul?"

He was clearly distracted. "Yes, I just need one more ..."

"Do you mind if I greet people?"

"Go right ahead. I'm nearly finished here."

An older couple she didn't know caught her eye as she plowed down the center aisle. The man leaned over. "Hello, Dr. Miles. I wanted to introduce myself. I'm Mike Kichline."

"Oh, how nice!" Erin shook his hand. "I guess we're related then."

His wife spoke up. "You are fifth cousins."

"Well, I'm very glad to meet you." She looked toward her family. "Can we chat later?"

He folded his beefy arms across his chest. "I'll be here."

The top of her head tingled. *A Kichline relative!* She fixed her eyes on the back of the room where Al and Pat Miles and her best friend stood, talking to Connie. Noticing Erin, they fell into a tangle of hugs and kisses until she came up smelling like the Philadelphia Flower Show.

"Is your mother coming?" Pat asked.

"Yes, and maybe my dad too."

Pat's eyes reflected her pleasure. "Well, I hope you saved us places."

She pointed. "I did, second row from the front."

"We'd better get moving," Al said. Then he winked at Erin. "You'd think the Pope was coming."

She hugged her father-in-law and, glancing over his shoulder, saw Tanya come through the door with her mother and Aunt Fran. "Well, hello!" she cried.

"Erin!" Audrey embraced and clung to her. "We could hardly find parking. I'm so proud of you."

"Thanks, Mom. Hi, Tanya." She shot a questioning look in her direction.

"Your dad had a stomach ache," she whispered. Then she brightened. "But Aunt Fran wanted to come."

"I wouldn't miss this," the elderly woman said.

"I'm so glad you're here, Aunt Fran. Uh, where's Allen?"

"Had to work. The kids all had sports today, so Alana and Kate aren't coming either."

"I understand." Erin directed them with words and gestures toward the saved seats, then went on to greet some of the George Taylor Chapter Daughters.

Connie approached her, touching her right arm. "Paul wants to run something by you. Oh, and our director will be introducing you."

On her way, Erin walked past the wooden chair from the old courthouse. *Grandfather Peter used this very chair.*

At the front, Paul handed her the remote control. "I had to change out mine for the museum's because mine had a glitch. Let me show you how this works."

After Erin figured out the device, Debbie Amato, director of the Northampton County Historical and Genealogical Society came over. "We're so happy to have you, Dr. Miles. And this crowd." She swept her arm as if she were a game show hostess about to reveal the grand prize. "Let's get going."

Erin was ready to break out of the starting gate but sat quietly next to Paul and waited her turn.

"Ladies and gentlemen, welcome to the Sigal Museum. I am delighted to see so many of you here this afternoon to hear Dr. Erin Miles, an Easton native and graduate of Lafayette College where she currently teaches history. She's also a member of the historical society."

Erin pursed her lips. Technically she'd grown up in P'burg, but she didn't mind. Would her family?

"Her doctoral dissertation was about Colonel Samuel Miles, Erin's late husband's ancestor, who became mayor of Philadelphia. Colonel, then

General, Miles was a friend of Colonel Peter Kichline's, Easton's illustrious Revolutionary War hero. Many of you have read her article in our historical society magazine, as well as the piece in last week's *Express-Times*. Please join me in welcoming Dr. Miles."

Erin shook hands with Debbie then placed her notes on the lectern and looked out over the capacity crowd. She broke into a huge grin when she spotted Herman Weinreich and marveled upon seeing Lafayette's president, Neil Drexler. "I'm delighted to be here with you today to talk about my ancestor, who poured his life into colonial and Revolutionary War-era Easton." She nodded toward Mike Kichline, and he smiled back. "Johann Peter Kichline's story begins in Germany in the year 1722 …"

The PowerPoint presentation had gone flawlessly, thanks to Paul. The applause made her ears ring and her arms tingle. Erin gathered her notes and was about to return to her seat when Debbie Amato came forward and held out her arm to stop her. "Don't go just yet."

Erin figured she was about to receive a book from the museum store or maybe a print or mug as a thank-you gift. She hoped the presentation would be quick—her knees were trembling.

"Dr. Miles, you've helped us understand this heroic man far better. We're proud of the way you've brought him back to our attention. You've also raised local awareness of the tavern he established where some of Northampton County's earliest courts were held. Forty-some years ago, many of our historical places began coming down in the name of progress, among them, your ancestor Peter Kichline Jr.'s Spring Brook Tavern. Those of us in the historical community don't want such things to happen anymore." She looked to the back of the room. "With us today are President Neil Drexler of Lafayette College and History Department Chairman Herman Weinreich. Would you gentlemen please come up here?"

Herman bear-hugged Erin, and Drexler shook her hand.

"President Drexler, I believe you have an announcement?"

Where had the reporter come from? Erin hadn't noticed her before.

"Yes, I do, Debbie." Drexler turned his lean face toward Erin. "Dr. Miles, when we learned about the impending sale of your ancestor's place, a few of us at Lafayette began investigating. As you know, in recent years the college has been moving some of its buildings and offices down here, creating a more synchronous relationship between 'town and gown.' Lafayette's history is intrinsically connected with Easton's, and we thought there should be a place where the two can uniquely come together. Therefore, I am announcing the purchase of the Kichline building, which will be restored to its original form and will operate as a center for the study of colonial Easton history."

He reached over and shook Erin's hand as she gawked shamelessly. He said something else, but she was too stunned to understand a word. Applause thundered throughout the room.

Herman stepped to the podium. "I have had the good pleasure of knowing Erin since her undergraduate years at Lafayette, and I am not too embarrassed to tell you, she's always been one of my top ten students." He smiled over at her. "While she's done a fine job teaching this year in our department, I think both of us have suspected she was meant for something just a little different. Yes?"

Erin closed her eyes and scrunched up her shoulders. Her cheeks burned.

"Dr. Drexler and I agree she belongs in our department, but not necessarily in our traditional classrooms." He turned to her. "Erin, we would like to offer you the position of Director of Lafayette's Kichline Center for Colonial Easton History."

When her jaw dropped, she didn't even try to close it.

From the back of the sanctuary, Erin waited for her cue along with four girls in colonial costumes and a half dozen boys in threadbare, "eighteenth century" clothes. The boys were poking each other.

"Psst!" Caught in the act, the kids started facing her and, getting the message, quieted. "Listen up," she whispered.

Pastor Stan spoke from the front. "On July 8, 1776, Robert Levers read the Declaration of Independence from Easton's courthouse steps. In agreement with the solemn pronouncement, many men from Easton pledged their lives, their fortunes, and their sacred honor to this great cause. Those men, led by Colonel Peter Kichline, marched to New York on a brutally hot summer morning at the end of August to engage the British."

Five-year-old Nolan Esteves yanked Erin's sleeve. "I have to pee!"

She leaned over. "Can you wait ten minutes?"

He nodded gravely. "But not a minute more."

Those in the back pews broke into titters. Pastor Stan pushed forward. Erin couldn't tell whether he'd heard or not. "Out of roughly three hundred members of the Northampton County Flying Camp, only a fraction returned. Many of the survivors had, along with their brave commander, been captured by the British and languished in makeshift prisons until they were released in February 1777. The story of what happened when they at last reached Easton is found among the chronicles of the Arndt and Kichline families." He craned his neck toward the back of the church, then nodded.

"There's our signal," Erin told the children. "After the girls and I reach the tables, you boys start down the aisles, slowly. Remember, pretend you just played soccer for five hours straight on a very hot day."

Pastor Stan stepped to the side and continued speaking while Erin and the girls took their places at rustic tables. They picked up pottery bowls and wooden spoons, pretending they were baking something. "I am reading parts of Thomas Jefferson Kichline's 1926 document:

> When the prisoners of Colonel Kichline's regiment were exchanged, they dragged their emaciated bodies to their Pennsylvania homes … Of the Reformed Church, Colonel Kichline was one of the founders and officers. He had aided to erect this building. He first saw it (again) as a hospital for his sick and wounded soldiers. When these poor fellows reached the little village of Easton, the women eagerly set to work to bake and cook for them.

The boys limped and moaned their way down the center aisle.

> … so famished were these maltreated men that they would snatch up and devour the raw dough.

The boys staggered up to the tables and grabbed pieces of bread dough from the bowls, stuffing them into their mouths, falling onto the floor as they ate. Erin wasn't sure what to expect from the audience, applause perhaps, as people often did when children performed. There was, however, no clapping. As she looked over the congregation, which included Paul, her mother, Allen, and Tanya, she saw tears slipping unabashedly down people's faces. One large man blew his nose like a trumpet. Stan Grube seemed to know exactly what to do.

"Let us rise to sing 'America the Beautiful.'"

She changed her colonial outfit at home in order to go to Maxim's with Paul. Ethan and Audrey went to Allen and Tanya's for lunch, and she didn't know why she and Paul just didn't go there too. Still, she went along with the plan to pick Ethan up there afterward.

In the kitchen, she lifted a bouquet of pink-tipped carnations from a vase on the table. "Before we go to lunch, might we have time to stop by the cemetery? I'd like to put these on Grandfather Peter's grave. I feel a need to be close to him after today's service, and everything else that's happened recently."

He kissed her cheek. "I love the idea. You certainly are on a roll."

"I know! I just feel as if my life is finally coming together again."

Paul didn't say anything.

The tundra-like ground crunched under their feet, a bracing wind flapping their coats open. Erin placed the carnations on a simple stone with its German engraving, then she straightened out the tangled American flag anchored by a Revolutionary War marker. "'*Ihr ruhe in Gott*,'" she read aloud.

"'You rest in God.'" Paul drew closer to her, putting his arm around her waist.

She felt the sting of tears. "How fitting." She looked up at him. "You know, I feel closer to him than I do some of my living relatives."

"Maybe you never talked with him as you sat by a fire in his home, but I believe there are other ways of knowing." He looked into her eyes. "He's part of you, Erin, part of what has gone into making you."

At Maxim's, Erin cupped her chapped hands around a mug of hot coffee while telling the waiter what she wanted. "I'll have the Berry Crepes with a side of Brussels sprouts."

The twenty-something guy's eyebrows elevated. "Are you sure? Grilled ham or Lyonnaise Potatoes might work better with the crepes."

"She's sure," Paul said, handing his menu to the guy. "And I'll have the Steak Frites with grilled asparagus."

When the waiter left, Erin glanced about the busy restaurant. "I remember coming here when this was Pomeroy's Department Store. The ceiling is about the only thing I recognize from those days." She leaned forward, her eyes dancing. "Can you believe, I bought my first record here. You do remember records, don't you?"

He smiled. "Yes, I'm vintage enough to remember. So, what was your first record?"

"'Dancing Queen' by Abba, one of my all-time favorites. What was your first record?"

"I'm not sure, but the song I listened to repeatedly was Boston's 'More Than a Feeling.'"

The waiter brought a bread basket, and the two of them tucked into the contents after a quiet prayer. Erin liked how Paul gently expressed his faith. "I feel hungry enough to eat some raw dough myself," she said with a chuckle before sobering up. "Then again, I've never been as hungry as my Grandfather Peter and his men."

Paul handed her the crock of butter. "You first." While she applied some to a roll, he said, "The play was really touching. You did a nice job."

"Thanks. I hope there wasn't anything disrespectful, except maybe when Nolan burst out about having to go to the bathroom."

He made a light huffing sound. "I must've missed that."

She told him the story, and they both laughed.

"I assure you, even if the entire congregation had heard Nolan, the effect of the play would've been the same. There wasn't a dry eye, as they say."

Erin leaned back in her chair, contented. "What an amazing meal."

He grinned. "So, the Brussels sprouts and berry crepes made a good combination?"

"For me, yes." She looked down at her lap, grateful a splotch of strawberry jam had landed on her napkin, rather than her skirt. "Thanks for not making fun of the way I eat."

"Like so many things about you, I find your food preferences endearing."

She caught and held his blue-eyed stare as the waiter reappeared. "Would you like more coffee with your dessert?"

"Oh, we didn't order dessert," she said.

The young man looked at Paul, who glanced at Erin. "I was hoping we could share their Bon Bon, which is too rich for one person."

"What's in a Bon Bon?"

The waiter repeated, "Triple layers of chocolate accompanied with vanilla ice cream from Bank Street."

"I can't argue with chocolate and ice cream, and I'll definitely need more coffee."

Paul winked at the waiter, who disappeared with a smile.

That was strange.

Paul rested his elbows on the table. "You've had quite a couple of weeks—the offer from Derek McCutcheon, the Sigal talk and your new job offer, not to mention pulling off a wonderful production this morning."

"I know. At the beginning of the year when Ethan got so sick, I was feeling pretty discouraged. I couldn't figure out why life wasn't just falling into place the way I expected when we moved here." She paused. "Do you ever second-guess yourself?"

He nodded his head, but there wasn't anything solemn about his expression. "Yes, though not lately. Now I'm very sure of myself."

"How nice! Actually, I'm feeling more confident, too."

"About what?"

"Oh, my work and, well, living here again."

"Anything else?"

She looked at him sideways, her cheeks flushing.

The server returned with the restaurant's signature chocolate dessert, which had been sliced into two portions. After placing them before Erin and Paul, he poured more coffee and handed something to Paul before walking away.

"I wonder why they cut the cake in half?"

Paul seemed not to have heard her. "This looks delicious."

She took a bite. "Oh, yum. Yum, yum, yum! My mouth is doing a happy dance."

He smiled and ate some as well.

A few moments later Erin exclaimed, "How strange!"

He leaned forward. "Is anything wrong?"

"I hit something hard with my fork. Somebody really messed up in the kitchen. I think we should tell the waiter." She put the fork onto the dish and turned her head to look for the guy. He wasn't anywhere in sight.

"Uh, before you do ..." Paul covered her hand with his. "... maybe you should try to figure out what's in there so you can tell him."

She drew in her head and upper body. "You think?

"Yes."

"Well, alright then." She poked around until she located the object, dragging the thing to the side with her fork. "Oh, look!" She picked away cake and icing with her fork until a tiny light twinkled. Taking her stained napkin, she rubbed away until a ring emerged. Erin giggled. "I think maybe I've found the Cracker Jack prize?"

Paul gazed at her, more mellow than she'd ever seen him before. "I definitely found the prize when I met you."

She opened her mouth, but nothing came out.

"Erin, I would hate for you to go on your new journey in life alone. I'd very much like to come along. I'd like to share your life, your son, your home—your bed."

A bolt of warmth shot through her body.

"I think the time is right for us." He took the ring from her and produced a wet cloth to clean the piece, revealing a square of tiny diamonds surrounding a medium-sized center stone set in platinum. He held the ring toward her. "Would you do me the honor of wearing this—of marrying me?"

She couldn't help but tease him. "I don't know. Did you speak to my father?"

"Actually, I did."

"You did?"

"Yes. He gave me his blessing."

She was feeling like a giddy teenager. "And did you ask Al?"

"I did."

"What did he say?"

"He said he was happy for us."

"Uh-huh." She crossed her arms. "And what about Ethan? I'm assuming you spoke to him as well."

"Yes."

"And what did Ethan have to say?"

"He said he's happy for us, and …" Paul's voice caught. "… he said his father would be too."

Erin closed her eyes, picturing Jim smiling. Sighing, she took off her wedding band and put the ring into her wallet for safekeeping. She reached out her hand, and Paul slipped the diamond onto her finger. She didn't see the waiter grinning from pierced ear to pierced ear. She only had eyes for Paul.

About the Author

At fifteen, Rebecca Price Janney faced-off with the editor of her local newspaper. She wanted to write for the paper; he nearly laughed her out of the office. Then she displayed her ace—a portfolio of celebrity interviews she'd written for a bigger publication's teen supplement. By the next month she was covering the Philadelphia Phillies. During Rebecca's senior year in high school, Seventeen published her first magazine article and in conjunction with the Columbia Scholastic Press Association, named her a runner-up in their teen-of-the-year contest. She's now the author of twenty-one published books including two mystery series, as well as hundreds of magazine and newspaper articles.

Her other books include: *Easton at the Forks*, *Easton in the Valley*, *Great Women in American History*, *Great Stories in American History*, *Great Events in American History*, and *Great Letters in American History*, along with *Harriet Tubman*, *Then Comes Marriage?* and *Who Goes There?* A popular speaker, Rebecca also appears on radio and TV shows. She's a graduate of Lafayette College and Princeton Theological Seminary, and she received her doctorate from Biblical Seminary where she focused on the role of women in American history. She lives with her husband and son in suburban Philadelphia.

GLOSSARY OF GERMAN WORDS AND EXPRESSIONS		
PAGE	GERMAN	ENGLISH
25	Frau	Mrs.
	Tochter	Daughter
	Guten abend	Good evening
	Danke	Thank you
	Deutsch	German
27	Bürsten Sie den Schnee vom Hut.	Brush the snow off the hat.
28	Ja	Yes
	Hausälterin	Housekeeper
	Vielen dank	Many thanks
	Bitte	You're welcome
	Apfel	Apple
31	Ich bin Stefanus Drunkenmiller.	I am Stefanus Drunkenmiller.
41	Bitte, nehmen Sie Platz?	Please, take a seat?
	Mann	Man
	Herr	Mr.
	Nein, dank	No, thank you
56	Mein	My
57	Beeile dich! Schneller! Schneller!	Hurry up! More quickly! More quickly!
	Nein! Es ist Frau Benner.	No, it is Mrs. Benner.
58	Ich werde nach ihm schicken, wenn es sein muss.	I will send for him if need be.
60	Wie kann ich Ihnen helfen?	How can I help you?
	Mein Junge ist nicht hier.	My boy is not here.
	Ist das dein Sklave?	Is that your slave?
	Ich kann nicht bezahlen.	I cannot pay.

GLOSSARY OF GERMAN WORDS AND EXPRESSIONS

PAGE	GERMAN	ENGLISH
	Ich möchte nicht, dass du denkst, ich stimme deiner Sache zu.	I do not like you to think I agree with your cause.
61	Liebling	Darling
73	Guten morgen	Good morning
	Alt	Old
75	Herr Kichline, Ich scheiße auf Sie.	Mr. Kichline, I s - - t on you.
87	Dieser Schurke sagte einige hasserfullte Dinge.	That rogue said some hateful things.
	Was ist falsch?	What is wrong?
	Schweine! Sie sind alle Schweine!	Pigs! They are all pigs!
123	Jawohl	Yes!
	Richt	Right
153	Kleines Mädchen	Little Girl
158	Danke schoen	Thank you very much
	Sie sind eine wundersame Frau.	You are a wondrous woman.
190	Schlage nicht! Ich bin Deutsche!	Do not strike! I am German!
	Deutsch	German
239	Hausfrauen	Housewives
246	Ihr ruhe in Gott	You rest in God

Easton Series Books

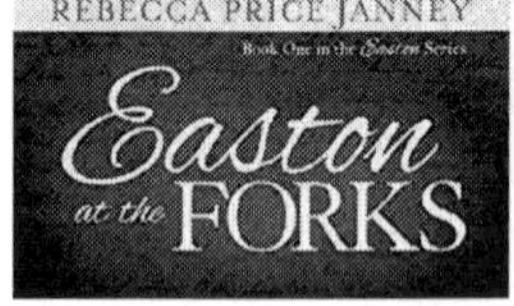

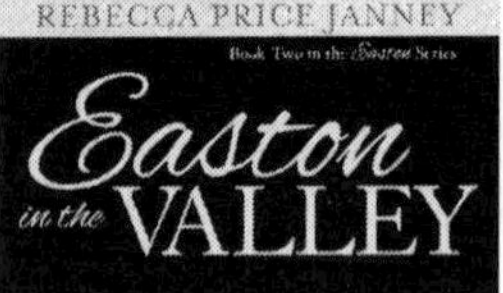

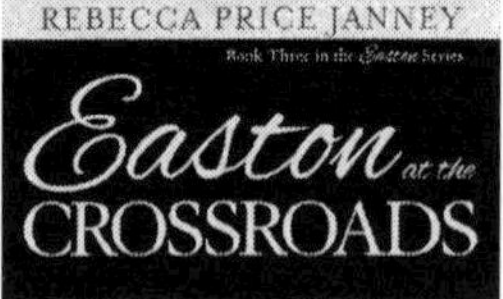

Dr. Rebecca Price Janney

Author of Twenty-One Published Books/Historian/Speaker
For more information visit www.rebeccapricejanney.com

Other Books by Rebecca Price Janney:

Great Events in American History (AMG)
Great Women in American History (Moody)
Great Stories in American History (Horizon)
Great Letters in American History (Heart of Dakota)

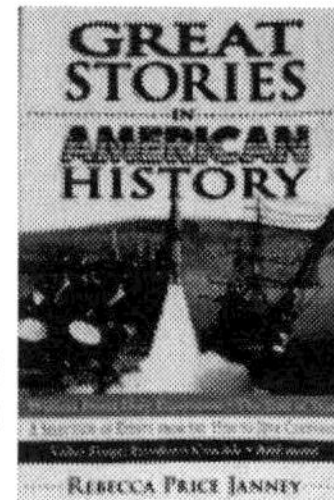

Harriet Tubman (Bethany House)
Who Goes There? (Moody)
Then Comes Marriage? (Moody)

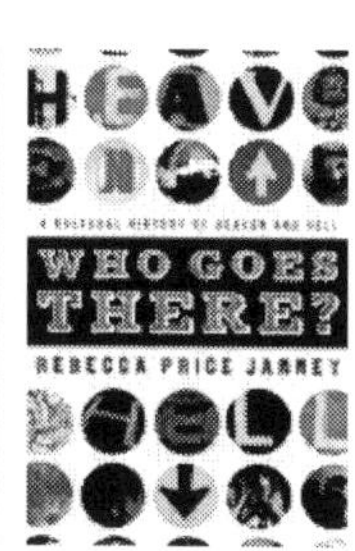

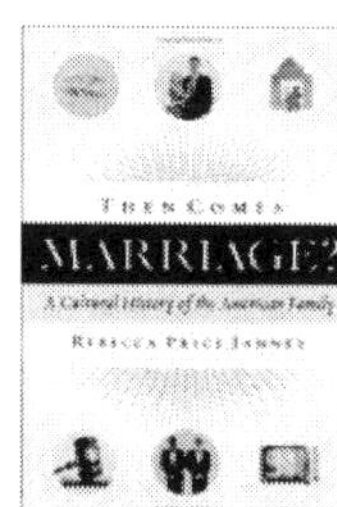

The Heather Reed Mystery Series (Word)
The Impossible Dreamers Series (Multnomah)

Made in the USA
Lexington, KY
01 October 2018